i gave
you
my heart,
but you
sold it
online

By Dixie Cash

I Gave You My Heart, but You Sold It Online
My Heart May Be Broken, but My Hair Still Looks Great
Since You're Leaving Anyway, Take Out the Trash

Coming Soon

Don't Make Me Choose Between You and My Shoes

Dixie Cash

i gave
you
my heart,
but you
sold it
online

A V O N

An Imprint of HarperCollins*Publishers*

FIRST EDITION

ISBN: 978-0-06-082972-8
ISBN-10: 0-06-082972-9

The William Morrow hardcover edition contains the following Library of Congress
Cataloging-in-Publication Data

Cash, Dixie.
  I gave you my heart, but you sold it online / Dixie Cash.—1st ed.
    p.   cm.
1. Beauty operators—Fiction.   2 Texas—Fiction.   I. Title.

PS3603.A864I15   2006
813'.6—dc22   2006043303

07 08 09 10 11 WBC/RRD 10 9 8 7 6 5 4 3 2 1

acknowledgments

Long before I shared the title of Dixie Cash, I was blessed with the title of Mom. My son is the center of my life and the reason behind everything I do. He has always made me proud, and now I can repay that honor by seeing pride in his eyes when he looks at me. Thank you, Brandon, for bringing your wife, Michelle, into our family and blessing me with Caleb, Joel, and Olivia; for being a better son than I deserve and a funnier comedian than I could ever hope to be. Never give up, or in, and always strive to make a hand.

To my mom, Joan Cumbie, for always being on the other end of the phone saying, "What's wrong?"

Thanks also to Joe Dunnam for his emotional support. He's the best PR man I could ask for. And Richard, for not scolding me for watching *Dancing with the Stars,* when I should have been writing.

To my gang at the office: Gary, Jim, Shanen, Laura, Tiffany, and Slim Katie. Y'all help make work fun and the days go faster.

And last but never least, Janis Gist and Dawn Hunter. Thanks so much for making my life in Abilene worth writing about.

—*Dixie Cash (Pam)*

one

On a sunny October afternoon, Quint Matthews's red Ford truck roared along the endless gray highway that stretched through the wide-open spaces of far West Texas. As he sped past tumbleweed forests, sparse mesquite trees stunted from lack of moisture, and scattered pumpjacks laboring against the horizon, Quint returned his cell phone to its cradle on his dash and cussed again. This was getting old, damned old.

The Visa customer-service representative had been polite, even sympathetic, just as she had been every time he had called and reported unauthorized charges on his credit card. His credit limit was "no limit" and the girls in his office always paid his bills on time. Canceling his card altogether was something the bank had already proved it was not eager to do. "Don't worry, sir," the customer-service rep said. "We'll cancel this card and issue another."

When he asked for help in identifying the unauthorized user, she suggested he speak to the bank's fraud and abuse department. Quint had talked to the fraud and abuse department a dozen times and gotten nothing but absurd excuses about how the charges hadn't been large enough to set off alarms and cause automatic action.

The credit-card abuse was aggravating enough, but the real blow was that deep down in his heart and ego, Quint believed he knew the abuser. Monica Hunter. It had to be her. The pieces he already knew about fit the borders of the jigsaw. What was missing was the rest of the puzzle.

Monica had entered his life like a tsunami swamping a sleeping sunbather. Just when he had been playing it safe, too.

And just when he had been vulnerable and recovering from an experience so horrible he couldn't bear to speak of it. He might not talk about it, he might try not to think about it, but he would never forget how a good-looking redhead had perpetrated an outrageous deception, fooled him completely, and publicly humiliated him. For months, tabloid newspapers and magazines blaring about the scandal had appeared beside the cash registers of every grocery store in Texas. And who knew where else?

Since that nightmare, Quint had limited his social life to hooking up with women through an exclusive—and expensive—Internet dating site that thoroughly screened all of its members. His relationships with the women he met on the Internet had amounted to nothing more than casual dinners and one-night stands. Then one evening as he surfed the

Net, Monica had come online and hit him harder than a rodeo arena floor. Up to then, he had been seeking nothing serious with the fairer sex. Monica had turned his world upside down. For ninety blissful days and nine ideal evenings, he had entertained the notion that he had found *The One*.

Then she disappeared.

What *had* appeared, on the other hand, and in a matter of hours, really, were myriad baffling charges on his Visa.

Well, he had no intention of shrugging it off and moving on. No intention whatsoever. He was no ordinary lovesick fool. What Monica didn't know, couldn't possibly know, was just how royally she had screwed up. In the world Quint Matthews had carefully carved for himself in years of living in the rough-and-tumble world of ProRodeo, he was the King. And everybody knew, you don't shit on the King. Nosiree, baby. You don't squat wearing spurs and you don't shit on Quint Matthews.

He picked up the phone again and keyed in another number that had been programmed into it for several years. On the third ring, he got an answer. He recognized the hello and a sense of relief flowed through him. The voice on the phone was the one he shouldn't have let get away. "Debbie Sue?" he said with a grin. "Hey, darlin', this is Quint. How you doin', sweetheart?"

"Why, Quint. What a surprise."

Debbie Sue Pratt was the only human alive he trusted to help him solve his current problem. "I've been thinking about you, darlin'. When I need somebody good-looking and clever, I always think of Debbie Sue Pratt."

"Why, thank you, Quint, but you know my name isn't Pratt anymore."

Shit. He did know that. He just didn't like to think of her being married to Buddy Overstreet. Buddy, who used to be the sheriff in Cabell County, had always looked at him with a jaundiced eye. These days the guy was a Texas state trooper, working toward becoming a Texas Ranger. Big deal.

"Sure, darlin'," he told the one who made him feel more alive than any woman he had ever known. "I heard you and Buddy got together again. But just because you got married, you wouldn't high-hat an old friend, would you?"

"Nope. Not for a minute."

"You and your pal up for taking on a new customer?"

She laughed. "You need a detective?"

Quint laughed, too. He loved the way nothing got past her.

When Debbie Sue and her partner, Edwina, had solved the mystery of Pearl Ann Carruthers's murder, a reputation for being experts at crime solving descended upon them. Quint had even read about them in *Texas Monthly.*

Debbie Sue had taken advantage of the publicity. Dragging her partner along, probably kicking and screaming, she had opened sort of a private investigation agency in one end of her beauty shop. The Domestic Equalizers, she had bragged in the article, specialized in spoiling the fun of philandering spouses and significant others.

Quint had neither, but when it came to his love life, he might be better off if he did.

"I do need a detective, darlin', and I need one now. Look,

I'm gonna be in Salt Lick on Saturday. You think Buddy would care if I stopped by your shop for a little visit?"

To Buddy Overstreet, Quint suspected, a visit to his wife by Quint Matthews would be about as welcome as a drunk driver traveling the wrong direction on I-20. Buddy didn't have to worry, though. Under the present circumstances, Quint's interest in Debbie Sue had to be more professional than carnal. He listened again as she told him to come on by the shop anytime.

"Hey, thanks, Debbie Sue. I'll call when I get into Salt Lick. You're the only one I can trust."

Why did he trust only her? Because she was honest and loyal to her old friends. She would keep what he told her in the strictest confidence. Despite their rocky history, he had no doubt she would take his best interest to heart.

Disconnecting, he felt better. There was just something about that woman's attitude that made him believe his problem was near an end.

Debbie Sue turned from the Styling Station's payout desk and looked at Edwina Perkins-Martin, her longtime friend and now her business partner.

A frown creased Edwina's brow. "Good Lord, who died?"

"You're not gonna believe who that was," Debbie Sue said.

"From the look on your face, I'd say it was the Angel of Death and you're next on his list."

"Quint. That was Quint Matthews. He's coming to see me."

"Bingo!" Edwina said. "I'm right again."

The driver of a plain, dark blue sedan slowed and switched to the right lane behind an eighteen-wheeler. Keeping sight of Quint Matthews's bright red one-ton truck was easy. It didn't blend in with the rest of the traffic, and if it should, the vanity license plate, RODOMAN, was easy to spot. Rodeo Man. The driver chuckled. It was hard to tell which was bigger, the rig that was in Quint's control or the ego that wasn't.

Following Quint stealthlike wasn't the ideal means to an end, but what choice was there? Being recognized could cause a confrontation and ruin everything. A clash with him could be ugly, even dangerous. Behind his public, successful-businessman facade Quint was still an ex-professional athlete, strong as the bulls he used to ride. He was capable of physical harm. His quick temper had erupted over smaller things than his public image.

The most important thing was to avoid identification. "Just keep a low profile," the driver mumbled to no one, "and have a little patience."

two

"M ommy, can I tell you something?"

Allison Barker's twelve-year-old daughter, Jill, never called her Mommy unless she wanted something badly or catastrophe was imminent. Allison swerved her attention from the Excel spreadsheet on her computer screen to the slender girl standing in the doorway.

"Don't freak out, okay?" Jill said in a tiny voice. "And promise me you'll go and try to have a good time."

Extracting a commitment from her mother before the end of a discussion was typical of Jill. "I don't like the sound of this already. What have you volunteered me for this time?"

The preteen stood in the doorway with a wide-eyed stare, a maneuver Allison recognized as one Jill resorted to in order to avoid tears. A feeling of foreboding crept through her. This was serious. She closed her laptop, stood up, and took a seat on the sofa. She patted the cushion beside herself. "Come sit down and tell me what's got you so upset."

"I can't. We don't have long and you need to get ready."

A tiny panic rose in Allison's chest. "What in the world are you talking about?"

"It's six-thirty. You've got a date in thirty minutes. A really nice man. He's coming to Salt Lick on business and he's coming to pick you up. Pul-leeze, Mommy, pleeeze. Promise me you'll go and have fun."

It was Allison's turn to stare wide-eyed. "Jillian Elaine Barker, what have you done?"

Words rushed from Jill's mouth. "He's perfect for you, Mommy. He's really nice. He lives on a ranch and he likes long walks on the beach and sharing a glass of wine with a special lady."

Long walks on the beach? . . . A glass of wine? Special lady? Concern replaced shock. "When and where did you meet this person?"

"Online," Jill said meekly.

"Good Lord, Jill. Tell me you didn't give him our address."

"How would he pick you up for a date if I didn't give him our address?"

Allison dropped her forehead to her hands. She was accustomed to her daughter's frequent comments about her needing to get out of the house and have a life beyond working twelve-hour days, but she hadn't dreamed the child was so concerned she would resort to arranging a blind date.

"Please, Mommy—"

"Honey, you just don't give out your address to perfect strangers, especially perfect strangers on the Internet." Allison got to her feet and went to her daughter, placed an arm around her narrow shoulders. "You don't know who or what someone really is. He could be a stalker. A rapist or a murderer. Haven't any of the talks we've had gotten through to you?"

Jill's posture stiffened. "I wouldn't give our address to just anyone."

"But, honey, apparently you already have. You don't know this person."

"Yes, I do. We've been talking online almost every day for a month."

"A whole month? Good Lord, where have I been?"

"Working."

The answer stung because it was true. Two years ago, Allison had moved herself and her daughter from the small West Texas town of Haskell to the smaller and even farther-west West Texas town of Salt Lick to help her mother salvage her dress shop, Almost the Rage. In reality, Almost the Rage was Almost the Bankrupt. At the time of the move, Allison had no idea the monumental task she had agreed to take on.

What she discovered, too late to back out, was that everything in her mom's store was outdated, starting with the fashions and ending with the hand-posted bookkeeping system. True, she had visited her mother in Salt Lick over the years, but she hadn't bothered to look deeply into the small dress shop's operation. The work that had to be done to save it had left little time for Jill and even less for herself.

"I know I've been in the dress shop a lot, but I'm doing this for us. You know our goal. I'm trying to build the store to be successful enough to move into a space at the mall in Midland. With the right clientele in Midland and Odessa—"

"I know, Mom, I know. I want that, too, but what I want more is for us to be a family. Before you know it, I'll be grown and gone. You say so yourself all the time." Jill's eyes glistened; her face began to pucker. "More than anything I want us to be a family." She burst into tears and ran from the room.

Allison rolled her eyes. So much drama, so little time. She trudged up the hallway and rapped gently on her daughter's bedroom door. "Jill? . . . Honey, I'm coming in."

Allison eased the door open and paused to watch her daughter as she sat at her computer, tapping at the keys between sniffles, her brown ponytail bobbing in time with the rhythm of her fingers. Many times Allison had questioned the wisdom of letting Jill have her own computer, her own TV in her room. She had seen the warnings. But a grandmother's determination to shower her only granddaughter with whatever she desired, even if Grandma couldn't afford it, had been hard to fight.

For a few seconds, Allison looked around Jill's bedroom. It held most of the symbols of a young girl in transition. Ageless Barbies sitting ignored, a toy-filled bookshelf huddled beneath a poster of a hot rock band. Where had the time gone? Wasn't it just yesterday that Jill was playing with dolls? Allison walked over, stopped behind Jill, and smoothed her hand over her daughter's brown hair.

She had raised Jill alone after being deserted at the age of eighteen by Jill's father. Most women had a scrapbook of memories from prom night—corsages pressed between the pages of a book, pictures of a smiling young couple. Allison had a crib and high chair . . . and a child now standing at the edge of adolescence. Until this moment she had viewed the "sperm donor's" departure as a blessed event. God, she hated having to question a belief she had clung to for so long.

Other mothers had warned her that adolescence brought a unique set of problems and situations. Allison had thought her and Jill's special relationship would make them immune. Had she been wrong? Had she been so busy making a living and patting herself on the back for raising Jill alone that she had failed to see the angst their lifestyle had instilled in her daughter? Now she felt guilty and helpless. "Sweetie, I didn't know you felt this way. I thought we were happy. I'm always here for you. You know that, don't you?"

"I'm happy," the morose girl said. "I just want us to be a family, a *real* family, Mom. I want a mother *and* a father. I want the three of us to go places and do things together. I'm the only one in my class that doesn't have a father."

Allison didn't question this. Jill's seventh-grade class was made up of only eighteen kids and Allison knew every parent. She also knew that some of them were miserable in their marriages but hell-bent on staying together. Their upbringing in Salt Lick demanded as much. Couples might not speak a civil word to each other, they might lie and cheat, but there were few divorces. Few stains on the family fabric under the spotlight of a small town.

The logic to that kind of life was lost on Allison, but she couldn't expect a twelve-year-old girl to understand that the two of them were better off as they were. At the moment, a greater worry nagged at her. Her daughter had been communicating with a stranger on the Internet. She had given him their home address. Allison stepped back and sank to the edge of Jill's pink frilly bed, taking a pink stuffed cat from its resting place and hugging it to her as she tried to sound calmer than she felt. "Tell me more about this person you've been communicating with. How did you come to meet him?"

Jill turned in her chair, facing her. "I joined an online dating service."

Allison could only blink. She didn't know her daughter even knew about online dating services. For that matter, she knew next to nothing about them herself. True, she had heard a couple of her customers speak of dating via the Internet. Well, this was just too absurd. "Those sites cost money. How did you do this?"

"Grandma's credit card. It's only for ninety days and the first month was free."

Allison's jaw clenched. Her mother's involvement was no surprise. Ten years after finding herself suddenly a widow, Lydia Barker, fifty-five years young, had rediscovered sex. Thanks to Allison taking over the dress shop, Mom had newfound freedom to explore life. She had joined a square-dance club for singles in Midland and for the past year had been do-si-doing with a plumber named Frank. She was loving life again and had told Allison numerous times that she should be doing the same. Unable to keep her eyes from narrowing, Allison asked, "How did you use your grandmother's credit card? Is she a part of this?"

"Grandma agrees with me," Jill said, "but she doesn't know about online dating. I told her I wanted to buy you a present. I didn't lie. Not really."

"You're twelve years old. How could you join a dating service?"

"I didn't. I mean, it's not, I'm not— Well . . ."

"Jill, please tell me you didn't enter *me* in this dating thing."

Jill didn't answer. Her face puckered again.

"Jill?"

"I scanned one of your pictures and answered a bunch of questions and stuff. I answered like I thought you would."

Dismay widened Allison's eyes. "Good grief, Jill—"

"You got a lot of responses and this guy was the best."

Allison sat up straighter. "I did? I got responses? Really? What picture did you scan?"

"My favorite. The one of you at your senior prom."

Dear God. The way Allison had looked in her new frilly pink dress twelve years ago had lured an irresponsible teenage jerk from hiding. What had it caught the attention of this time? "Good Lord, Jill. I was a child. What is this guy, eighteen? Or worse yet, a pedophile?"

Allison thought she could actually hear the clatter of Jill's eyes rolling in her head.

"No, Mother. He's old. Thirty-five or something like that. What's a pedophile?"

"Never mind. How could he not know he was talking to a child?"

"Mother. I'll be thirteen in ten months. I can carry on a conversation like an adult."

Allison had to agree. She and her mother had always treated Jill as an adult. Consequently, the child was comfortable in adult company and was years more mature than her peers. But a single, thirty-five-year-old man looking for "companionship" had to be *really* looking for sex.

"Did he ever mention, uh, I mean, has he ever brought up the subject of, uh—"

"Sex?" Jill asked. "Once. But I told him I didn't like talking about that stuff. He wrote back that I was sweet and he liked that I was naive."

While Allison wondered if she should call the sheriff, Jill turned back to her computer. "Want to see his picture?"

"Heavens, no. I don't care what he looks like. I'm not going out with him."

Jill struck a key on the keyboard and turned to face her mother again while a sheet of paper slowly rolled out of the printer. "But, Mom, you're never going to meet anyone in this town. The only people you're around all day are women. The only men you see are the ones shopping for their wives. I've heard you say it a hundred times."

True. Allison had spoken at various times about the lack of men in her life. And at this moment, she wished she had used more discretion in letting Jill hear her.

Her daughter's expression grew more serious. The drama queen again. "You know, Mom, you're not getting any younger. Grandma says you'll never be any better looking than you are right now."

"Hmm. I'll have to thank Grandma personally for that one. What else has your grandmother told you?"

"She said you're so jaded by your past experience you've forgotten how to live. What does jaded mean, Mom?"

"It means I'm *definitely* going to have a talk with your grandma."

Jill thrust the black-and-white printout toward her mother. "Here, look at his picture. Isn't he cute?"

"It doesn't matter," Allison said, glancing down at the printout now in her hand. A cowboy. Great. She had been surrounded by them all her life. They were a living, breathing, hard-partying part of the West Texas social scene. The romantic notion of a hero on horseback rescuing her from her dull existence had died years ago. Not that cowboys weren't fun. Tight butts in tighter Wranglers had been the downfall of many a well-intentioned female. Allison was so glad she had matured beyond that.

The picture was a little grainy and the black-and-white print didn't reveal a lot of detail. "I swear I've seen him somewhere. Probably on *America's Most Wanted*. Or in a wedding announcement in the newspaper."

Allison studied the photo that looked so familiar more carefully. But how could she have seen him before? "How do we know this is even his real picture?"

Jill's face brightened. "Maybe he's famous and rich! Maybe the only way he can meet someone that isn't after his fame and money is to find someone who doesn't know who he really is." The twelve-year-old closed her eyes and lifted her shoulders. A dreamy smile played across her lips. "Isn't that romantic?"

Allison's brow knitted as she continued to study the print-out. She had definitely seen this man before . . . And, damn, he was really cute. "Do you even know his name?"

"Just his online name. Desperado."

Oh my God! Allison had a driving urge to close the curtains and bolt the doors. "Jill, when he gets here, *if* he gets here, I'm going to tell him the whole story and send him on his way. I'm not—"

"Noooo," Jill wailed, as if in pain. "Puh-leeze, Mommy. Just talk to him. He's nice. He used to be in rodeos. He rode bulls. He doesn't have any kids and he said he'd like to have a home and family. He might *like* you." She fell against her mother with a fierce hug and began to sob. "He might want *us,* Mom."

Allison felt like a heartless shrew. She supposed she could meet the guy outside on the porch, sit down and have a conversation. Lord knew, in her younger, wilder days she had met men in riskier situations . . . Hadn't she? "Shh, now. Quit crying. I'll meet him. But only for a little while, okay?"

I'm also keeping a baseball bat near the porch swing in case I need to defend myself.

Jill's tears dried at once. She leaped to her feet, grabbed Allison's hand, and began to tug her up the hall. "C'mon, Mom, I'll help you find something to wear."

The thought flitted through Allison's head that she really should get this kid into acting classes.

★　★　★

While the mouthwatering aromas of meat slowly searing over smoldering mesquite coals, fresh ears of corn steaming to tender, golden perfection, and tangy coleslaw tossed with pecans in a secret dressing swirled around him, Tag Freeman tasted a pungent barbecue sauce. He took a few seconds to savor the flavors—fresh chilies, chili powder, honey, vinegar, tomato sauce, even a little strong coffee. He gave his cook, Rafael, a thumbs-up.

From the very beginning of the cooking process, Tag kept an eye on the food served in his restaurant. His strict oversight began when he purchased a prime beef or pork carcass from a purveyor of fine meats. His attention went from there to the butchering and trimming of said carcass, to the secret seasoning he rubbed and massaged into the meat by hand, to the moment a rasher of tender, succulent brisket or a glistening rack of ribs was lovingly laid on a heavy white crockery plate.

Most of the time, every item on the menu of Tag Freeman's Double-Kicker Barbecue & Beer had his personal seal of approval before being served to the ever-growing crowds of customers frequenting his dining establishment. At one point, he had been so particular he had done his own butchering. A poor meat-cutting job could ruin a good piece of beef quicker than a cut cat.

While Tag knew the food was delicious, he also realized that as much as the quality food he served, the crowd attractor was himself. His customers wanted to see him and talk to him. He didn't mind a bit. He intended to capitalize on his fame as one of ProRodeo's greatest bullfighters while it was still in the forefront of the public's memories.

Nor was his business harmed by the fact that on any given night, a country music star or a ProRodeo champion might drop in and give customers a chance to rub shoulders with celebrity. Tonight, one of his oldest and best friends from his rodeo days, Quint Matthews, had called and said he was coming for dinner. Typically, with Quint, that could mean he might show up within the hour, in a day, or sometime this year, but the guy had also said he had a date in Salt Lick. Knowing how Quint was about women, Tag had a hunch he would stick to his schedule tonight.

Untying his apron and pulling it over his head, Tag winked at Rafael. "I'm gonna leave 'er to ya, compadre. I'm stepping out front, but I'll be back to help you out if you need it."

"No problema, jefe."

No problem, boss. Tag laughed at the young man's confidence. Only a twenty-year-old kid could undertake a new task with such a devil-may-care attitude. Tag had been twenty years old once himself—nearly twenty years ago.

And he had once walked without a limp, he thought as he rounded the long stainless-steel counter on his way to the dining room. A freak accident had ended his rodeo career and changed his life. He had been standing in the wrong place when, with no warning, a top shelf collapsed in a Save-A-Buck Discount City retail store and an avalanche of John Deere hedge trimmers, leaf blowers, and chain saws had struck him and fractured his back and hip. If he hadn't had lightning-quick reflexes honed by the years in his profession, he might have been hurt worse. Or he might not have survived.

In the early days after the accident, there had been a fear he wouldn't walk again, but Tag's iron will and a blessing from God spared him from being wheelchair-bound for the rest of his life. Every day he said a silent prayer of thanksgiving.

He'd had to sue, of course. His medical bills were enormous, his livelihood destroyed. He would never again step inside a rodeo arena as a bullfighter. He would never again bring home an enviable paycheck. He still collected a few endorsement fees from flush sponsors, but that well would dry up soon.

In the Midland courtroom, his lawyer had shown videos of him throwing his body between bull and rider, a superb athlete performing unthinkable feats with amazing agility. The video then switched to images of him in physical therapy learning to walk again. His lawyer had followed up by pointing out to the jurors that the same thing could have happened to any of them or their loved ones. The panel found "gross negligence," and the judge had ordered the giant retailer to pay handsomely.

Tag missed his former profession—the adrenaline rush that went with matching wits with a wily animal ten times his weight, the satisfaction accompanying the knowledge that he had saved some young man from being seriously mauled, maimed, or even killed. He missed the kinship of

ProRodeo, the rough and raucous camaraderie of cowboys. He missed the excitement of the crowds and the attention of the ladies.

But he had already faced the fact that Tag Freeman's days as a ProRodeo bullfighter were over. Now he caressed a safer and less violent mistress: cooking.

three

Debbie Sue Overstreet pulled her truck behind the Styling Station. In the nearly five years she had owned and operated the beauty salon, she had made this wide sweeping turn into this parking space more times than she could count, yet she still looked forward to doing it every day. She owed the feeling in large part to her partner and best friend, Edwina Perkins-Martin.

Edwina was more than her best friend; she was also her therapist, often applying the cold, hard slap of reality to Debbie Sue's stubborn chin. And she provided comic relief that kept Debbie Sue and the Styling Station's customers laughing.

Debbie Sue gathered her insulated lunch box, a stack of magazines, and her purse and slid from behind the steering wheel. Entering the Styling Station's back door, she heard Edwina's voice. "Well, Darlene, if that's what you want to do, that's fine. Last I heard, cash was still accepted in most places, so I don't think the Domestic Equalizers should be any different."

Mentally running through a list of the Darlenes she knew, Debbie Sue determined Edwina was on the phone with Darlene Duncan, the latest Domestic Equalizers client. They had helped the poor woman locate the focus of her cheating husband's diverted attention. The person with whom he had been canoodling had resided right under Darlene's nose all along—her brother's wife. It hadn't taken Perry Mason to figure that one out.

As Edwina hung up, Debbie Sue set her armload down on her workstation. "What did Darlene want, a refund?"

"Naw, she was just asking if she could pay us in quarters. She's been saving them up for a while from her vending machine route. I told her not to worry about it. Quarters spend just like real money."

"Ed, her fee was three hundred dollars. What are we gonna do with all that change? Did you tell her we accept credit and debit cards?"

"Sure did, but she says she cut up all of her credit cards," Edwina answered between gum smacks. "She's afraid of identity theft. Said she's been learning about it from TV news." The hairdresser blew a bubble the size of a baseball. She had taken up chewing wads of bubble gum to distract her from smoking.

"Why would anyone want to steal Darlene Duncan's identity?" Debbie Sue asked as she headed toward the storeroom refrigerator with her lunch. "Most people don't want to claim they even know her."

Edwina laughed.

Debbie Sue returned to the salon's front room, buttoning a bright blue smock. "Speaking of identity theft, did you see the newsletter from the bank? Stolen credit cards and identity theft are a big deal."

"I read it. Living where we personally know everybody who hands us a credit card, you just don't think about stuff like that happening. But Vic knows a lot about it."

"Naturally," Debbie Sue said. Edwina's husband, Vic Martin, was a retired navy SEAL. He knew a lot about *everything*.

"Well, he does know a lot," Edwina said with a touch of prideful indignation. "Just because he's retired doesn't mean he forgot everything or doesn't keep up. He says credit-card fraud is one of the ways terrorists get money to blow up stuff.

"He told me something else, too. You know how waiters and waitresses in the city restaurants always want you to give them your credit card and tell you they'll be your cashiers? Vic says there's this little electronic gadget where they can store a credit-card number when somebody gives them one to pay for a meal. Then they can use the number to buy things and get money."

"Wow," Debbie Sue said, frowning and mentally deciding to pay cash in restaurants in Odessa and Midland from now on. How unprofessional would it look if a private investigator had her identity stolen?

"It's so scary," she said. "Just last week I saw on the news where they arrested this guy in Dallas. He stole nearly a million dollars using other people's credit cards. He was in prison, mind you, and a bank had prisoners processing credit cards. When he got out, he had all these people's numbers and the secret codes. In prison, they taught him how to beat the system."

"I don't have to worry," Edwina said. "Anybody steals one of my credit cards, they're SOL. Every piece of plastic I've got is within about ten dollars of being maxed out."

"On TV, they said a lot of people have stopped using credit cards. Have you noticed a drop in customers paying us that way?"

"Maybe a little, but I just assumed they couldn't use them because they hadn't paid their bill."

"Hmm. Well, just remember, since you didn't get a credit card from Darlene, when she hauls that bushel of quarters in here"—Debbie Sue pointed a finger at Edwina—"*you* have to roll 'em."

"Me? Why the hell should I be left with that job?"

"Because *you* told her we'd take 'em." Debbie Sue gave her an evil grin. "Of course, it could be worse. She could have asked us to take one of those goats she raises. Then it would be you and Vic who would have to keep it in your backyard. Rocket Man would not like to share his pasture with a goat."

Edwina jammed her fists against her hips. "Well, I'll be go-to-hell. If I'd told her to pay us in chicken-fried steak, you'd be the first in line for that, wouldn't you?"

"Only if there's lots of peppered country gravy, Ed. Lots of peppered country gravy. And only if there's enough to share with Buddy."

Quint glanced at his watch again. He was an hour behind schedule. A long-winded auctioneer at the Abilene cattle auction had kept him cornered too long. He had intended to leave the auction early enough to get to Salt Lick and sit down with Debbie Sue before meeting his date. Now he was out of time. He plucked the cell phone from the dash and keyed in her beauty shop's number.

A voice answered on the first ring. "Domestic Equalizers. Don't get even, get evidence."

That twangier-than-usual Texas twang would belong to Debbie Sue's zany friend and partner, Edwina. He identified himself.

"Why, as I live and breathe," Edwina drawled. "Quint Matthews. The last time I saw you, sugar, you were squiring a redheaded piece of arm candy around Las Vegas."

The skinny brunette cackled louder than a flock of guinea hens and Quint had to hold the phone away from his ear.

Shit. He would never live it down, especially with people like Edwina, who was as full of bull as any woman he had ever met. "Is Debbie Sue around?"

"Sure, sweet lips. Just hang on. To the phone, that is." She guffawed again.

While Quint waited for Debbie Sue to come on the line, his mind spun backward to two years ago and the reason for

Edwina's raucous laughter. He had made Debbie Sue an offer she shouldn't have been able to refuse, but she had turned
him down and gone back to her ex-husband. On the re-
bound, Quint had involved himself in a very public affair
with a gorgeous redhead named Janine Grubbs. The spotlight's glare generated by a rodeo cowboy dating a Las Vegas
beauty was blinding.

The glorious publicity distracted him from the fact that
she kept putting him off when it came to sex. At the time he
had given that part of their relationship little thought because for him, finding sex had never been difficult. But good
press and photo ops were rare as duck lips. In his mind, the
front-page exposure made up for missed opportunities for
fornication.

Thinking of the experience, he cringed. Janine had not been
a sweet, cream-filled bonbon. Instead, he/she/it turned out to
be a sugar-free, artificially flavored surprise, complete with
nuts. In the testosterone-steeped world of rodeo competition,
an affair with a transsexual was more disastrous than having a
bad case of diarrhea when you had drawn a rank bull.

"Quint, is that you?"

Debbie Sue came on the line at last. "It's me, darlin'. I'm
running late."

The dark blue sedan followed Quint's red pickup as they
breezed past the Salt Lick city-limits sign that rose bravely
from its arid surroundings. *Oh, no!* Quint was turning into
the Styling Station's parking lot. If the two hairdressers who

worked there came outside, remaining undetected would be impossible. Those women probably knew every car and truck in Salt Lick. They just might take notice of an unfamiliar one. Attempting to look nonchalant by reading a map or a newspaper or talking on a cell phone would stand out like a rain cloud in the West Texas sky. Even amateur detectives would recognize the ruse.

"Just stay out of sight," the sedan driver mumbled. "Don't talk to anyone and wait for the right moment."

Reaching Salt Lick, Quint began to think of his blind date for the evening, Allison Barker. A question formed in his mind. Was someone he had met on the Internet really a blind date?

From the very first e-mails they had exchanged, he'd had doubts about their compatibility. Though sweet and demure might be desirable attributes for preachers' wives and schoolteachers, such traits didn't excite Quint Matthews. But she had seemed to be in such awe of him, his ego had overtaken his good sense, as it often did, he privately acknowledged, and he had arranged to meet her. After what he had been through, he reasoned, hero worship might be just what he needed.

She had a twelve-year-old daughter. Children weren't high on Quint's list of requisites. He had to consider, though, that having a kid proved she had the right female parts, an asset of which he was acutely aware these days. Not that they'd had a conversation about anatomy. She had been unwilling even to discuss sex and that intrigued him. Perhaps she was just inexperienced. If that were the case, it was a deficiency he was able and eager to remedy.

For a reason he couldn't name and for the first time in a long time, he felt happy and relaxed. All week he'd had a feeling something good was on the horizon. In fact, just today, before leaving Abilene, he felt so upbeat he had dared to stop at Luskey's Western Wear and had given the Luskey's employees and customers a chance to see a three-time world-champion rodeo star up close and personal.

What his fans would never know was that turning into Luskey's parking lot had taken the guts he used to call on back when he straddled two thousand pounds of pissed-off bull in the rodeo arena. Why? Because the last time he had been in Luskey's, on the life-size cardboard cutout of him that usually stood tall in the boot department, someone had painted eye shadow on his eyelids and lipstick on his lips. They had even drawn earrings on his earlobes.

Today, to his relief, the vandalized cutout was gone, replaced by a newer one in pristine condition. He had even signed a few autographs for the folks milling around the store. Yes, sir, it was starting to feel good again to be Quint Matthews.

Allison slipped her arms into yet another blouse. "How's this one?"

Jill shook her head. "No, Mom. With that dumb collar, you look like a nun."

Allison thought the navy long straight skirt and white long-sleeved blouse fit her well. She thought all the other outfits had looked fine, too, but Jill had vetoed every one of them. Now she didn't know if she was dressing to impress or repel. This whole evening had taken on a surreal feeling, as if she were auditioning for a reality TV show.

"I'm going to go see what Grandma has in her closet," the twelve-year-old said.

"Oh no you don't. I'm not going out in my mother's clothes . . . Besides, they won't fit. I'm four inches taller than Mom and my boobs are bigger and . . . well, I've tried most of them on already. They're too small."

"But her clothes are cool. I'll bet I can find something."

"No, I'm wearing this. I'm tired of trying on. This skirt and blouse are fine. There are worse things than looking like a nun."

Jill groaned. "Then can I help with your hair? Add a little gel? Fix it like Edwina does when you go see her?"

Allison's hair was her best attribute, a thick swath of lustrous auburn. Kept trimmed to chin length by Edwina at the Styling Station, it required little additional help. Running a brush through it was mostly all Allison ever did. But Edwina could improve any hairdo and did so when Allison went to see her. "Okay, I'll let you do that and I'll even wear those dangly gold earrings you gave me for Mother's Day."

"Those are perfect. Oh, Mom, you're going to be so beautiful. Even if you are dressed like a nun."

★ ★ ★

Just as Quint feared, the Styling Station was dark and the Closed sign hung behind the glass in the front door. He was glad he hadn't scheduled a time. Debbie Sue would have waited for him and showing up late would have meant a tongue-lashing. He had never known a woman who could dish it out like Debbie Sue. That had always been part of her appeal. She took no b.s. from him.

After driving another block, he slowed as he approached the dress shop of the woman with whom he had been communicating for the past month. Almost the Rage. Catchy name for a dress shop. Funny, but in all of his trips to Salt Lick, he had never noticed the shop. Not that he had been looking for women's clothing, but he had a keen eye, and in a town of less than two thousand, seeing all of Main Street didn't take many trips.

The front of Almost the Rage looked as if it had been freshly painted. Pale yellow. A dark blue-and-yellow striped awning shaded the two large display windows on each side of the entrance. The clothing, displayed without mannequins, looked stylish. Being a clotheshorse, Quint considered himself an excellent judge.

But the most important thing was that the business really existed and was really located there on the main street of town, just as Allison had told him. So far, so good.

He gave a quick glance at his sideview mirror and noticed the dark blue Neon again. He had spotted it earlier on the highway and it had stayed with him all the way from Abilene. Was he being tailed? *Shit. Not again.* He tapped his brake and slowed, watching in the side mirror for the Neon driver's reaction.

The sedan slowed, too, turned left onto a residential street, then disappeared in a cloud of caliche dust. Relieved, Quint chuckled at himself. He didn't want to become one of those paranoid losers who saw someone lurking in every shadow, but what the press had put him through gave him justification. For months after the Janine Grubbs fiasco, the ever-prying reporters had hounded him, as if there were no other celebrities to fill the pages of their sleazy tabloids.

The bastards were worse than vultures landing on roadkill, tearing meat from the carcass and fighting over the bones. They had dug up information he had long forgotten. One had even been able to solicit a "no comment" from his ex-wife, Christine, who had once been Miss Rodeo America. It was the first time he had known her to keep her mouth shut when asked for an opinion. That uncharacteristic behavior had fueled wagging tongues and even more tell-all articles.

Glancing again at the address he had written on a piece of notepaper, Quint made a quick turn, drove two blocks, and parked in front of the first house on the left. It was just as she had described. Nothing fancy. Low-slung, redbrick, well-kept lawn, and two carved jack-o'-lanterns on the front porch.

He had considered picking up a bouquet of fall flowers as he passed through Midland but decided against it.

No point in going overboard. This might turn out to be one of those meetings he would just as soon forget. Be-sides, showing up with flowers would be overkill. He was Quint Matthews. He always made a good first impression.

four

The driver of the dark blue sedan drove onto a deserted side street, pulled to a stop, and released a great breath. God, that was a close call!

The sudden appearance of Quint's brake lights and his hard glare reflected in his truck's side mirror had sent a chill of terror up the sedan driver's spine. It wasn't clear which body part was about to give way—tear glands or bladder and bowels.

But the sedan driver couldn't give up. Too much was at stake. *Be calm. All you have to do is be at the right place at the right time and catch the egotistical hero when he falls.*

Maybe a different vehicle would be a good idea. If only an Enterprise car rental existed in Salt Lick. The pathetic Dodge Neon could be exchanged for a car of another make and color, as well as one that had more than four cylinders.

Compared with Quint's big diesel, a four-cylinder automobile was a roller skate.

But a car rental business in Salt Lick was wishful thinking to the extreme. Salt Lick was such a small backward place and it was full of hicks. Most of the residents probably didn't even know how to drive anything but a truck.

Hmm, the sedan driver thought. Before continuing, maybe a trip to Midland or Odessa was called for. Perhaps renting a truck and blending into the surroundings made more sense.

The sound of the doorbell sent Allison's blood pressure skyward. Good Lord, he had actually shown up. She had a sudden urge to pee. "Jill, do not open that door until I get back."

"But, Mom, he'll leave."

"If he leaves, he leaves. Do not open that door."

From the bathroom, she heard Jill shout, "My mom'll be right out. She had to take a leak."

Well, that bit of news must have eliminated the possibility of ever meeting this stranger. He had surely bolted. Besides that, even the neighbors must have heard Jill's yell. Allison closed her eyes and shook her head.

As she entered the living room, through the opaque glass in the front door, she saw a silhouette of a figure wearing a cowboy hat. So he hadn't left. A mix of relief and dread coursed through her. "Best to just get this over with," she mumbled.

She opened the door and got her first look at "Desperado."

He was holding one of the jack-o'-lanterns she and Jill had carved, peering into it. He quickly clapped the top back onto the pumpkin, set it back on the porch, and brushed his hands together. With a huge smile, he swept the hat from his head and held it in front of himself. "Ma'am," he said.

His self-assurance spanned the distance between them. He looked even more familiar in person than he did in the black-and-white printout from Jill's computer. But Allison's mind was whirling and she couldn't collect her thoughts enough to decide why.

He had a square jaw, sky-blue eyes, and Brad Pitt hair that looked mussed and sexy, even after wearing a hat. "Uh, how do you do," she managed, and stuck out her right hand.

"You must be Allison," he said in a rich deep voice with a thick Texas drawl.

Good grief! This stranger, this person on whom she had never laid eyes, knew her name. The reality of what her daughter had done washed over her. What else had Jill told him besides her name? "Allison? I mean, uh . . . yes, Allison. That's me. You must be . . ."

Good Lord, she didn't know *his* name.

He laughed, an easy confident chuckle. Charisma. He had buckets of it. In spite of her anxiety, she couldn't keep from grinning like a loon.

"We never did get around to my name, did we? Quint. My name's Quint. May I come in?"

She felt like Scarlett O'Hara. What Southern belle, living

or dead, had ever been able to resist cowboy charm? What the heck, she decided. She didn't want to make a snap judgment, but she just might owe her daughter an apology. "Oh, forgive me, Clint. I'm so sorry. Of course, come in, please." She stood back to allow him entrance.

"It's Quint, ma'am," he said, stepping through the doorway. "Not Clint. My name is *Quint*."

So much for meeting him and talking to him out on the front porch. Now she worried over how her house must look. She hadn't had the time or inclination to care earlier. It hadn't once occurred to her she might want to carry this thing further, but the temptation was now almost irresistible.

He wasn't a big man, she noticed as he passed in front of her. Only a few inches taller than her five feet eight, but it was hard to tell his exact height when he was wearing a huge hat and . . .

Her eyes traveled to his feet and full-quill ostrich boots. Oh, yes, cowboy boots. If she knew cowboys, even if he couldn't buy groceries, he had probably spent several hundred dollars on his boots.

"Oh, Quint. I'm so sorry. I misunderstood. Um, is that short for something?"

Looking closer, she could see he was dressed in the latest Western garb—stiffly starched Wranglers that hugged his muscular-looking legs like gloves, a tan leather jacket that showed off broad shoulders. It partially covered a green-and-tan plaid shirt. His belt buckle was silver with gold inlay. The pale gray hat in his hand appeared to be beaver, no doubt the

100X grade. Her knowledge of fashion told her it had cost more than a monthly house payment. She had no way of knowing if he had money in the bank, but she could see he had made a sizable deposit in his clothing.

"Yes, ma'am. Quinton. Quinton William Matthews. Quint Matthews. That's me, *Quint* Matthews."

Allison arched her brow as she closed the door behind him. He didn't seem nervous or ill at ease, so why had he felt the need to mention his name over and over? "Uh, please have a seat. May I offer you something to drink? Iced tea, water? Perhaps a cup of coffee?" She had nothing else in the house.

"Coffee would be just fine, ma'am, if you've got it made. Evenings are getting a little cooler. Something warm would be welcome."

Blinking and staring and trying to remember the last time a man had addressed her as "ma'am," Allison nodded, then excused herself.

In the kitchen, she found Jill already adding scoops of dark coffee to the Mr. Coffee. The twelve-year-old began to talk in a rush. "He's cute, isn't he, Mom? I think he's *real* cute. Do you like him? Are you gonna go out? Aren't you glad I did this now? Did you see what he's driving? I love his jacket. I'll bet it's real leather."

"Whoa. Keep your voice down. He's cute, okay? I told you I'd talk to him. I'm not promising anything. Not *anything*."

Punching the coffeemaker's on switch, Jill babbled on, unaffected by her mother's skepticism. "You could have a country wedding on his ranch. I could be in it. A brides-maid. And I could wear a long dress. And high heels. And I could wear makeup. Can daughters be bridesmaids?"

Allison stopped reaching for cups and grasped her daughter's shoulders, forcing her to turn toward her. "Honey. Looks and clothes aren't everything. You need to know someone's heart before you give him yours."

"Well, you have to admit he's better than that last guy you went out with."

Allison made a mental sigh. Jill referred to Vernon Hobson, Salt Lick's only accountant. When Allison had gone out with him, he was newly divorced.

The only good thing that could be said about Vernon was he wasn't a twin. It hadn't been so bad that he had taken her to dinner at Hogg's Drive-in. After all, Hogg's was a little like a museum and just being there was entertaining. Barr Hogg, the owner, claimed Elvis had eaten there once. The place was filled with Elvis memorabilia and the jukebox played only Elvis's recordings.

Besides, what choices were there in Salt Lick? Kay's Koffee Kup had closed, which left the Sunrise Donut & Sushi Bar that an Asian couple from California had just opened. Allison hadn't yet acquired a taste for sushi and somehow the combination of doughnuts and raw fish seemed un-nerving.

No, the problem with Vernon had become apparent when he paid for dinner with a "buy one, get one free" coupon. She didn't know if it was her meal or his that the "free" part of the coupon covered, but it was just too much that he didn't think she was worth the Hogg's Chuck Wagon Meal, which was a four-dollar burger plate. The last straw had been when the conversation throughout the meal turned out to be a debate with himself about whether the evening's expense was tax deductible. Frugal was one thing, but stingy was another. "I'll admit he's better than Vernon. So far."

"Yes!" Jill made a fist and pumped her arm. "Just think, Mom. He may be your knight in shining armor."

"Let's just wait and see, okay? Aluminum foil is shiny, too, but it can be crinkled."

Quint shifted in the chair, attempting to hear the conversation going on in the other room. Maybe Allison was talking to her daughter. Or, the way his luck had been running lately, the voice could belong to a second personality that lived in her psyche.

Before his rambling thoughts could take him down that path, Allison appeared in the doorway. "I forgot to ask how you like your coffee."

Quint shot up from his seat, feeling guilty for eavesdropping. "Black, thanks. I sure hope I'm not putting you to too much trouble."

"Don't be silly. I'll only be a minute."

She had startling green eyes, he noticed, and shiny roan-colored hair. It made a big swoop over one eye, sexy as all get out. He made a quick scan of her body. She didn't look like the former Olympic athlete she had told him she was online. Still, Quint thought as she left the room, she was a damn fine-looking woman. He liked that she was tall and slender. Despite a blouse with an oversize collar, he could see she was big-boobed and he imagined strong, athletic legs beneath her long skirt.

He returned to his seat, hearing more talking and, this time, laughter. Unless she was a ventriloquist, two people were in the kitchen.

She returned to the living room with a younger version of herself in tow. She handed the steaming mug of coffee to him and set her own on the table opposite him.

"Quint, this is my daughter, Jill." She looked to her side, but a child was not to be seen.

Quint leaned and looked around her. The kid was standing so close to her mother's backside it appeared they were Velcro-'d together.

"Jill?" Allison took the girl by the wrist and led her to her side as if she were a balky horse. "Honey, let me introduce you to someone. Jill, say hello to Mr. Matthews."

The girl stared at the floor and mumbled a hello.

Why, bless her heart, she was shy. Quint bent and ducked his head attempting to make eye contact. "Well, hello, pretty little lady." When Jill said no more, he looked back at Allison. "So this is your budding actress?"

A puzzled expression crossed Allison's face, but he bent again and spoke to the daughter. "Your mom's told me so much about you. She's real proud of your accomplishments. Are you excited about going to New York City?"

"New York City?" Allison echoed.

"Oops, did I let the cat out of the bag?" Quint switched looks between daughter and mother.

"No, no, not at all," Allison said. "I just forgot I had mentioned it to you. Jill, honey, why don't you tell Mr. Matthews about your trip to New York."

"It's nothing, really," Jill mumbled, still looking at the floor.

"Nothing?" Quint said. "Why, I'd hardly call a summer program for gifted teens nothing."

"Oh, me either," Allison agreed.

"I guess you can appreciate how nervous she is," Quint said to Allison. "You weren't much older than her when you tried out for the Olympics, were you?"

Allison looked at him, her eyes blinking. Did she have a tic or something? Or had he hit a nerve? Even after all these years, losing the opportunity to participate in the Olympic Games had to be devastating. Being an athlete himself, he could appreciate the lingering pain. "I'm sorry if I said something wrong—"

"Oh, no, you haven't said anything wrong." Allison released her daughter's wrist. "Excuse me. I'm going to get some cookies from the kitchen."

Shit. Cookies usually had nuts. His last allergic reaction to nuts had occurred in this very town and had sent him to an Odessa hospital. "Thanks, but I never eat cookies." He patted his stomach. "Gotta watch my weight."

"Well, I eat cookies," Allison said through a stiff smile, "and it's time I had one. Jill, why don't you come into the kitchen and help me?"

"I'm fine here," Jill said, plopping into a chair.

Still smiling, Allison gripped her daughter by the upper arm and pulled her to her feet. "Come on, Meryl Streep. I need your help."

"Ow, ow," the kid wailed. Then: "Who's Meryl Streep?"

"Never mind." Allison guided her daughter out of the room, speaking to Quint over her shoulder. "Quint, we'll be right back."

He had another sip of coffee as he stared after them. Both of them were a little uptight, but things seemed to be going okay. It was probably his fault. He'd messed up, mentioning the Olympic trials. He made a mental note to watch what he said and refrain from mentioning her being forced to give up the Miss Texas title, too.

As soon as Allison guided Jill into the kitchen, the girl yanked her arm free and made a beeline toward the back door that opened to the yard. "I'm going to see if Susan Kay is home yet."

"Get back here now," Allison said sternly. "Tell me what other fabrications you've told this man."

Jill's eyes welled up with tears. "I told him those things in the beginning, Mom. When we were first talking. I didn't think he'd ever come here."

"It wasn't right to lie to him, Jill. He seems like a nice person." Allison leaned against the cabinet and brushed her hair from her brow. "Now I don't know what to do."

"You aren't going to tell him the truth, are you? He'll

think I'm a psycho. A total dweeb. He'll leave and never come back." Jill began to sniffle.

"Tell me right now what other stories you've told him. I can handle anything, but I have to know about it first."

"I told him just one more thing," Jill said meekly.

"What? What is it?"

"I told him you had to give up your crown as Miss Texas when you got pregnant with me."

Allison's jaw dropped and she gasped. "My Lord, Jill. What made you go to those extremes?"

"I had to, Mom! I didn't have anything else to tell him. Our life's so dull. The truth is, Mom, he's famous. I thought you'd recognize him when I showed you his picture. He's been World Champion All-Around Cowboy lots of times. He advertises stuff everywhere. He knows George Strait. I couldn't let him think we're losers."

Losers? Allison was stunned. She had no idea Jill viewed their lives in such a negative way. But she couldn't dwell on the worry because a lightbulb moment flashed in her head and distracted her. "My God. That's Quint Matthews."

five

Debbie Sue left the Styling Station not just tired and worn out, but tense. She headed home with odd emotions confusing her thoughts. Memories of her long-ago relationship with Quint Matthews and her years in rodeo roiled in her mind. She had met Quint at sixteen, and from the first, he had affected her in an unsettling way.

Ten miles later she reached the cattle-guard entrance to the home she shared with her husband, Buddy Overstreet. In almost all ways, no two men could be more opposite than Quint and Buddy, she thought as she eased up the long caliche driveway. Quint was smart, exciting, and good-looking. He was fun and crazy, always shooting for the stars . . . But a woman—*any* woman—would be downright foolish to let herself believe half the words that fell from his mouth.

Buddy was plenty smart, too, but the difference was Buddy was steady and loyal. No matter the circumstances,

Debbie Sue never doubted his affection. He was more truthful than George Washington; his word was a bond and he just instinctively knew the difference between right and wrong. Wherever he went, he commanded respect. Besides that, he was big and tough, and hands down, he was the best-looking man in Texas.

On the far side of the twenty-five-acre pasture, she saw Rocket Man grazing; he was her horse from her rodeoing days. Another part of her brain noted the sparse, dry pasture and wondered if he had enough to eat. She regarded the paint gelding as a best friend. He had made her a barrel-racing champion in ProRodeo and he deserved to spend the rest of his life grazing and lazing in the sun.

In a matter of minutes she was rewarded with the best sight on earth—the old, modest dwelling where she had grown up and where she and Buddy now resided. There were grander and newer houses to be had, even in Salt Lick, but they were houses, not homes. Nothing compared to the warmth, serenity, and pure happiness she associated with this place.

She pulled her pickup under a carport attached to one side of the house, grabbed her purse from the passenger's seat, and scooted out. Three dogs met her with energetic enthusiasm. Each of the mixed-breed strays had found his way to her home and into her heart since she and Buddy had moved here two years earlier. Jim Beam, Jack Daniel's, and José Cuervo—or commonly called Jim, Jack, and Joe—seemed to appreciate their good fortune and yapped and jumped and ran about in a frenzy. Debbie Sue laughed. "Settle down, boys, settle down. You're acting like I've been gone a week."

She reached inside the back door for the bag of dog biscuits she kept on a shelf and tossed each mutt a treat. After giving each of them a loving scratch behind the ears, she went into the house with Quint still on her mind.

On the one hand, she was relieved he hadn't made it to the salon before she closed. She felt guilty enough that she hadn't already told Buddy her ex-lover had called a few days ago. She hadn't told him because she didn't look forward to opening up old wounds. Still, no way was she going to keep a conversation with Quint a secret from Buddy, either. Her husband was her soul mate. They had made promises to each other when they remarried. She wouldn't jeopardize that trust—not for Quint, not for anyone.

On the other hand, her nosy side was dying to know the mess her old friend might have gotten himself into this time and how he thought the Domestic Equalizers could help him.

The only logical conclusion was that his problems involved a woman. In that area, the possibilities were endless— married, separated, divorced, engaged, underage, or another gold digger. Poor ol' Quint had been through them all. Even someone confused about his/her sexual identity or preference wasn't off-limits to Quint. Where women were concerned, there hadn't been a man so intent on his own self-destruction as Quint Matthews since Adam took a bite out of that apple.

She had agreed to talk to him because if she had a flaw

in her character, it was undying loyalty—even when it went undeserved—to those who had crossed the threshold of her life and left footprints.

Together, she and Quint had been rough-and-ready teenagers chasing the rodeo circuit and the dreams it offered. On her seventeenth birthday she had given him her virginity behind a horse trailer at a rodeo in Lubbock and nothing could change that.

In the ensuing years she had seen sides of him that most people hadn't. The cockiness he never failed to show masked a host of insecurities. He had grown up with disinterested parents. His dad had been consumed with making money. His mom was determined to spend his dad's every penny. Golfing, shopping, day spas, and jetting from one fad watering hole to the next was her life. Debbie Sue had always believed that Quint's desire to show he was no slouch at making money himself was an effort to prove something to his dad.

Basically, Quint was a good person. A real heart beat inside his chest, faint at times, but still there.

When she was divorced from Buddy, Quint had come closer than anyone to winning her over, but thank God she and Buddy had mended their fences. Living apart from him wasn't a formula for her continued happiness.

But that didn't mean she couldn't care about Quint's well-being, did it?

Oh, shit, here she was again, making seemingly rational decisions based on worthless assumptions. Hmm. Maybe she had *two* character flaws.

Well, she would hear Quint out. Rodeo people always had been and still were Quint's family. And just because neither he nor she performed in the arena anymore didn't mean they didn't have the mud and the blood in their veins. Just ask Garth Brooks. He sang a perfect song about it. In the end, more than likely, she would try to help Quint the best she knew how and deal with the fit Buddy would have.

She made her way to the bathroom up the hall from the master bedroom and shed her clothes. A day's worth of permanent solution, hair dye, and cigarette smoke propelled her to the shower. Midway into her second shampoo a large masculine hand appeared inside the plastic shower curtain. She giggled and dodged as the hand reached and finally found her breast. "Did you find what you're looking for?" she shouted over the roar of the water.

"Not really," a deep voice answered. "I was hoping to find my wife, but this doesn't feel like her."

"Oh, yeah? And just who does it feel like?"

"My wife's kinda flat-chested. This feels like Dolly Parton. But I can't figure out what she's doing in Salt Lick and, stranger yet, inside my shower."

On a laugh, Debbie Sue swept back the shower curtain and confronted her husband. He was as naked as she was. "Fuck you, Buddy Overstreet."

He gave her a leering grin and stepped into the shower. "That's kinda what I had in mind."

Debbie Sue wrapped her arms around his waist and pressed her face against his solid chest. *Happy* wasn't the word to describe how she felt with Buddy. In his arms was where she belonged. She hadn't planned on this approach for delivering her news about Quint, but she wasn't above taking advantage of the situation either.

Almost an hour later, definitely less tense than she had been earlier, Debbie Sue snuggled closer to the warmth of Buddy's big body in their king-size bed. "I think it's my turn to cook supper," she murmured, nuzzling his neck. "I need to go."

His hold tightened on her waist. "Hmm, I could eat a horse."

"Don't say that after what we went through with Rocket Man." Debbie Sue still hadn't forgotten how, in a daring night raid, she, Edwina, and Paige McBride-Atwater had rescued Rocket Man from a horse thief and the slaughter-house. Buddy hadn't forgotten it either, though she wished he would. It had been a little bit of a fiasco.

"Let's stay here ten more minutes," Buddy said. "Then I'll help you cook."

As the minutes passed Quint's phone call niggled at her. Finally, she said, "Hey, guess who called the Domestic Equalizers?" It sounded better to say he called the business instead of calling her personally.

"A bill collector."

"No, silly. These days, I'm keeping the bills paid."

"I give up. Who called?"

"Quint." There. It was out. She held her breath waiting for the outburst.

"Matthews? Quint Matthews called you?" Buddy moved

her away from him and looked into her face, his deep brown eyes boring a hole all the way to her soul.

"Not me. He called the Domestic Equalizers. There's a difference."

"Not as far as I'm concerned. There's no reason the son of a bitch should be calling you."

"Don't get upset. He wants to talk to Edwina and me when he's in town about—"

"He's coming to town?" Buddy pushed her farther away. "He's coming to town to talk to *you*?"

"No. He said—"

"I don't care what he said." A muscle in Buddy's square jaw clenched and Debbie Sue recognized the warning. "You're not gonna talk to him."

"It's business," she countered. "He needs help with a problem and he called us. That's why we started the Equalizers, Buddy, to help people. You know I don't care about Quint in the way you're thinking."

"What I know is that you did once. And how he still feels about you is what bothers me. He tried to take you away from me. He's not getting the chance to do it again."

"You're being silly, Buddy. I've never loved anyone but you, and besides, we were divorced when I went out with Quint. It's not like I was cheating on you."

Buddy swung his feet to the floor and stood up. Both hands went to his hips and he glared down at her. She had a hard time not laughing. The angry look on his face was scarcely one she would expect to see on a naked man when she was naked, too.

"Debbie Sue, I'm not gonna argue with you. I forbid you to see him and that's it. End of discussion."

Somewhere in the silent immense universe, a bell rang and a part of her over which she had no control crouched and put up fists, poised to come out fighting. "You forbid? . . . You? Forbid?"

She sprang to her feet, stood up in the middle of the mattress, and glared down at him, her body language mirroring his. "Buddy, you know damn well you're not supposed to *forbid* me to do anything. You promised you wouldn't do that to me again."

He flung a hand in the air. "Okay, maybe *forbid* was the wrong word. I don't and won't forbid you to do anything. It's just that I can't stand that skirt-chasing lowlife. I don't trust him. Plain and simple, I don't want you seeing him."

She leaned toward him, tapping her collarbone with her fingertips. "What about me? Don't you trust me?"

"You know I do." Buddy reached up for her, but she took a step backward, the unsteady mattress surface almost tripping her.

"Then listen to yourself. If you really trusted me you wouldn't be afraid of Quint."

"I'm not afraid of him," Buddy said. "It's just that he's always strutted around like he's the only rooster in the chicken coop. And now he's got all that damn money. I never liked him, even before y'all got together."

Debbie Sue gave him the squint eye. "So you're saying that any good, paying customer the Domestic Equalizers gets you have to like first?"

"You know that's not what I'm saying. I have good reason not to want Quint around. Trouble follows him everywhere he goes. I don't want you getting caught in the middle of it."

"I'm flattered you're jealous, Buddy, but—"

"How would you feel if Kathy called me up out of the blue and asked me to help her? How would that set with you?"

While she and Buddy had been divorced he had been seriously involved with a schoolteacher from Odessa, a fact that still irked. Debbie Sue had an old score to settle with Kathy Boczkowski and would love nothing better than a chance to scratch her eyes out. That aside, Buddy's argument made sense, but Debbie Sue couldn't relent too easily. "That's different," she said.

"Why is it different?" Buddy made a quick lunge, grabbed her around the knees, and hauled her over his shoulder. Her long hair cascaded down his back.

"Stop," she said, squirming to free herself. "Put me down. Where are you taking me?"

He trekked toward the bathroom. "Why is it different?" he asked again.

"Because you're civilized. With Quint, you'd conduct yourself like a decent human being. I, on the other hand, would snatch Kathy's fucking head bald and paint it like an Easter egg. Where are you taking me?"

They arrived in the bathroom and Buddy turned on the shower. He let go of a deep laugh. "I'm gonna wash your mouth out with soap. And I'm not gonna stop there."

He placed her inside the shower and stepped in after her. Debbie Sue wrapped her arms around him and spoke into his chest. "I love you, Buddy. I'll always love you and nothing, nothing can ever change that."

Buddy tilted her chin up and looked down into her eyes. She could see how much he loved her, and just knowing that a man as honest and good as Buddy had such feeling for her made her heart swell.

"Okay," he said. "Do what you think you have to, Flash. Just promise me you'll be careful. Don't get into something over your head and don't give that bastard a chance to get you alone. Keep Edwina with you when you're in his company."

Debbie Sue giggled. "You say that like it's an option. I promise I'll be careful, and if it'll make you feel better, for Quint, I'll up our standard fee."

"That'll work," Buddy said, and began to wash her between her thighs.

Later, after Buddy left the bathroom, Debbie Sue stood in front of the vanity mirror drying her hair. Telling Buddy hadn't been as bad as she had thought. So why did she still feel uneasy? The answer was simple. Buddy was right. Trouble and Quint were tied together like twisted vines and already she could feel the tendrils of a persistent invisible runner crawling up her leg.

six

Was the woman baking those damn cookies?

Quint could hear a whispery conversation coming from the kitchen. At least she was still in the house and hadn't slipped out a back door. He glanced at his wristwatch and saw that little time had passed since he arrived. So why did he feel as if he had been sitting here an hour?

Allison stumped him. She was either very good at playing games or just flat-out not impressed with Quint Matthews. There had been a few times when a gal hadn't been taken with him and all he had to offer. That hadn't bothered him in the past because, usually, he wasn't interested either. One disinterest canceled out the other.

This time was different. This time, he *was* interested. He didn't know if the challenge of her not being overwhelmed by his presence struck a competitive chord or if he was just tired of being alone. Though in many ways his life had been richer than most men's dreams, it had been poor in substance and he knew that. For a while now he had been feeling a need to seek out something meaningful with a nice woman like Allison Barker appeared to be.

Then again, maybe he was just horny.

Well, the reason didn't matter. The evening's outcome was what he would concentrate on. If he knew anything from experience, he knew how the evening would end. So, dammit, he would sit here and wait for those damn cookies. And hope they didn't have nuts.

As if she had been waiting in the wings for a cue, Allison reappeared, empty-handed. "I'm awfully sorry," she said. "I thought I had cookies, but I was wrong."

Quint stood up and showered her with his best dazzling smile. "That's okay. We're going out to eat, aren't we? Why spoil dinner?"

There it was again. That befuddled expression on her face. Maybe she had a memory problem. Maybe she was just so busy with being a single mom, running her own business, and trying to get from day to day she had forgotten the plans they had made.

Or, wait a minute. Maybe she was e-mailing so many other men she had gotten her facts and dates mixed up.

Competition. The very thought made him stand a little taller. If there was anything into which he could sink his teeth, it was competition. In his opinion, a more potent driving force didn't exist in man or animal. Viagra might jump-start the sexual juices, but there was no drug in existence that could instill the desire to win. He could almost taste the adrenaline coursing through his system. "Now don't be telling me you can't make it, darlin'. I drove all this way to take the prettiest gal in Texas out to dinner. You wouldn't disappoint me, would you?"

She bit down on her lower lip. He took this as a good sign. At least she was thinking about it.

"Look," she said. "You wouldn't be too disappointed if we just stayed here and visited a little more, would you?"

"You mean, like talk?"

She laughed, a warm and sincere laugh.

Damn, she had a pretty smile, though she didn't look much like the picture she had posted online. Of course, he had always known the picture wasn't current. She said she was thirty-one and the picture was of a teenage kid. A woman's age didn't matter anyway. Women were women. He liked them all.

"Why, yes, talk," she said. "We could get to know each other better."

He was getting hungry and he had been visiting with her for a month now. What the hell else did she need to know? "Get to know each other better?" he repeated.

"Exactly. I'm not in the habit of leaving the house with a man I don't know. I just wouldn't be comfortable."

He sighed mentally, but he wasn't ready to yield. "But you've known me for a month."

"Talking online isn't the same thing as meeting in person. Let's just visit a little longer. Perhaps we could go out to dinner another night."

"Tell you what. I've got a friend in this town who can vouch for me. Debbie Sue Pr— Overstreet. Know her?"

"Yes. Yes, I do."

He plucked his phone from his belt and began to scroll through his phone index for Debbie Sue's number. "I'll give her a call. She can tell you I'm okay."

A knowing expression came into her eyes. "That isn't necessary. I see Debbie Sue and Edwina often. If she thinks you're okay, that's good enough for me. But I thought you had business in Salt Lick."

"I do, but it can wait. I decided it was time I met you, and I'm glad I did. I'd be honored for you and Jill to join me tonight for dinner. I want you to meet one of my old friends."

"You want Jill to come, too? That's wonderful."

Quint knew the tried-and-true trail to a single mother's heart was through her kid. Inviting Jill hadn't been planned, but he had yet to meet the woman who didn't love having her little darling noticed and even invited. It made major points, though he also believed that most of the time, women didn't really want to drag along their offspring.

He waited for her answer. The ball was in her court. Since she seemed to be floundering, he decided to put some top-spin on the delivery. "I have a confession. Jill's responsible for bringing us together."

"Oh? I mean, uh, well . . . uh—"

"Once I found out you had a child, I was immediately interested in you. I love kids and I can't think of a harder job than raising one alone. I admire women who do it, especially when there are other options nowadays. It takes strength of character to shoulder that much responsibility."

Her sigh was nearly audible. "Ohhh! That's so sweet of you. It *can* be hard sometimes. You know, I'm sure Jill would enjoy going to dinner, but she's spending the night with her best friend. In fact, she just went out the back door to her house. She lives only a couple of doors down."

"Maybe another time, then," Quint said. "I can count on you, though, can't I? I won't keep you out too late."

"What else can I say? I'd love to. Am I dressed all right?"

"You're dressed just fine. You might want to take a jacket. It's a little cool outside."

"Excuse me while I get one."

As Allison made an exit from the living room, Quint couldn't hold back a grin. Piece of cake. He clapped his hat back on his head and waited for her return.

Maybe this whole mess would turn out all right, Allison thought, pulling her Santa Fe jacket from the closet. She had to admit Quint's manners were impeccable. His looks were nothing to complain about either, and perhaps most important, he liked Jill. That alone made him worth getting to know. She had gone out with men who barely acknowledged Jill's presence in the room, much less her existence in Allison's life. She shrugged into the jacket and cleared her hair from the collar. So, yes, she would go to dinner with this stranger and keep two things open—her mind and her eyes. But her heart was still off-limits.

She glanced in the mirror one more time. The jacket's red-and-yellow blanket design coordinated nicely with her navy-blue skirt. She checked the battery on her cell phone, picked up her purse, and returned to the living room.

"Let me leave Jill a note." She walked over to the stack of computer printouts she had been studying earlier, tore a sheet of paper from its spiral rings, and scribbled a note. She signed it *Miss Texas*. As she drew a tiny heart over the letter *I* in *Miss,* her daughter's imagination brought a smile to her face. *Good grief, Jill, Miss Texas?* . . .

"Okay, I'm ready," she said to her escort. "Do you have a restaurant in mind or would you like me to suggest one?"

"Actually, I have a friend of more years than I want to confess who's just opened his own place in Midland. You ever hear of Tag Freeman?"

"Why, yes. Tag Freeman's Double-Kicker Barbecue and Beer. My mom and her friend eat there a lot. They keep fussing at me to try it, but I haven't had the time."

"It's settled, then. Tonight we're making the time."

"Great," she said.

Outside, Allison eyed Quint's bright red pickup with apprehension. Not even a running jump would enable her to hoist herself into the cab. "Oh, my goodness. It certainly is . . . well, tall, isn't it?"

His deep laugh came from behind her. "It's a King Ranch edition," he said, as if that explained everything. "Skinny skirts and tight jeans can make getting into it a challenge. Let me help."

Before she could protest, he gripped her waist and lifted her into the passenger side of the cab. For the briefest moment her face was an eyelash length from his and all she could see were his lips. And all she could smell was something sexy and alluring. A thought flitted through her head.

Besides being masculine and muscular and smelling like the most expensive cologne at a perfume counter, this man was good-looking and available. And he was rich. She might have already decided to keep her mind open, but she had to remind herself to keep her thighs closed.

Nestling into the buttery leather seat, she watched as he rounded the front of the truck and climbed behind the steering wheel. She hadn't made much of an effort to impress him, had made little attempt at conversation, and had not used the ability to charm that many told her she possessed. She couldn't let go of the notion she had held for years, the notion that men were rats. Too many of the males in her life had been of less than exemplary character. Even her dad had been distant and cold. He had worked hard, provided for the family, and left child rearing to his wife.

Forget all that baggage, she told herself, looking at Quint's profile as he backed out of the driveway. Tonight her mother was out of town and Jill was tucked safely away at her neighbor's house. Tonight was going to be about *her*, Allison Barker. Not the dress shop, not her mom's financial future, not even Jill. Tonight, she, Allison Barker, intended to relax and have fun. She had a driving urge to lower her window and present her arm in a stiff wave befitting a queen. A wave befitting Miss Texas.

As they motored toward Midland, Allison thought of what she had read in *Cosmopolitan* about making a man interested on the first date. She had read the articles, had even passed the test at the end. Rule number one: Be a good listener. A man loves when a woman urges him to talk about himself. She was trying to do that very thing, but all Quint wanted to do was ask questions about her—her life, her upbringing, everything related to her.

This was particularly nerve-racking because Jill had already supplied so many details, most of which Allison didn't know. Oh, well, if she stumbled, she would deal with it, and if necessary, she would simply tell him the truth. She never had liked charades.

"So," Quint said, "you're from Haskell?"

"Yes. Everyone has to be from somewhere."

"You said the doctor in your hometown gave you a job when you were only eighteen? And pregnant? Pretty nice of him to do that."

Mental gasp. *Jill, my darling daughter, I will absolutely strangle you when I get home.*

Allison didn't talk about her unplanned teenage pregnancy. The decision to become an unwed mother might have been hers, but that didn't mean it was her choice. A cottage with the white picket fence, a dog sleeping on the front porch, and a minivan in the driveway were what she had imagined. When reality fell short, she had learned to deal with it.

In fact, "deal with it" had become her mantra. When her friends left for college, leaving her, the valedictorian, behind, she had dealt with it. When Mom had inherited from her older sister a dress shop called Almost the Rage in an outpost named Salt Lick, Mom had moved from Haskell to start her life anew. Allison had dealt with it. Several times a year, she had dutifully driven from Haskell to Salt Lick so that, at the very least, Jill would know the only grandparent who acknowledged her existence. Years later when Mom called, crying and despondent over the dress shop's imminent failure, Allison had packed everything she and Jill owned, and moved west to deal with it.

"I know. I was very lucky."

Apparently Quint wasn't ready to put the subject to rest. "Jill's father helped you, right?"

No one ever so openly asked about her past. She considered a lie, but then thought better of it. After all, she wasn't responsible for Jill's father's reputation. "He went to prison shortly before Jill was born."

Quint's gaze jerked in her direction. "No sh— I mean, really? What'd he do?"

The only answer she could give Quint, or anyone, was none at all. How could she defend someone whose answer for quick wealth was to counterfeit money in seventy-five-dollar bills? The U.S. government had never seen fit to print bills in that denomination, so why did John Billy Anderson think *he* could? Seconds ticked off while she silently watched the fence posts fly past.

"It must have been something pretty bad," Quint said. "Did he kill somebody? Plot a terrorist attack? He was just a kid, too, wasn't he?"

Allison swallowed hard, her mind racing. Finally, a deep sigh left her lips. She supposed she had to tell him *something*. "He had just turned nineteen. What he did was so stupid I'm embarrassed for him. Could we change the subject?"

She turned her attention to Quint. "Do you know Tag Freeman from the rodeo? Was he a bull rider, too?"

"You don't follow rodeo?"

"I used to when I was younger, but I haven't been to one in years."

"Tag wasn't a bull *rider*. He was a bull *fighter*. The best in the business. He's saved more cowboys than Alcoholics Anonymous. Stepped in front of a roarin' tornado more than once for me. I flat-out might not be here today if it wasn't for him. Now he's an investor in some of my bulls."

"How can you be an investor in something that doesn't cost any more than a bull?"

"Darlin', a good bucking bull is worth more than a hundred thousand dollars. A breeding cow that throws a tough animal can be worth five or ten thousand."

"My goodness, I didn't know rodeo animals cost so much money."

"Rodeo's become big business. I've got all kinds of rodeo stock, but my specialty is bulls. The bigger and badder, the better. That's my motto. I've got plenty of good cows, but the high-powered bulls are scattered all over the country. I rely on Tag for some consulting work."

"Consulting?"

"I can't be everywhere at once, so he does some of the traveling. We might have to collect ejaculate from a super-bull in Nebraska to be implanted into one of my high-strung cows in Texas."

"And that's called consulting?"

"Well, yeah. Sorta. We can't always get a bull and a cow together in the flesh when the cow's ready, if you know what I mean. Did you forget I'm a stock contractor?"

If only. She couldn't think why she had asked the question or gotten into this discussion. The last conversation she wanted to have with a perfect stranger was one about animals breeding. "I wish I had," she muttered.

"What was that again?"

"I, uh, guess I did."

Allison made a mental note to remember this moment when Jill was grown. She wouldn't retaliate against a child, but she couldn't wait to become her daughter's burdensome elderly mother.

"Here we are," Quint announced, and let out a low whistle. "Man, he told me it was easy to spot and he wasn't kidding."

"Oh, my gosh!"

Allison stared at the building, visible in its entirety from their parking spot in a far corner of an immense lot. She thought immediately of a circus. The low-slung structure's clapboard siding was painted a vivid red. Hanging from the roof were red, white, and blue inverted fans of bunting, held in place by yellow stars outlined in neon tubes. Atop the building a realistic Brahma bull charged a barrel, from which a clown periodically popped up his head. Pulsating lights gave the image animation. She had seen pictures of the restaurant, but they hadn't prepared her for the visual assault.

"It's too bad Jill couldn't come with us," Allison said. "She should see this."

"Who?" Quint asked.

"Jill. My daughter?"

"Oh, of course. Jill. Sorry, I was just trying to take it all in."

"You mean you haven't seen it before?"

"Naw. I missed his grand opening."

"Well, it has family appeal, I'll say that. Your friend must like kids."

"Yeah. At rodeos, he was always surrounded by a bunch of rug rats."

Allison sent him a glare, concluding that he didn't really like children at all.

If he noticed how his remark about kids had put her off, he didn't show it. "Well, pretty lady," he said, giving her a Hollywood smile. "Ready to check it out?"

"Well, that *is* why we made the drive." She reached for the door latch and hopped to the ground, thankful she hadn't worn spike heels. Quint hurried around the front of the pickup and grabbed the door and she realized she should have waited for him to open it and help her out. She hadn't been on a date with a gentleman in so long she had forgotten that chivalry still existed. She felt her face flush and she gave him a self-conscious laugh. "Sorry. I guess I'm a little too independent sometimes."

"That's all right, darlin'. I'll take independent any day of the week. Weak women bring out the worst in me. A strong woman challenges me, especially if she's the prettiest gal in Texas to boot. Guess I'm still an ol' adrenaline junkie." His mouth tipped into a bad-boy grin. "Just promise me I can help you get back in. I kinda liked that part."

As they ambled toward the restaurant's entrance he looped an arm around her shoulders and she didn't pull away. It felt good being treated like a woman again.

"Why did he name it Double-Kicker?" she asked. "Is the food spicy?"

"Not if he's still cooking the way he used to. *Double-kicker's* a rodeo word. That's what we call a bull that kicks up with his hind legs, walks on the front legs, then kicks again with his hind legs before his feet touch the ground. An ol' bull like that's real tough on riders."

Allison recognized the description of the move, but didn't realize it had a name. She had been with Quint less than two hours and already she knew more than she had ever wanted to know about bulls . . . not to mention bullshit.

seven

In the restaurant's entryway, they were greeted by a lifelike statue of a Brahma bull and George Strait's mellow voice crooning "If It Wasn't for Texas." What could be more appropriate in a Texas barbecue joint?

As a hostess led them into the noisy dining room, Allison looked around, absorbing as much as possible. She wanted to describe all of it to Jill later. The first thing she spotted was a mechanical bull and a teenager hanging on desperately. The machine's steady rocking and spinning finally tossed him onto the surrounding red, white, and blue floor mats. His friends and spectators on the sidelines jeered.

From behind her, Quint laughed. "I'd say that boy's got a long way to go before he gets to the pros."

"I suppose so," she replied, shunting her gaze to the shiny wooden picnic-style tables that marched down the center of the huge room. They were occupied by diners of every age and description. To the right she saw a small dance floor, barely enough room for the half-dozen couples shuffling to the music coming from the jukebox in the corner. A karaoke machine sat to the side, along with a handmade sign that read EVERY NIGHT IS KARAOKE NIGHT!

Everywhere she looked, she saw laughter. Groups stood in knots throughout the room, holding mugs of beer, salty margarita glasses, or quart-size plastic glasses of iced tea. *Fun* was the word that came to Allison's mind.

The atmosphere reminded her of a scaled-back Billy Bob's, the Fort Worth honky-tonk of all honky-tonks that was now being promoted as a family-friendly hangout. Exactly whose family she didn't know. Blending adult activity with underage children might be an everyday event in Fort Worth, but not in West Texas. Here, when it came to having a good time, choices were few and well defined—either church- and school-sponsored events or bars and dance halls. Water and oil. From the looks of her present environs, Quint's friend had managed somewhat to bridge the two.

She looked forward to meeting this Tag Freeman, who had put this business together. He obviously had good marketing skills and she was always anxious to learn new ideas.

A man with a limp was headed in their direction. His gait thrust his hip to one side, almost in rhythm to the music. As he moved in and out of tables, slapping backs and shaking hands, his baritone voice carried across the room.

She couldn't keep from watching him. His limp didn't detract from his appearance. He was tall and slender, but also muscular. His carved-in-granite features belonged on a roadside billboard reminding every passerby how a real man should look. From the big grin on his face when he looked their way, she knew this was Tag Freeman.

In terms of appealing men, she had thought her luck had changed when she saw Quint in her living room a couple of hours earlier, but now, if this was indeed Tag Freeman, she had hit the mother lode. Meeting one attractive eligible man a year was all a single woman could hope for or dream of. Meeting two would be a dream all right, but in this case, it was a nightmare, because the two most desirable men she had met in years were best friends with a long history.

Mental sigh. Oh, well, what difference did it make? Tag Freeman was surely married. Good. Married men were off-limits. She could relax. The evening and her good time were saved.

As Tag Freeman made his way toward his old friend, Quint Matthews, he couldn't take his eyes off the good-looking woman with him. No, *good-looking* wasn't the right word. Make that beautiful. Redheads had always caught his eye.

He stopped the waitress bearing down on the couple, her hands filled with large menus and silverware bound in napkins. "Tracy, I'll take care of this one."

He reached Quint and his date, extending his right hand. "Matthews! Glad you could make it, buddy."

Quint grabbed his hand in a test-of-strength handshake. "Hey, Dink. Damn, man, you're lookin' good."

Tag laughed. *Dink*. At the beginning of his career in rodeo, Quint had hung that handle on him.

Quint's introduction of the woman with him came almost as an afterthought. Allison. Tag liked that name.

"So how's the old hip doing?" Quint asked.

"Coming along. You know how it is. Can't let a few deer keep me down."

Allison's brow furrowed. "Deer? I thought you were a rodeo clown?"

Tag looked into her remarkable green eyes, eyes like he had never seen. "No disrespect to rodeo clowns, ma'am, but I'm a bullfighter. I never did consider myself much of a clown."

"Unless you count the times he took on a snot-slinger and lost," Quint said on a chuckle.

Allison laughed then, a sincere, self-deprecating laugh that lit up an already bright face. "Forgive me for being so naive," she said, "but I thought a bullfighter was a matador."

"That's down in Mexico. Up here, we don't kill any bulls. If we did, the SPCA would shut us down in a heartbeat. They're already mad at us all the time anyway," he said on a laugh. Then, as an afterthought, he added, "In rodeo, the difference between a clown and a bullfighter is sort of like the difference between bar whiskey and Royal Crown."

"Sorry," she said, "but that doesn't tell me much."

Tag chuckled again. "Clowns entertain the crowd. Bullfighters entertain the bull. I did do some clowning a long time ago. Still do on occasion. Get Quint to bring you to my house sometime and I'll show you some tapes. Then you'll know the difference between clowning and bull-fighting."

"Oh, okay. But I'm still confused. You said a few deer? You had an accident with deer?"

Quint interjected the story of the freak accident and Tag's injuries.

"Oh, my goodness." A frown of concern knit her brow. "That must have been awful. You must have suffered terribly. And losing a career in the prime of your life had to have been devastating."

Devastating? An empty, meaningless word considering the multiple surgeries, the endless months of rehabilitation, and the depression into which Tag had sunk after the prognosis had been handed down. His career in the rodeo arena was over. *Devastating* didn't come close to describing the state of mind in which Tag had functioned for the five ensuing years. More than once he had considered taking a shotgun to himself. Even now he couldn't recall how or explain why he hadn't.

His only answer was that he had visited Walter Reed Hospital in Washington and seen those kids who had come home from the Middle East, some of them missing multiple limbs. He had seen their courage, admired their fortitude, and envied their upbeat attitudes. After that, he knew that many a man and woman lived with worse handicaps than his and for a more noble reason. After that, Tag Freeman chose life.

Allison's hand touched his forearm and gave it a gentle squeeze. "I hope you're doing better now."

Tag was impressed. Most pretty women, upon hearing the circumstances surrounding his accident, steered the conversation toward asking if he had gotten a lot of money from a lawsuit, their mental cash registers tallying up the loot. He sensed that this woman might be different. She seemed to care and understand what he had been through. Where in the hell had Quint met this incredible female?

And why in the fuck did he have to bring her here?

Three hours later Allison realized her earlier presumption had been wrong. Tag had been married; now he was divorced. But she could still relax. The only commitment he was ready to make was to remain uncommitted. The stream of females of all ages that flowed through the restaurant and stopped by their table—Wrangler-clad hotties with firm bottoms and exposed navel rings—gave her a clear picture of just how active his social life was. Having made that observation, why was she still drawn to him? Her life was too complicated for additional complications.

Still, she was having fun. She couldn't remember the last time she had laughed so much. Both men entertained her with hilarious stories, and with each one, another frosty mug of beer appeared in Quint's hand. The restaurant's customers were eager to buy the rodeo celebrities a drink and Quint and Tag lifted mugs and nodded thank you to each one. The only difference was that Quint drank his while Tag sipped on one and motioned a waitress to remove the others from in front of him. It wasn't lost on Allison that he remained in total control of himself and his surroundings.

The same was not true of the world champion, Quint Matthews. Soon he had consumed way beyond what the law allowed the driver of a motor vehicle.

Now, while Quint manned the karaoke machine, singing along loudly and off-key, Allison turned to Tag. "Quint said you two have been friends for more years than he wanted to admit," she shouted to be heard.

"That's a fact," Tag said, leaning so close she could see the dark stubble on his jaw and smell his scent—musky man and cologne she believed to be one of her favorites. Hugo Boss. Yum. "We go all the way back to the beginning of both our careers," he added.

"I heard him call you 'Dink.' "

"He's the only man who's ever called me that. Or who ever will."

"Most nicknames like that have a special meaning, so I assume that one does, too."

Tag laughed as he pulled one of the untouched beers toward him and sipped. "It's something just between us two. A dink is a bull that doesn't live up to his fierce image. Or perform as expected and desired in competition. Maybe he doesn't buck hard enough. Or maybe he just runs around the arena. A dink's worthless in competition. He poses a threat to only two things—a stock producer's blood pressure and a rodeo cowboy's wallet. A weak-performing bull don't get asked back and those entry fees ain't refundable."

"Oh," she said, feeling her face flush. "Guess I've got a lot to learn."

"Hey, don't worry about it." He leaned in close again. "It's an industry word. Not even most rodeo fans know what it means."

She cocked her head and looked at him, appreciating his effort to make her feel at ease and studying his expressive brown eyes. "So how does it apply to you?"

"In the beginning, I guess I was somewhat of a dink. It took a while to get that fearless bullfighter reputation. It started when a certain young comer got bucked off a man-hating Brahma and got hung up in his bull rigging."

"Quint?"

"Yep."

"Well, don't stop there."

He hesitated, his gaze leveled on her face. Even in the dim lighting, she saw a spark in his eye and she resisted the urge to lick her lips.

"You really want to hear this?" he asked.

"Of course I do."

He paused a moment longer, just looking at her. "Okay," he said finally, turning back to his beer. "We were both just kids. A rodeo in Green River, Wyoming, is where we were. Tough stock. Bunch of mustangs for broncs. I don't know *where* they got them bulls, but they were rank sons-a-bitches. Quint was a skinny little fart, but he was tougher'n whang leather. He'd made it to the finals on sheer guts. That ol' bull—Cyclone they called him—bucked him off right out of the chute.

"I didn't know what I was doing and neither did Quint. Ol' Cyclone was throwing him around like a rag doll and dragging him all over the arena."

Tag began to use his hands to accompany the story and Allison felt herself getting caught up in the drama.

"Quint kept trying to get himself loose, but that ol' bull was so strong, Quint couldn't get a hold. All I could see was danger and destruction. When that hard-charger ran past me, I vaulted up on his back and hung on with one hand. With the other, I finally got Quint's rigging loose. End of story. We've been friends ever since."

"Was Quint hurt?"

"Oh, yeah. I forget now exactly what got broke. I'm sure he got hurt just as bad many times after that. Being hurt is just part of bull riding. That's why bull riders gotta be tough and hardheaded."

"Gosh," Allison said with a smile and a wish that it was Tag Freeman who would be taking her home. "You really are a hero."

"Nope. Just doing my job. But you get the picture. Without bullfighters, bull riding would be a lot more dangerous. A lot of cowboys might not survive it. You see, that's what I meant when I said it ain't clowning. Bullfighting can be a matter of life and death."

Quint had just started a rendition of "Mamas, Don't Let Your Babies Grow Up to Be Cowboys." Allison looked toward the karaoke machine. "Speaking of life and death, my escort shouldn't be driving. I'm not sure how we're going to get home."

"I thought he'd had a little too much hooch a couple of hours ago, but I figured you'd drive."

"His pickup's so big. And I can't drive a stick shift. Between the clutching and the braking and the shifting, I'd be hours making it home." She laughed. "Can I drive all the way to Salt Lick in first gear?"

"Well, you could," Tag said with a chuckle, "but I wouldn't recommend it."

A frown tugged at her brow. "I think I'm in a bit of a bind."

Tag knew there was only one solution, only one *logical* solution. For him, as the owner of the restaurant and bar, to allow Quint to drive away in his present condition would be an irresponsible act. Driving Quint home was the least Tag could do as a friend. Quint would do the same for him.

But as a man with a strong attraction to the woman Quint had brought with him, it was a dubious undertaking. Just the thought of sitting close to Allison in the intimacy of a truck cab kicked up his pulse.

Despite all of his misgivings, he was compelled to do something. "I might be able to help you out," he said. "How far is it to Salt Lick? Sixty miles?"

eight

An orchestra of bass drums thundered in Quint's head. He wished he could just lie still with his eyes closed, but he felt a presence and heard motion. Then something cold and wet touched his neck. He opened one eye and saw a black dog the size of a small calf shimmying and whining. The monster let out an earsplitting bark and both of Quint's eyes sprang open.

Where the hell was he? He vaguely remembered lying in the backseat of his truck while someone else drove.

As the dog continued to dance about, a male voice spoke. "Jake! Sit or I'll make you go outside."

That voice belonged to Tag.

"Mornin', sunshine."

That voice, too, belonged to Tag. Quint rolled his eyes toward the voice. His old friend was leaning a shoulder against the doorjamb, his bare feet crossed at the ankles.

"I hope you don't feel as bad as you look," the voice said, and the body that went with it walked over and scruffed the dog's ears.

"What time is it?" Quint asked.

"Just after ten. You gonna sleep the day away? I've been up for hours."

The dog was now prancing and barking loud enough to send a shudder through Quint's whole body. He glared at the beast. "What's with your dog? Am I in his bed or something?"

"It's probably that baloney sandwich you're sleeping on."

"What?" Quint raised his head from the pillow just enough for inspection and felt the sandwich firmly pressed against his cheek. "Fuck. What am I doing sleeping with a baloney sandwich?"

"Baloney was the only sandwich stuff I had in the fridge. You never did get around to eating dinner at the joint last night."

Quint peeled the remains of the sandwich from his cheek and tossed it to the salivating animal.

Tag guffawed. "Matthews, you're just the picture of class and good breeding."

"I am, ain't I?" Quint sat up and looked around. He felt a serious need for a shower. "What happened to Allison? Did she get to eat supper? Did I pay for it? She's not here, is she?"

"The meal's no problem. We took her home last night. Then I drove you back here. She said to tell you she had a good time."

Quint had wanted to make a good impression on Allison. Judging from his rumpled, slept-in clothing, someone other than himself driving her home, and now, waking up on an unfamiliar couch, he felt sure he had made one hell of a bad one. "She's a nice gal. Guess I better give her a call."

The aroma of brewing coffee wafted from the kitchen. "I hope that's fresh coffee I smell. If I'm gonna eat crow this early in the morning, I need something to wash it down." Quint got to his feet but failed to gain his balance and fell back on the leather couch's soft cushions.

"Just sit tight. I'll get it," Tag said.

As he walked to the kitchen Tag was troubled by what Quint had said about giving Allison a call. Not that Quint shouldn't apologize for getting drunk, leaving the woman he had brought with him stranded, and, in general, acting like an ass, but Allison Barker was the only woman who had aroused an interest in Tag in a long time. In fact, she interested him enough for him to remember her last name. He didn't like the idea of a cock hound like Quint having further contact with her.

Jake had followed him into the kitchen, so he opened the back door and put the dog outside to amuse himself chasing chickens from the backyard.

As Tag reached into the cabinet for a mug his mind took him back to last night and how he had enjoyed Quint's date's company. It had been a long time since he'd had that feeling of connecting with a woman. Allison was so down-to-earth, he could have talked to her all night. She looked into his eyes when he spoke, actually listening and holding on to his every word. She had a way of crinkling her nose when she laughed and she did that often. Laughter was so important. Too weird that she lived in Salt Lick. That close all this time, yet ushered into his life by an old friend. Unfortunately, as the date of an old friend.

He poured a mug of coffee for Quint, refilled his own mug, and reentered the family room. Quint was still sitting on the couch holding his head in his hands.

"You really like this woman, do you? What I mean is, she sounds like more than just a little poontang you picked up." Tag didn't mind speaking frankly. Quint's reputation with the ladies was what it was and they both knew it. He handed Quint the mug of coffee.

"Yeah, I like her. She's got some ambition and spunk. I like that." Quint blew on the coffee and sipped. "But she's got this kid. Twelve years old, I think. *That,* I'm not crazy about, but I guess it wouldn't be so bad. Twelve's more than half-grown. She'll soon be out of the house and on her own."

Tag remembered how Allison's face had brightened when she talked about her daughter. The kid was clearly the center of her universe and he felt an annoyance at Quint for not appreciating this. He only wished he had seen his ex-wife just once with that expression on her face when it came to talk about kids. He had always assumed all women had strong maternal instincts, but his ex-wife had taught him different.

As he looked out the window at Jake playing in the big grassy backyard, for the first time in a long time he envisioned kids playing in it, too—a little boy and a little girl running and romping with Jake, their mom nearby watching and laughing.

With Allison nearby watching and laughing.

He blinked away the image. *Whoa, hoss. You haven't known this woman twenty-four hours and you got her giving birth to your kids.*

And don't forget, you've given up women.

This attraction to Allison was nothing more than a little old-fashioned lust. It had been too long since he had given in to the lust.

And at the end of the day, wasn't the lust all he had ever pursued? Was he any better than Quint?

Though the question and its answer made him feel guilty, he readily acknowledged that anything more than a little physical gratification could prove disastrous to him. His phobia against commitment had formed a shell that protected his heart. In the past, when he'd had these harebrained attractions, an old cowboy adage had always seen him through: *There never was a bull that couldn't be rode, never a cowboy that couldn't be throwed . . .*

. . . And, he had added, *there never was a commitment to a woman that you didn't regret.*

He had best not forget that. His braver friend Quint Matthews could drift into that murky water that was filled with undercurrents and alligators, but Tag Freeman would stay in safety on the bank, holding a life preserver.

★   ★   ★

As Allison sipped her orange juice she reveled in the Sunday-morning solitude. She had the house to herself. Her mom was out of town on a trip with Frank. Still at her friend Susan Kay's house, Jill wouldn't be home until noon. She always went to Sunday school with Susan Kay's family.

The idea of that gave Allison a pang of guilt. She should be taking Jill to Sunday school herself, but, she rationalized, she needed a few moments at some point during the week to get reacquainted with herself. With Almost the Rage open six days a week, Sundays were her only downtime, a day when she could simply shower and wash her hair without styling it, put on an old pair of jeans, and go without makeup. Sometimes she even cooked something great on Sundays.

She placed her glass in the dishwasher and headed for the shower. As she shampooed her hair her thoughts drifted to the extraordinary events of yesterday afternoon and night. Her mother would be ecstatic that she had gone out on a Saturday night with one eligible man and returned home with two. If Jill knew, she would already be plotting her next move and Susan Kay would be helping her.

Would Quint call today? she wondered as she dried her hair. His behavior last night had been off-putting, but in his defense, every time he came close to finishing a drink, someone bought him another one, compliments of a herd of admiring fans.

Despite his drinking, she'd enjoyed herself. She couldn't remember the last time, if ever, she had been deluged with male attention. And the endless stream of stories from him and his friend Tag had made the lack of luster in her life more apparent than ever. She hadn't failed to note that any amusing anecdotes from her were centered on something Jill had done or said.

Tag was such an attractive man in a rugged way. Cowboy through and through, but he seemed good-natured and he had been such a gentleman. In fact, he had been so attentive she felt he was interested in her. Was the interest genuine or was he just being polite to his old friend's date? Probably the latter. He was good at PR. She had learned that much from watching him with his customers.

As wicked as she felt for wishing it, Tag was the man she wanted to hear from. But she might as well forget such a pie-in-the-sky notion. She had watched and listened as Quint teased him throughout the evening about his fear of commitment and his determination to stay single. Tag offered no defense, no examples to prove Quint wrong. He had only laughed and agreed.

It was just as well he had that attitude, she thought ruefully as she pulled on old jeans. A man like him would never find dull Allison Barker appealing. Good grief, he rubbed shoulders with celebrities, had probably dated some, probably knew dozens of people with exciting lives. He was sure to have a bevy of females to choose from. He was simply out of Allison Barker's league.

Now, if only she could get him out of her head.

After Quint showered and shaved, he hauled his duffel from his truck and put on clean clothes, trying to return himself to the land of the living. Mornings like this made him wonder why he didn't give up alcohol altogether.

Tag treated him to a breakfast of sausage and cream gravy, freshly baked biscuits, and cantaloupe. Tag Freeman would make somebody a good wife. They spent the afternoon alternately napping and watching the PBR competition from Mesquite on TV and analyzing each bull's performance. He and Tag were partners in one of the PBR's current superstars, a big white Brahma they had bred and raised on Quint's ranch. Quint felt guilty. He should be in Mesquite with his bulls instead of roaming the West Texas highways chasing a whirlwind.

"I like ol' Double Trouble's performances more every time I see him," he told Tag. "He looks a little like Bodacious, don't he?"

Tag agreed.

"He's one hell of an athlete," Quint added. "Riding him's a real challenge for those young guys. Every time I drew a bull that spins like he does, I knew I had my work cut out for me."

"And I believe the older he gets, the better he'll be," Tag said. "We should start collecting his semen. He's got qualities worth passing on."

As evening neared, Quint gave in to Tag's goading to get up and do something. He found the nerve to crack a can of beer and walked out on the large wooden porch that wrapped around the house. There he found his host checking the heat in a stainless-steel grill that looked bigger and better than a lot of entire kitchens. Two plate-sized T-bones lay on a platter nearby.

Quint looked over Tag's backyard, mentally comparing it with his own home in Seguin. For shade trees, Tag had only a few puny mesquites, stunted from lack of moisture. In reality, West Texas was a high desert. South Texas, where Quint lived, was semitropical, with low elevation and a lot of moisture. On his ranch, trees grew and the plants and pastures were lush and green. When it came to heat and humidity, hell had nothing on the summers, but the surroundings were pretty to look at.

Still, even if Quint found the Midland landscape lacking, he had to admit he liked the weather. This fall evening was as perfect as you could get. Not too warm, not to cool. Just enough breeze to notice the touch on your skin.

"You look like you're feeling better," Tag said. "I told you you'd heal up faster if you moved around."

"I'm all right. I don't drink like I used to. It doesn't take much to get me shit-faced. And it takes me longer to get over it."

What he didn't say was that lately he had been taking a long, hard look at his frequent copious consumption of alcohol and made a decision to go in another direction. He had no intention of letting Quint Matthews become one of those cowboy stereotypes. Nobody would ever be able to call Quint Matthews "just another drunk cowboy."

"Potatoes should be nearly done," Tag said, poking inside the oven. "Big ol' Idaho russets right out of the field. I've got a friend up there who ships 'em down to me. We'll load 'em up with all the fixings."

Quint didn't know an Idaho russet potato from any other, but he knew Tag did. "Great."

"I brought some sourdough bread home from the restaurant and some of our specialty peach cobbler."

That menu might be just plain cooking to some, but coming from Tag's restaurant, it would be a mouthwatering delight. Quint's stomach reacted as the steaks began to sizzle. He was hungry as a baby pig. "Sounds good. That's more food than I usually eat, you know."

"Who's doing your cooking and housekeeping these days?"

"I got a Mexican woman. She takes care of everything. Cooking, cleaning, the whole thing. The girls in my office pay all the bills. I don't worry about any of it. And that suits me fine. Only thing is, I don't get much American food. I eat a lot of tacos."

Tag laughed like he was amused, but Quint was sure Tag would never be content letting someone else run his personal life to that extent. Tag was a homebody and always had been.

"Listen, thanks for letting me bunk at your house, Dink. I've got to go to Salt Lick tomorrow on business. If things go the way I want them to, I may have to stick around for a few days if you don't mind."

"Heck, no. You're welcome to come and go as you please. There's just me and Jake here."

At the mention of his name the dog rose from his spot and ambled to his owner.

"You and your animals," Quint said, squinting in the late-day sunlight and looking at his old friend. "You've always had some stray critter trailing behind you. Dog, cat, goat—it was always something lost that needed a home."

"Well, somebody's got to take care of the lost ones. Where'd any of us be if we didn't watch each other's backs? Ain't that right, Jake?" The dog rested his body against Tag's leg and looked up at him with adoring brown eyes. Tag bent over and patted the dog's head. "You and me just roam this big ol' house all by ourselves, don't we, boy?"

As Tag turned the steaks Quint looked back at the two-story house. "I always wondered why'd you buy such a big-ass house for just you? This place must be, what, five thousand square feet?"

"Four thousand four hundred and twenty-seven," Tag answered.

"Like I said. Why so big?"

"When I had it built, it wasn't just me. Me and Diann had just got married. I thought we'd have some kids. I wanted a home big enough to live in, entertain in, and eventually grow old in. Something our kids, their friends, and someday our grandkids would all want to come to. She was on board for the entertaining part, but she never bought into the other. When we got divorced, she didn't even want the house. I bought out her half."

Quint looked down and away at the mention of Tag's ex-wife. Though he and Tag had been friends for years, they had never discussed the reasons for the breakup of Tag's marriage. Quint had deliberately avoided it. He suspected he knew without being told. Men had always liked Diann Freeman and she liked them back. Long ago, after more Royal Crown than any one man needed, Quint had spent a night with her in a motel in Oklahoma City. He wasn't proud of it, but the fact that she shared her time with many more than him was the balm he had used for years to soothe the guilt he felt. "Whatever became of her?" he asked, hoping the casual tone sounded genuine.

"Last I heard she was working for a music producer in Nashville. She used to call me up when her bed was empty." Tag laughed. "She hasn't called me in a while."

"Right," Quint said. *And amen.* He wanted to change the subject and quick.

Tag plated up the steaks and dug the baked potatoes from the oven. Quint walked back into the house and returned with another can of beer. Rodeo gossip filled the next hour. Rodeo people, though not always congenial with one another or functional in their relationships, were a tightly knit family with a common understanding of "the life." For sure, the ProRodeo community had been Quint's family.

He and Tag were exchanging notes on who was still married or not and who was sleeping with whom when Tag suddenly asked, "How'd you meet Allison?"

Quint had dreaded that question. Joining an online dating service was beneath him somehow and fessing up to it embarrassed him. In the past he hadn't had to work at meeting women. He certainly had never paid a service to orchestrate an encounter.

Discussing how he had met Allison would inevitably lead to a conversation about him and Janine Grubbs. Or whatever her/his name was. Though he and Tag had a long trail behind them, that whole story made Quint uncomfortable.

Fidgeting with the remnants of the baked potato he had just devoured, he finally said, "You remember a couple of years ago, that wild story going around about me and a woman that was really a man?"

Tag's laugh boomed loud enough to make Jake wake up and raise his head. "Yeah, I heard it. One night at the coliseum in Fort Worth I knocked a guy flat on his ass for repeating it. I was curious, but I never would have asked you about it. I figured if you wanted to tell me, you would."

Quint shook his head. "It was the damnedest thing I ever got into, Dink. After it was over, I was wore out. I didn't care if I never saw another woman. But eventually I got lonesome, so I decided to give this Internet dating a try. I figured if I got a look at some gal's picture first and talked to her for a while, I'd be able to tell if she was crazy. If she didn't answer my questions right, I wouldn't even let her get in my truck, much less my bed."

Tag stood, gathered the plates, and headed inside. Quint followed him, watching as Tag began rinsing the dishes under the faucet.

"Then you must have been pretty impressed with Allison," Tag said. "I can't believe you came all the way up to Salt Lick just to take her out to dinner."

"She's not the main reason I came. What I'm really up here for is to talk to Debbie Sue Overstreet about doing some investigative work. You remember her. She ran the barrels a few years back. Won some titles. She quit the rodeo, you know. Now her and a friend have a detective agency in Salt Lick."

"The Domestic Equalizers. I read about them and how they got started." Tag turned off the faucet and began putting the dishes into the dishwasher. "But they claim they spy on cheating husbands and wives. What are they doing for you?"

Quint paced the kitchen and repeated the story about his identity theft and his suspicions, concluding with, "If anyone can locate that woman that played me for a fool, those two can."

"How does Allison figure in?" Tag asked, bracing a hand on the counter.

"Well, she doesn't. I just thought that since I was in Salt Lick anyway, I might mix some pleasure with business. Online, she came across as a real nice gal. You know how it is, ol' buddy. When you get bucked off, you get up, dust off your backside, and crawl back on to ride again. You'll never be a winner any other way."

Tag laughed and started back to the porch. "God knows I've seen you do that enough times. I just never had that much faith in that process, I guess."

"Faith and good luck. The keys to success, buddy."

"That might work for you," Tag said, "but I sleep better at night with the truth, based on cold hard facts. And I don't believe in luck."

Quint looked back at the old dog sitting by the door. "You believe in luck, don't you, boy? You got pretty lucky when you showed up here." He offered the dog the stripped bone from his steak.

The dog met his outstretched hand and accepted the offer, then lay down again. Wrapping his paws around the bone, he let out a sigh of utter contentment.

The Internet. Quint had found Allison on the Internet. That answered one of Tag's questions. From the beginning he hadn't seen her as the barhopping bucklebunny who usually fell for Quint.

Quint had guts. Tag would never post his picture and personal profile on the Internet. He would hop a fence and face a mad bull, but the thought of putting himself out there for everyone and anyone to examine was too . . . well, too invasive. Too personal.

Beyond that, he was too old for dating and didn't have time anyway. If a female ever entered his life again in a serious way, it would have to be through the door of his restaurant, because of late that's where he spent his waking hours. A woman would have to catch his eye and heart from across the dining room. But he wasn't going to be looking, so if it happened it would have to go down just that way.

Then it dawned on him. That's how he had met Allison Barker.

nine

Monday morning, Debbie Sue was the first to arrive at the Styling Station. The other beauty salon in Salt Lick didn't open on Mondays. From the beginning, she had planned on getting ahead of the competition by being open bright and early every Monday. Edwina agreed with the strategy.

Now, standing in the Styling Station's doorway, she watched Edwina wrestle, one-handed, her huge cowhide purse—the thing was big enough for its own zip code—and another oversize satchel from her car. In the opposite hand she carried a quart-size cup of Dr Pepper. Debbie Sue flung the door open and Edwina stumbled into the salon on pink stiletto spike heels.

She was wearing a dark green sweater coat and she was shaped like a bowling pin. Debbie Sue couldn't imagine what she could be wearing under that sweater. With a lollipop stick protruding from her mouth and mirrored sun-glasses reflecting the salon lights, her pal and partner looked like a living, breathing Christmas tree. The sight was a Ko-dak moment, for sure. Debbie Sue burst into laughter. "A Christmas tree! How original. Add a bad case of dandruff and you'd look like you were flocked."

"Vic flocked me this morning, but I didn't think it showed." Edwina tilted back her head and cackled as she plopped her purse and the striped satchel on her work-station. "But I'm not a Christmas tree. I'm a New York City ballerina. The original Nutcracker."

She threw open her sweater and revealed a stiff pink net tutu tied around a pink bodysuit. The spandex top flattened her bosom even more than Mother Nature had done. The pink tights, straining to cover her mile-long skinny legs, broke all records for elasticity. Edwina peeled off the sweater, tossed it across the room, and struck a pose—head thrown back, arms looped above her head.

"You're a nutcracker all right," Debbie Sue said, "and you've got three ex-husbands to prove it."

Edwina dug into her satchel. "Wait'll you see what I brought to do you."

"What makes you think I want to be done?"

" 'Cause it's Halloween, dearie, and you know this after-noon all the little darlings in town will come by dressed in their costumes to get trick-or-treat goodies. You don't want them to see you looking like your ordinary old self, do you?"

Debbie Sue laughed. This was the flavor of her and Edwina's friendship, unpredictable and salty with a touch of sweetness. Never-ending fun was something Edwina had brought into Debbie Sue's life. Not that Debbie Sue didn't have fun on her own, but Edwina's zaniness gave "fun" character. "Well, hurry up," Debbie Sue said. "I've got a trim at ten."

The next thing she knew, her long thick hair was pinned up in a bun and her face was covered with white greasepaint. "This reminds me of your mom's new song," Edwina said as she painted a big red grin on Debbie Sue's mouth.

Debbie Sue's mom, Virginia, was having great success in Nashville as a composer of country-western songs. "Which one?"

"The one Gretchen Wilson recorded, 'She's Left Lipstick Traces in Too Many Places.' "

"Oh, yeah," Debbie Sue said. "I really like that one. And Gretchen did a great job with it."

"Do you think she wrote that about me?" Edwina asked, frowning.

"I don't think so, Ed."

Edwina finished off Debbie Sue's face with heavy black eyeliner and stuck an orange ball on the tip of her nose.

"Yikes! I look like a real clown," Debbie Sue said as she stared at the finished image in the mirror.

"Not quite yet." Edwina dragged from her satchel a red yarn wig, baggy pants and suspenders, a T-shirt, a bow tie, and a pair of Vic's size 15 combat boots.

Debbie Sue changed into the clothing and boots and clapped on the red wig.

"Nooowww," Edwina said, "you look like a rodeo clown."

And the day began.

A gray Ford pickup pulled to a stop in a roadside park. The driver adjusted the rearview mirror again and peered up the highway, waiting for the red mini–rocket ship Quint Matthews called transportation to appear. There was no way of knowing if Quint would be traveling this road today, but this was the only highway connecting Midland to Salt Lick, and Quint's big red Ford had been back and forth three times just yesterday.

Saturday's epic trips—228 miles from Abilene to Salt Lick, 60 miles Saturday night from Salt Lick to Midland; another 60 miles back to Salt Lick from Midland, then back to Midland again—were taxing to more than body and mind. With "regular" gasoline at over two dollars per gallon, more than 400 miles in one day was hell on the pocketbook. When renting the pickup, the driver hadn't known about its lousy gas mileage.

How did a region from where a vast amount of oil was sucked account for its high price of gasoline? The answer wasn't forthcoming, but one thing was: the gray pickup was going to take a respite at this roadside park and watch from afar as Quint's truck ran up and down the highway. Quint was rich. He could afford to buy fuel for a gas guzzler.

As those thoughts jelled, the roar of a familiar engine came from the north.

✶ ★ ✶

This was a heck of a way to begin the week. Allison gave up and plopped her backside on the floor. She had been in a squatting position folding and rearranging Almost the Rage's display of T-shirts and jeans for so long her knees and back begged for relief. The kids were out of school today and a swarm of teenage girls had hit the store like hungry grass-hoppers. They left the two dressing rooms filled with re-jected garments, some on hangers, some barely on hangers, but most lying in a heap on the floor. She had lectured Jill more times than she could count about not leaving this kind of mess in a store for some worker to straighten.

Just then, the front door's chimes drew Allison's attention. She craned her neck to see who had entered. All she saw over the racks of clothing was a cowboy hat, but she could smell something heavenly, a mix of leather and cologne. *Tag!* Why he was the first person she thought of she didn't know, because a cowboy-hat-wearing customer could be any num-ber of men from this area. Stetsons were practically issued at birth.

"Be with you in a sec," she called out, then mumbled to herself, "I just have to get up off the floor."

"Need some help, pretty lady?"

Allison jerked her head around so quickly she could have suffered whiplash. "Quint." He was among the first men she should have considered but the last she expected. "No, no. I'm fine. I was just trying to put things back in order here."

She accepted his outstretched hand and felt a rush in her

pulse as he pulled her to her feet. She still wasn't sure how she felt about Quint, but for some reason she wanted to impress upon him that she wasn't just a hick from a small town, though that's what she was. Nothing but pride and vanity, she told herself, but deep down, she knew it was more personal. Quint and his celebrity intimidated her. She felt like the pimply-faced high-schooler the football hero had suddenly taken an interest in. She was unable to keep from tittering as she smoothed her clothing. "Goodness, you surprised me."

"You here alone?" he asked, looking around the shop and continuing to hold her hand.

She lifted her hand from his and used it to sweep her hair off her forehead. "My mom's usually here, but she and her boyfriend have been out of town since Saturday."

"Your mom's got something going on with a boyfriend, does she?"

Allison felt her face flame red-hot, confused because she felt embarrassed. She was happy for her mom to find someone and Frank was a man to be adored. Having him hanging around Almost the Rage, as well as the house, was like having a handyman on the payroll for free.

She rolled her eyes in an attempt to appear exasperated. "You'd think at her age she'd be past that"—she crimped the air with two fingers for emphasis—"'I've got a crush' phase. I swear, they're worse than rab—" Her hand flew to her mouth.

A laugh burst from Quint. "Rabbits? Hey, that's great. If there's an age limit on a little lust, I haven't heard about it."

He lifted off his hat and gave her a little-boy grin she felt certain was meant to melt her heart. He leaned in close enough to make her heartbeat quicken and fixed her with an ice-blue gaze. "How about you? Don't you ever have any lusty thoughts?"

Allison felt hypnotized. Lust had been off her radar screen for so long she had almost forgotten the word. "Uh, very rarely."

He tucked back his chin and frowned. "No kidding?"

"When you live alone and no prospects are looming on the horizon, letting your mind wander in that direction is kind of a waste of time."

His gaze seared through her clothing. "And whose fault is that?"

Unable to think of a clever answer, Allison looked at the floor. Good grief. Her twelve-year-old daughter could handle this conversation better than she. "I guess it's mine," she finally replied.

He set his hat back on his head and shrugged. Oh, no. Was he giving up?

"Look," he said, "I'm sorry I didn't call yesterday, but you know, you never did give me your home phone number."

"I didn't?" Allison blinked and hooked her hair behind one ear. "Well, there you go. That's why I'm still single. I missed that important step."

"No big deal. I spent yesterday mostly trying to get over the night before anyway. But I did want to tell you I'm sorry I drank so much. I don't usually act like that when I'm with a beautiful woman."

Allison's eye began to twitch. Beautiful? He had said

beautiful, hadn't he? She picked up another T-shirt and began to fold it. "Oh? And how do you treat women you take out that you *don't* think are beautiful?"

"That's just it. I don't go out with women I don't think are beautiful." He reached toward her with one hand and touched the earring that dangled from her left earlobe. His fingertips brushed her neck and she felt a tiny frisson race down her spine.

Oh, he was smooth. Too smooth. Allison made a gulp she was sure he heard. "Don't worry about it. I got home okay. Tag saw to it. He was good company. How is he, by the way? I mean, uh—he's fine, I'm sure. He's, uh, a nice person. I really enjoyed meeting him."

Inside, Allison cringed at how strained the effort to sound casual came off. She was sweating so profusely she was tempted to wipe her face with the cotton T-shirt in her hand. Good grief, she was as bad as her mom and Frank.

"He's fine. Good man, Tag. Hardest-working guy I've ever known. He's got something big going on tonight. He was gone from the house before I woke up." Quint casually walked around the dress shop, looking at garments as if to give his approval.

"You're staying at Tag's house?"

"Didn't I tell you? I'm surprised he didn't mention it. Yeah, I'm there till I get some business settled up here. I live down in Seguin, but it's four hundred miles from here. No point running back and forth."

"Yeah, staying in Midland does make sense. I didn't know you lived so far away. Tag has a big date tonight?" In her head, she replayed her and Tag's conversation driving home. He hadn't mentioned seeing anyone.

"Must be. But I really don't know."

A sour taste came into her mouth at the thought of Tag with a woman. Her mind flashed back to Saturday night and the dim interior of the pickup cab and studying his profile while he watched the road and spoke of his home located on the edge of the city. She had been touched by how lovingly he described it. He was a man focused on living his dream. Nonetheless, she thought she had heard a strain of melancholy in his tone, like something was missing. But he gave no clue what.

"So, would you like to?"

Quint's voice brought her back to reality. "Huh? I'm so sorry. I was thinking of something else. I've got a lot on my plate today. What did you say?"

"I asked if you'd like to go to dinner tonight?"

Allison was caught short. She had wondered if she would hear from Quint again, but she hadn't counted on another invitation so soon.

"Tonight? Oh, I wish I could, but I'm busy tonight. I'm taking Jill and some of her friends trick-or-treating. I figure they'll be too old after this year, so I want to take them. We're going to some homes here in town, then to the festivities in the mall in Midland."

"No problem. I'll grab something . . . somewhere."

He sounded disappointed. Rejection was something with which she was all too familiar and hearing it in someone else's voice affected her. "Say, why don't you join us? It's going to be fun. Jill and her friends would get a kick out of you being our guest."

Quint reset his hat and rubbed his chin. "Go trick-or-treating with y'all? I don't know—"

"Oh, come on. I mean, if you don't have something else to do. The kids are going to meet at my house about six. You come, too. We'll do the trick-or-treating, then get something to eat later. Since we're going to be in Midland, maybe we'll go to Tag's place for some barbecue. I think the kids would love the atmosphere."

"Well . . . I guess I could do that. Okay, sure. I'll be there." He started for the door but stopped and turned, wearing a devilish grin. "I don't have to wear a costume, do I?"

Lord, he was cute. Really. What was the matter with her? Here stood a great catch by anyone's standards, and what did she do? Think about another man. Another man who probably had an important date tonight. Another man who showed no greater interest in her than he had shown in every customer in his restaurant. And worse yet, who was the best friend of the only appealing man who had asked her out in years. How dumb could she be?

And in that split second she made a decision. She would give Quint the chance for which he seemed to be asking. Yes, indeed. She would devote her attention to the warm body that was at hand instead of the lukewarm daydream that wasn't. She laughed. "Absolutely not."

The pressing question now was where was the *Cosmopolitan* article to get her out of this dilemma of suddenly having two men in her life and being attracted to the wrong one.

★　★　★

Cradling the phone under his chin, Tag hung his change of clothes behind the door in the employees' break room and busied himself smoothing wrinkles from the purple fabric with his palms. "Sounds good to me, Vanessa. I'll see you tonight. I'll get there around five-thirty or six."

He was excited about this evening. It had been a while since he had done something just for the fun of it. Lately it seemed that his every move had a purpose or goal. No time for fun. The closest he had come to having a really good time had been Saturday night, and he had been thinking about it ever since.

Reliving the same old stories for the hundredth time with Quint was pleasant enough, but being alone with Allison had been the best. They had talked and joked as if they'd known each other for years instead of hours. Tag loved the camaraderie of his old friends, but there was nothing to compare to having a good time with a woman. The question was, under the circumstances, what the hell would he do about it?

ten

Debbie Sue fought the urge to scratch her face as she shifted boxes in the Styling Station's cramped storage space, looking for coconut-scented shampoo. The white greasepaint on her face irritated. For all she knew, when she washed it off, she might find that her whole head had turned into one big zit.

Though the makeup was a pain, all day the beauty salon's customers had raved over her and Edwina's costumes. And they must have loved the pumpkin cookies Vic had baked and the orange Kool-Aid Debbie Sue had contributed because they scarfed up every crumb and drop. One nice thing about Salt Lick was that to celebrate something, no one expected fancy food. Homemade cookies and Kool-Aid worked just fine.

For the kids, Debbie Sue had bought packages of candy wrapped in Halloween-decorated papers. Soon dozens of them would drop by for trick-or-treat goodies. They, too, would get a kick out of her and Edwina. What little girl didn't want to be a ballerina and what kid didn't like a clown?

In truth, as much as she had fun with the kids, she also dreaded having them come by. She couldn't keep from thinking that if life weren't so cruel, she would have a son she might dress up in cowboy regalia and take trick-or-treating. The child she and Buddy had lost was conceived on Halloween. She wondered if Buddy, too, would be thinking about that today. And she wondered, as she often did, if they should try to have another child. They weren't getting any younger. She was past thirty now and Buddy would soon be thirty-four.

She found the shampoo and replaced the boxes just as the jangle of the sleigh bells tied to the front doorknob announced someone's arrival. Her one o'clock appointment.

"Debbie Sue," Edwina yelled. "You're not gonna believe who's here!"

"Dammit, Ed," she yelled back. "I had that intercom system installed so you could talk to me when I'm back here and not wake the dead by yelling."

Edwina's mocking, sultry voice in an exaggerated Southern drawl came over the intercom. "Miizzz Overstreeet, could you pleeezzze come to the front?"

Debbie Sue parted the curtain dividing the storage area from the shop. "Now, is that so hard?"

"Damn, girl," Quint Matthews drawled, "you didn't have to get all dressed up just for me."

Debbie Sue froze. She had expected Quint to show up eventually, but he had said he would call when he got to town. She had hoped he wouldn't come today. Not that she didn't want to see him. She just didn't want him to see *her* looking like a clown. She was no different from every other woman alive, she figured. She wanted an old flame to regret what he lost, not thank God for the lucky break.

She could see Quint struggling to keep a straight face. She yanked off the red yarn wig. "It's Halloween, ass-hole," she told him. "We're dressed as something we'd like to be."

He clapped his hat back on his head and jammed his fists against his waist, his mouth turned up in a big Quint grin. "Awww. Well, darlin', if you needed to dress up as a fantasy, you could have come as Mrs. Quint Matthews."

"Oh, yeah? I thought about it, but I couldn't figure out how to grow a pair of balls."

The grin fell from Quint's face and instantly she regretted having said something so mean. She laid her armload of supplies on her workstation counter and placed a hand on his shoulder. "Oh, Quint, I didn't mean to hurt your feelings. I never would've said that, but you gave me an opening I couldn't pass up."

"That's all right," he said, his head hanging and shoulders slumped forward. "Guess I had it coming."

She could see his pride was still smarting. She continued to pat his shoulder. "C'mon, now. Perk up. You know I was kidding. Look, you probably don't have all day and I don't either. My one o'clock appointment and those kids in their costumes will be here any minute. Let's get down to business. What did you want to talk to us about?"

Quint was the type to take complete charge of his surroundings, but now he looked around the room in obvious discomfort. For a moment Debbie Sue thought he might bolt. Missing was his overinflated ego. Whatever his problem, it must have changed him. "What's wrong, Quint? I've never seen you like this."

"Hell, hon," Edwina said to him, her brow drawn into a frown of concern, "if somebody hollered boo you'd leave a vapor trail."

He sighed, pushed his hat back with his thumb, and rubbed his brow. "Sorry, girls, but you don't know what the last year's been like for me. Those damn reporters from those rag magazines made a fool out of me. I think one of 'em's still following me around even now. I just haven't caught him yet. But when I do . . ." He made a fist and shook it three times.

"Well, rest assured he's not in here," Edwina said, taking an exaggerated look around the room.

Quint looked at the floor and shook his head. "After that bullshit with that Janine—"

"Yeah, what's become of Eugene/Janine?" Edwina asked, plopping into her styling chair, her pink tutu sticking up around her like a turkey's ruff. "No one's seen hide nor hair of him since y'all broke up."

Quint scowled. "Dammit," he said, stabbing the air with his finger, "we did *not* break up. We were never together. I've told this story a dozen times. I was only with him, er . . . her—I was only with her for the photo ops. She was good-looking. It made good press."

"Yeah," Edwina said. "I read some of that good press. Fame's a bitch. Look what it did to Elvis. You know, I had a dream about him the other night—"

"Could we get back to my problem?" Quint gave her a withering glare.

"Hush, Ed," Debbie Sue said. "Let him talk."

Quint turned to Debbie Sue. "Like I was saying, I just thought he was a good-looking woman. I wasn't interested in her, uh, him, sexually."

"That may be the first break your libido ever gave you," Edwina said.

"Ed," Debbie Sue said. "Let. Him. Talk."

"Edwina, you don't like me much, do you?" Quint said.

"That's not true, Quint. I don't have anything against you personally. You're just always leaving yourself so wide open. Go ahead with your story. I'll keep quiet."

Quint sank into Debbie Sue's styling chair and began the story of his experience with the Internet dating service. After several slow starts online, he had finally met a woman from Fort Worth. Monica. She seemed to be what he wanted—smart, funny, and as uninhibited in bed as he was.

Though his ranch was more than a two-hour drive from Fort Worth, without a complaint, he made nine trips up to see her and take her out to the places she wanted to go. They had attended concerts at Bass Hall, spent weekends at the Worthington Hotel, dined in the Reata and other good downtown restaurants. He had to admit he enjoyed the performances at Bass Hall and he liked staying in the luxurious Worthington. The food downtown had been great.

He had, however, found it odd that Monica never wanted him to come to her home. They had always met at a location of her choice. The only phone number he had for her was for a cell. He told himself a young woman being cautious was only natural these days, but after three months and nine dates, her constant vigilance began to worry him.

Debbie Sue, too, sat down in a dryer seat to hear the rest of the story.

When unauthorized charges began appearing on his bank-card bills he hadn't connected them to Monica. Visa's customer-service rep had sent him information on identity theft but told him she doubted that was his problem. She had suggested he look at those "closest to him" for the possibility of a use without permission.

Then, three weeks ago, Quint casually mentioned his predicament during dinner with Monica. She had been sympathetic and caring. He ended by joking and saying to her, "For all I know, it might be you. You're pretty secretive."

She had laughed, excused herself to go to the ladies' room, and he hadn't seen her since. She vanished into the night, leaving a maze of confusion in his head and a wounded heart in his chest.

And a badly bruised ego, Debbie Sue thought. "My God, Quint," she said. "That girl's stolen your identity."

"Damn, Quint," Edwina followed up, "didn't you call

the police? Something bad could have happened to her. She could have been abducted by aliens or something."

Debbie Sue shot her a "shut your mouth" glare.

Quint ignored her. "I called her cell number and she answered. Told me she was okay, that it was all wrong between us and I should forget about her. Just that, nothing else. Every call I've made to her cell since, I get a 'no longer in service' message."

"And that's where we come in?" Debbie Sue asked.

"I want y'all to help me find her. If she's done this to me, she could've done it to someone else, or will soon."

"But besides her stealing your identity, you cared for her," Debbie Sue said, studying him intently. He really did seem to be distraught.

Quint looked down. "Yeah, I cared. I'm capable of caring for somebody. But I care about my reputation more."

Ah, Debbie Sue thought, the real Quint was back.

"We're not talking enough money for me to lose sleep over," he said. "Not yet, anyway. I want to know why she did it. I thought we had something. But most of all, I want to make sure she doesn't sell the story to the tabloids. It'd make me madder'n a peeled rattler seeing her make money off making an ass out of me."

"Why would she expose herself to the press?" Debbie Sue asked him. "If she's done what you said, she could face charges."

"The people she'd be dealing with at those rags would protect her identity if they thought they'd sell a bunch of magazines. You think these assholes who leave anonymous tips with scandal mongers don't get paid well?"

"I guess I never thought about it," Edwina remarked. "Man, Quint, this is some serious karma. In some other life you must have really pissed somebody off."

Quint ran his fingers through his skillfully layered blond hair, a somber expression marring his handsome face. He looked intently at Debbie Sue. "Will you help me? I'll pay you double your usual fee."

The look of desperation in his eyes was more than she could stand. Out the window went her plan and her promise to Buddy to double the fee. Edwina opened her mouth, but Debbie Sue spoke up first. "You don't have to do that, Quint. We'll help you. We just need all the information you can give us. Dates, phone numbers, anything."

Quint nodded. "I've got all the information in my suitcase and some of it on my laptop. I'll bring it to you tomorrow."

"You've brought a suitcase?" Edwina said. "You planning on sleeping on Salt Lick's one park bench?"

"I'm staying at a friend's house in Midland. I want to be close by in case you dig up something for me."

"What's her name and number?" Debbie Sue said, rising and walking over to the reception desk and taking a pencil from a coffee mug.

"What's whose name and number?" Quint asked.

"The woman you're staying with in Midland. You know, in case I need you and you're not answering your phone."

"It's not a her. It's Tag Freeman. I don't have his number

on me, but you can reach him if you need to at his restaurant."

"Well, I'll be damned," Debbie Sue said. "I remember Tag. The last time I saw him was in Oklahoma City. Buddy and I've been to his place to eat a couple of times, but we haven't run into him. Sorry. I just assumed you were staying with a woman."

Edwina tsked. "Poor guy. Been scared off women altogether, have you?"

Debbie Sue felt like kicking Edwina for her sarcasm. Quint was obviously in pain.

"Not entirely," he answered. "In fact, I'm leaving here to visit a lady friend here in town. You might know her. Allison Barker?"

"Allison at the dress shop?" Debbie Sue asked. "Sure, we know her."

Edwina gasped. "That poor little thing never leaves that shop. She's innocent as a lamb. How the hell did *you* meet her?"

Quint glared at her, then turned back to Debbie Sue. "I'll get back to y'all tomorrow with everything you need to get things rolling. I want to do this in a professional way. I expect a daily report. I'm not gonna rest until this is taken care of." He touched the brim of his hat with his finger. "Thanks, girls, I really do appreciate it."

He walked out, but stuck his head back through the doorway. "If your face wasn't all screwed up, I'd kiss you."

"Get outta here," Debbie Sue yelled.

He laughed and shut the door.

She and Edwina stood in the doorway and watched as the Domestic Equalizers' latest customer climbed into his truck.

"That's the biggest, brightest red pickup I ever saw," Edwina said.

"It's a truck, Ed. A one-ton dually. He uses it to pull a stock trailer."

"Two miles to the gallon, I'm guessing."

"I can't believe it," Debbie Sue said, shaking her head. "We just had a conversation about identity theft a couple of days ago and now we've got our first case. And the victim is Quint Matthews, of all people."

"You'd think a person would have been smarter than to pick someone as well-known as Quint."

"Or as stubborn. When he sets his mind to something, he never lets go. That hard head went a long way toward making him a champion."

"My keen ear picked up that his heart is being stubborn, too." Edwina turned from the doorway and stepped back into the salon. "I couldn't help but notice, baby girl. You gave him a pass on doubling the fee."

Debbie Sue could feel her brow furrowed and she remembered the latest magazine article she had read about frowning causing wrinkles. "I know. And after I told Buddy I would, too."

"How do you think he met Allison?" Edwina asked.

"I don't know. If I were going to put two people together, I'd put her with Tag, not Quint."

"I don't think I know this Tag."

"He used to be a rodeo bullfighter. The best ever. He got hurt and got a big settlement from a lawsuit."

"A bull got him, huh?"

"No, shopping got him. He was in a store and a bunch of equipment fell on top of him from about fifty feet up."

"Lawsuit city," Edwina said.

"Yep."

"Speaking of Quint, I suppose it's already occurred to you that Buddy's gonna scream like a mashed cat when he finds out you're seeing or talking to Quint every day."

For the first time ever Debbie Sue dreaded seeing Buddy when she got home. "He already did, but I tried to help him get over it."

Edwina gave her an arch look. "Oh, really? In the usual way?"

Debbie Sue couldn't stop the grin that sneaked across her mouth as she remembered yesterday's confession to Buddy, the argument that followed, and the mind-numbing resolution. Buddy Overstreet knew how to end an argument. "The usual. I'll have to decide later the best way to drop the news about the daily contact."

Edwina gave a mischievous chuckle. "Well, you could always—"

"Cut it out, Ed." Debbie Sue knew what Edwina was going to suggest and it was, well, no one's damn business what went on between her and Buddy.

Edwina opened her palms, her face a picture of wounded innocence. "What'd I say? Anyway, after you've dropped the rest of the news, while you've got him weak and trembling, maybe you could get him to fix that speeding ticket I got over in Odessa last week."

"For your information, Ed, Buddy and I don't settle all our disagreements in bed."

Edwina gave her another arch look. "Really? Since when?"

eleven

"Trick-or-treat? Mom, I'm twelve. I'd die if someone saw me. Besides, I'm not eating carbs. I don't want my face to break out from all that yucky sweet stuff."

Allison stared at her daughter, who had always been an eating machine, especially when it came to sweets. When had she become enlightened about carbohydrates? "What about the mall? Are we still going to the mall, then out to dinner? I've invited Quint and told him that's what we're doing."

"Quint? Quint Matthews is coming? Ohmigod. This is so cool. I can't wait to tell Susan Kay. I knew he'd like you, Mom. Can I take some friends? Can I pick the place to eat? Pleeeze?"

"I was thinking—"

"Could we please go to Tag Freeman's? A bunch of kids from school are gonna be there. Pleeeze?"

The thought of seeing Tag made Allison's pulse quicken. But somehow, feeling attracted to him while she was being escorted by Quint didn't seem right. "I guess so," she said, hoping her eagerness didn't show. "Yes, I guess we could go there."

"Yes!" Jill made a fist and pumped her arm. "How many friends can I take?" She grabbed up the phone and began keying in a number.

Allison smiled, glad to see her daughter so happy and so animated, but she gently removed the phone from Jill's hand. "Just hold on. There are only so many seats in Quint's pickup. I believe two extra guests would be enough. Think you can find two on such short notice?"

"No problem." Jill grabbed the phone again and dashed from the room, but she returned just as quickly. She wrapped her arms around Allison and kissed her on each cheek. "Thanks, Mommy. You're the best."

She was "Mommy" again. The word touched Allison's heart as she watched her daughter leave the room for the second time. Allison would walk through a bed of burning coals for that kid, but truly, going out with Quint again wasn't such a sacrifice to make.

Thirty minutes later she was slipping into a pair of jeans and listening to the giggling and chatter coming from her daughter's bedroom. Jill and her friends sounded like a bevy of squawking hens. She couldn't remember giggling that much when she was their age. Maybe she should talk to them before they left about appropriate behavior.

She walked up the hallway. "Jill?" She opened the door to

her daughter's bedroom and stopped. Jill and her two friends were there, or at least she *thought* that's who they were. Apparently the girls had used the time between hysterical laughter and breathless banter to add ten pounds of makeup to each of their faces.

"Honey, why the heavy makeup? You said you weren't going to be trick-or-treating tonight."

"Mother," Jill said, stamping one foot. "We're not made up for Halloween. You said I could wear makeup."

"I said *some* makeup. A little bit. You know, blush or some lip gloss? You've got more junk on your faces than the front row of a church revival. You look like—"

"Hookers?" Casee Thompson said.

Jill and Susan Kay giggled.

"Cool," Casee added.

Allison rolled her eyes. "Come on. Right now. All of you go into the bathroom and wash that stuff off. You're prettier girls without it."

The three girls dragged past her with the enthusiasm of death-row inmates meeting their doom.

"Use soap and try to remember, eye shadow is meant to work as a highlighter to complement the face. Never, ever wear any color on your entire eyelid, especially green, blue, and"—she looked straight at Casee—"definitely not black."

Watching the girls lather their faces, Allison thought about her own appearance and Quint's. He would be dressed impeccably. Now she wished she had bought more of the stylish clothing she stocked in the dress shop. Looking fashionable might help sales. She remembered something Tag had said about impressing the customers. She made a mental note to work on that, starting tomorrow.

Before she could return to her own bedroom to rethink her jeans and white starched shirt, the doorbell rang. The subdued trio in the bathroom returned to near-hysterical giggling. She reached into the bathroom for the doorknob. "Girls, try to act like young ladies tonight," she said as she closed the door on their prattle. She doubted her words would be heeded, but she needed to say them.

Opening the front door, she broke into laughter herself. Just as she thought, Quint was perfectly groomed. But beneath the soft gray cowboy hat he was wearing an eerily lifelike rubber mask of President George W. Bush.

"Good evening, Mr. President," she said on a laugh. "Sorry I don't have a recording of 'Hail to the Chief.' No Secret Service agents with you tonight?"

"I ditched 'em about two miles back. Pesky bastards. A man can't take a leak without them standing outside the door."

"And Laura?" Allison asked, still laughing.

"She's outside in the rig, facedown in a sack of Snickers. Taking advantage of the private moment. It's hell being in the public eye all the time."

Allison laughed more. She could like Quint if she could stop thinking about Tag. What a delicious predicament. "Come in. Where in the world did you find that mask?"

"Some store off the interstate selling Halloween garb. Looks like him, doesn't it?"

"I'll say. There are constant reports of George W. sightings in Midland. Now I know why."

Quint had removed the mask and was combing his hair with his fingers when Jill and her friends came in. Their freshly scrubbed faces gleamed as they pushed and shoved, jockeying for a position.

"Whoa," Quint said with a big grin. "I thought we were taking some little kids trick-or-treating. Who are these beautiful ladies? You girls waiting for dates?"

The trio blushed, gushed, and all but swooned.

"You remember Jill?" Allison said. "And these are two of her friends, Casee Thompson and Susan Kay. Girls, this is Quint Matthews. He's a world-champion bull rider."

Casee and Kay wiggled their fingers in greeting. Casee pulled a felt-tip pen from her back pocket, then boldly stepped forward, lifted her shirt, and exposed her midriff. "Will you sign my tummy?"

Allison was stunned to silence. This girl definitely had a future. It just wasn't clear if it was in a sleazy trailer park with babies on her hip or as the head of a major corporation.

Without blinking an eye, Quint stuffed the rubber mask in his jacket pocket and replied, "Let me sign your forearm instead. Then everyone can see it."

The less-than-thrilled girl made an exaggerated eye roll.

Grinning, he lifted Casee's arm and scrawled his name. Jill and Susan Kay extended their arms for the same.

"Girls, go get your jackets," Allison said. As they made their exit she turned to Quint. "You handled that so well. I suppose you've had incidents like that before? Overanxious fans? Aggressive women?"

"Oh, yeah. It's those underage ones you gotta watch out for. Nowadays it's harder and harder to tell how old they are. In a few years that Casee will be exposing a breast when she asks for an autograph."

"Yikes, let's go before that happens." Allison picked up her purse from the chair near the door.

"Hold on. I thought we were going trick-or-treating. Door-to-door stuff. They're not in costume. Have the plans changed?"

"Only just a little. Until Jill informed me, I didn't realize twelve-year-old girls don't trick-or-treat anymore. I promised them the mall, then a meal. They want to see some friends at Tag's place, if that's okay with you."

"Sure." Quint replaced his mask and positioned his hat on his head. "I'm game for anything."

Edwina pulled a pan from the oven and sighed. "Vic, I want you to promise me you won't leave me."

She stood in her kitchen doorway holding a pan of chicken breasts that looked like lumps of coal. Every Monday night was her night to prepare dinner and here it was, Monday night again.

Her husband, Vic, being a well-traveled man, an ex–navy SEAL, and a gourmet cook, had been urging her to learn to cook. What was the big deal? Using her less-than-bragging-rights skills in the kitchen, she had raised three daughters and none of them had died.

Vic enjoyed creating meals so much he was convinced that it was something they would enjoy doing together. *Bullshit.* She knew what she enjoyed their doing together and she had heard no complaints in that department.

He rose from his king-size recliner. The grin on his face did nothing to improve her nasty mood. She didn't understand why he was so hell-bent on this project, but because she loved him, she wouldn't refuse to try cooking. Her hard-headed attitude in the past was part of the reason for her three divorces. That plus three lousy choices in men and a dozen "other women."

Vic came to her and placed a kiss on her forehead. "Tell me what you were going for here, Mama Doll."

"What I *should* have been going for was a take-out order from Hogg's. Trying to bake this damn chicken is where I went wrong."

Vic poked a finger at a chicken breast that had been charred into a rock-hard mass. "How high did you set the oven and how long did you let it cook?"

"Five-fifty for about an hour and a half. I like steak a little rare, but I can't stand the thought of rare chicken."

"Well, you did a real fine job of taking care of that, hon. It's not rare, that's for sure. But what I'm more worried about is the fire in the microwave.

"What!" Edwina whirled and saw a flame in the microwave oven.

"Don't open it," Vic said. He quickly reached for the box of salt in the cupboard and poured his hand full. He opened the oven door and threw in the salt. The flame died away.

"I'll be damned," Edwina said. "How'd you know to do that? You didn't learn that in the navy."

"Just a little kitchen trick. Now, how much longer before Debbie Sue and Buddy get here?"

"An hour or so."

"Good. That gives me plenty of time. I'll clean up this mess and you run up to City Grocery and get some more chicken. I'll cook it."

"You got a deal." Edwina set the pan of chicken on the counter. "I'll be back before you miss me."

Damn plastic-and-wire twisty ties, Edwina thought as she drove the short distance to town. She kept forgetting about those when she put things in the microwave straight from the fridge. She had added bread to her list of items to buy at the grocery store.

She lit a cigarette the minute she lost sight of their double-wide trailer. God, it felt good to suck the smoke into her lungs. Oh, sure, she had quit smoking once. Vic had asked her to try and she had. Tried, that is. Her habit had been cut back severely and she could even feel the physical benefits. But stopping altogether was like learning to cook. It was going to take time and it was going to take patience on Vic's part.

You might know Debbie Sue would beg her to invite her and Buddy to supper on her Monday night to cook. That girl's relationship with Buddy was something else. Most women would kneel and kiss Buddy Overstreet's boots every day if he cared about them as much as he cared about Debbie Sue. But Debbie Sue, as much as she loved him, was always doing something, either deliberately or accidentally, that pissed him off. Or for that matter, something that would piss most men off.

Tonight Debbie Sue wanted to discuss with Buddy, with Edwina present, working with Quint on a daily basis to solve his mystery. Buddy might already know the Domestic Equalizers were taking on Quint's case, but he would balk for sure at the daily contact part. Debbie Sue's logic was that if Buddy heard from Edwina's own lips that she would be there, too, he might be more accepting.

As she sat waiting for Salt Lick's one traffic light to go from red to green, Quint's big red truck passed, driven by . . . *George Bush*?

Hmm, so that was Quint's new approach. Incognito. She'd have thought Quint clever enough to come up with a disguise other than the current president of the United States. But who was she to judge?

Edwina recognized Allison Barker in the passenger seat and she saw three heads in the back. She made a mental note to clue Allison in about Quint at her first chance. She didn't know how they had gotten started, but she knew how they would end.

Concentrating on her thoughts, Edwina almost missed the green light. A pickup was approaching, so she made a sharp, death-defying turn in front of it, causing her tires to squeal and narrowly missing being broadsided.

She stomped on the brake, not because the gray pickup's horn had blasted, but because that driver appeared to be someone she knew. Not someone she ever expected to see again, and dammit, not someone she could remember.

Well, the name would come to her later.

The driver of the gray Ford pickup couldn't believe that the classic Mustang had turned in front of a speeding vehicle. What was that person thinking? Did they have coupons that were about to expire? A blue-light special on canning jars? Damn small-town drivers.

The chore of staying far enough behind Quint to be undetected was proving difficult in the sparse traffic. The only way not to be recognized was to follow at a distance, and the driver of the vintage Mustang had almost ruined everything.

Quint had gone into the same house he had been to Saturday night. This time he was wearing a mask of the president's face, and when he came out, he had an adult woman and three girls with him. What was that about? Was the entertainment-starved Quint going in for group sessions now? Was he filming an episode of *Girls Gone Wild*? Answers weren't apparent, but two things were: keeping an eye on Quint Matthews wasn't easy and knowing when to make the right move wouldn't be either.

twelve

The ride to Midland in Quint's luxurious pickup passed quickly. Allison had made the trip so many times she knew every scrubby bush and pump jack by heart. Quint answered the girls' questions with extreme patience. Yes, he knew Kenny Chesney. Yes, Shania Twain was as pretty in person as she was in her videos, and no, he didn't plan on starting a singing career. The girls shrieked with laughter when he gave them a demonstration of his inability to carry a tune.

Allison joined the girls in their banter. It was good to be in the company of happy people, good to get out of Salt Lick for an evening, good to hear the laughter of a male. Her daily world was, for the most part, filled with women. All in all, Jill's impetuous move to improve her life seemed to be working. For the first time ever, she had a man by her side and one in her head. She had to wonder if either one of them would end up in her heart.

Quint had to admit to having a good time. He hadn't looked forward to the evening—hauling a bunch of kids around from door to door, begging for candy. He had never been allowed to do that as a child. His father said it was a "disgraceful display of vagrancy." He didn't know what his mother had thought; once his father had spoken, no one else's opinion mattered.

He stole a glance in Allison's direction. A ready-made family wouldn't be so bad. A twelve-year-old wouldn't be the same as having a baby and being saddled eighteen or more years with a kid in the house. Jill would be eighteen in only six more years.

Tag Freeman was happier than a flea in a pet store. He was in the Zone, at the peak of his point of comfort and wallowing in sheer delight. Music, laughter, sticky fingers, and adoring looks from ecstatic young faces surrounded him.

The minute Vanessa Parker, manager of the Lone Star Mall in Midland, called and asked if he'd dress in clown costume and help entertain children at the shopping mall's Halloween festival, he had jumped at the chance. The mall would be packed with parents, teens, and children looking for a substitute for the door-to-door practice of his childhood days and that was fine with him.

One of the most rewarding parts of his bullfighting years had been the interaction with an audience, especially the kids. He had taught himself to do simple juggling and a few simple but corny magic tricks that evoked peals of laughter from them.

Some of the youngest ones shied away, not sure about the tall man in the funny clothes. But the ones who had run to greet him with a hug around the knees, a tiny hand on the face, a kiss blown on departing . . . well, those were the ones who made it all worthwhile.

He was shaping his umpteenth balloon animal and elaborate balloon party hat when he spotted Quint.

And Allison.

Three young girls appeared to be with them. They circled him and Allison like moons drawn to their planet. One girl in particular bore a striking resemblance to Allison. *Jill.*

Quint being surrounded by women wasn't an unusual sight, but seeing him escorting a group so young was. And this shopping mall was the last place in the universe Tag would ever have expected to see him. Quint must care more about this woman than he was willing to say, was Tag's first thought.

Allison looked beautiful. Understated and simple in jeans and a white shirt. She walked with the ease and confidence of a woman happy in her own skin, not into making an impression or stealing somebody else's thunder.

The palms of his hands had started to sweat and it wasn't from the big white gloves he wore. He recognized the symptoms of adrenaline rush. He was fighting the urge to flee. *Not good, buddy, just not good.*

Thank God for the face makeup, protruding teeth, rubber

nose, and oversize glasses hooked on oversize ears. They and the cap with an attached purple wig made him unrecognizable. At times in the past, people he had known for years had watched his performance without realizing they were looking at someone they knew. One of his favorite jokes was to call out the name of a friend who knew him and watch the look of slow dawning. Priceless.

A young female artist seated near him was painting Halloween scenes on faces—black cats, grinning jack-o'-lanterns, or ghostly shapes running from temple to chin. A sprinkling of glitter on the wet paint made a pretty picture. Practically every young girl who passed fancied the look, and the three accompanying Quint were no different.

"Y'all look," said the one he believed to be Jill, tugging on her mom's arm. "Let's get our faces painted! I love the pumpkin. Can I get my face painted, Mom?"

The other girls joined in, each declaring a choice with enthusiasm equal to Jill's.

"Wait, girls," Allison said. "Let's find out what it costs. Do any of you have money with you?"

Jill said she had ten dollars she had earned, another girl produced a ten and some change, and the one dressed as if she were twenty-five dug a plastic card from her jeans pocket.

"Your mom trusted you with her credit card?" Allison said to her.

"It's not her credit card. It's mine," the girl said. "And it's a debit. No big deal. My account only has fifty dollars in it at a time."

Allison smoothed her hand down the length of the young girl's hair. "Well, be careful and don't lose it. I'd hate to see your evening spoiled."

Tag was close enough to hear the conversation and smiled as he turned away. Allison's message to the young girl was delivered with a sweet, motherly tone.

He was glad for the distraction the face-painting artist provided. Quint's group showed no interest in him as he busied himself with some gawking three-year-olds.

"Hey," Quint called out close to Tag's elbow, "y'all come over here and check out these hats this clown's making."

Tag turned and looked into his old friend's eyes and saw no indication that Quint recognized him, which was surprising in a way. Tag had worn this costume early in his career, before bullfighting became as popular an athletic event as the bull rides themselves. He had expected his longtime friend to remember it, but Quint just looked away, toward Allison and the girls, apparently clueless.

This was an opportunity for some fun and Tag couldn't resist. While the girls took turns having their faces painted, he constructed a huge cowboy hat from a dozen elongated balloons. He tapped his unsuspecting friend's shoulder, quickly lifted off his Stetson, and replaced it with a pink latex substitute, producing great laughter in the group that had gathered.

Quint enhanced the comedic effect by grabbing one of the balloons and blowing it up to its full length. He handed the balloon over to Tag, blew up another, and then challenged him to a mock sword fight. They jabbed and poked at each other until Quint suddenly stopped. With a quizzical stare, he loosened his hold on the balloon, allowing it to float to the floor.

Oh, hell. Something was amiss. Red whelps and streaks were forming on Quint's face and neck. He began to tug at his collar. Quint's allergies rushed into Tag's memory. Tag dropped his own balloons and grasped his friend's shoulders. "Quint? Quint—hey, buddy."

Quint's eyes cut to Tag in obvious bewilderment. "Twag? Twag, ith 'at 'oo, man? I din't weckanithe 'oo."

"You're having a reaction, buddy," Tag said.

Quint yanked the balloon hat from his head and began clawing at the fresh whelps. "Fug. Watex. I'm awergic to watex. I shou'n't o' bwone up tho' bwoons."

Allison came between him and Quint, looking worried. "What's wrong? Quint, you've got red marks all over your face."

Tag focused his gaze on Quint. "Apparently he's having an allergic reaction to the balloons. I forgot all about his allergies." He turned to Allison. "Do you know if he's got his medication with him?"

Allison's brow creased into a frown and she gave him a squint-eyed look. "Tag?"

"Medication. Does he have—"

"In my twug," Quint interjected. "I kee in my twug. Inna gwuf bos."

"How far away did y'all park?" Tag asked Allison.

"The mall has a valet service tonight," she answered, a bewildered look darting between Quint and Tag. "We couldn't find a place to park, so we gave the keys to the valet."

Tag reached into his bag of tricks and retrieved a walkie-talkie. "I'm calling mall security. We can't wait."

"No," Quint exclaimed. "They a caw a amwance! Fug!"

"Sorry, dude, but we gotta do something. You're looking worse by the minute."

"Eeeew, yuck," Casee exclaimed, pushing her way between Tag and Allison for a better view. "What's wrong with his face?"

Quint leveled a look in her direction that should have stunted her growth. "Wee me awone!"

The girl burst into uncontrolled laughter.

"Casee, you and the girls go to the food court and get something to drink." Allison turned the girl around and gave her a little push of encouragement. "I'll find you in a little bit."

Tag's call to mall security produced quick results. Security personnel were quickly on hand. Just as Quint had feared, they immediately placed a 911 call.

In less than ten minutes two EMTs appeared on the scene and a Pamela Anderson look-alike was taking Quint's blood pressure and pulse. The red letters EMT stretched across her ample chest. Her name badge read OLIVIA.

Quint gave her a lopsided grin. "Owiwia. Wha a wuwy name." He dug his truck keys from his pocket. "Twag, ta' the wa'ees back oo Sal' Wick when they're fwu. I know the dwill. I goin' oo the waspi'al."

Another female paramedic, her appearance startlingly opposite that of her coworker, was drawing a syringe of clear-colored liquid from a small vial. She had full command of the situation, delivering orders in military fashion.

"Is he right?" Tag asked her. "Does he have to go to the hospital? Won't that medicine straighten him out?"

"Yes, sir, it'll do the trick, all right. But if we administer medication, sir, we're required to take him to the hospital. The docs have to give him a once-over and sign off on the release. It's policy, sir. Liability concerns, you know. Now, please step back, sir, and let me take care of my patient."

"We'll go with you, Quint," Allison said as the EMT prepared Quint's arm and injected him.

"No, Awison. Tas a wong time. Thot'll work wick, but sy'sem won't." Quint smiled up at the blond goddess.

"What did he say?" Tag asked.

"I think he said the shot will work quick, but the system won't," Allison answered.

The EMT in charge nodded. "He's right, ma'am. He'll be fine by the time we get to the hospital, but allergic reactions are serious. They'll triage him. He'll probably have to wait awhile. Lots of activity in the hospital tonight. Say, isn't that Quint Matthews, the bull rider?"

"Uh, yes. Yes, it is," Allison replied.

The fair-haired angel of mercy took Quint's hand and pressed his arm into her cleavage. "Let me help you, Mr. Matthews. I wouldn't want anything more to happen to you."

Tag resisted rolling his eyes. But then, why was he surprised? All the years he had known Quint, he had seen women behave this way toward him.

Quint was helped by the two women to the gurney. The blonde clucked and fussed over him. He took his position on the stretcher as one well rehearsed in the process. Tag could see he was now in more than capable hands, so he picked up Quint's Stetson and laid it on his stomach.

As the EMTs rolled the gurney toward the mall exit, Allison called out, "I'm so sorry, Quint. Give me a call tomorrow and let me know how you're doing." She turned to Tag and shrugged. "I think we're stranded again. Do you mind being stuck with me and the girls?"

Tag didn't even try to restrain a grin.

Allison watched the EMT staff wheel Quint into the cool West Texas night. She felt guilty not following him or offering reassurance of some kind. It had all happened so fast.

It wasn't that she was unconcerned for his well-being, but she had worked in a doctor's office long enough to know that the true emergency was over and what followed was just paperwork.

That is, unless he got someone to complete the task of collecting personal information so that he would be free to collect the blonde's personal information. Allison hadn't missed the "reassurance" he received from the tall, attractive female taking his blood pressure, nor had she missed Quint's response. She knew she held no claim on the man—in fact, she hardly knew him—but she had noticed his roving eye each time they had been together.

Tag was different.

Just then, he asked her to have a seat nearby while he finished out the hour. She did just that.

He kept looking in her direction and smiling or winking. She enjoyed watching him interact with the crowd. Both young and old enjoyed his tricks and antics.

A young mother with twin daughters, who looked to be about six months old, approached Tag and asked if he would hold the girls while she snapped a picture. The moment the mother stepped away, the infants let out a howl.

Tag, a baby cradled in each arm, cooed and jiggled to no avail. He shot Allison a look of helplessness. She rose from her seat, moved forward, and took one of the babies in her arms. She rocked from side to side, talking in a soothing voice, and the infant soon became quiet. The sister in Tag's arms stopped crying, too.

For a brief moment her eyes locked on Tag's and a surreal feeling overtook her. She felt as if she had lived this moment before. It seemed so natural, so real. All she could do was keep smiling like a loon. Tag returned the smile.

He leaned toward her. Allison felt he was going to ask her a question, but she would have loved for him to kiss her. She leaned forward, too, but was yanked from her reverie by a female voice.

"My God. Tag Freeman, is that you? You're a sight for sore eyes."

Allison swung her gaze to the woman.

"Gone back to clowning, huh?" a beautiful petite blonde said. "And with a baby in your arms?"

Allison looked up at Tag. Even his heavy makeup failed to hide his shock.

"Are these yours?" the female asked, swinging a finger back and forth between the twins. Before Tag could reply, the woman turned to Allison and looked her up and down. Allison felt as if she had been undressed. "They're sweet, honey."

"Thank you, but I'm not the mother." Allison pointed toward the young woman with the camera. "She's over there."

"Oh. Okay. I was about to tell you to not give up. You'd get your prebaby body back soon. Sorry."

Allison felt her spine go rigid. She had just been insulted by a pro. No fear, no intimidation, no concern for the effect of the message. Yet she put out her right hand, smiling the forced smile she had honed from years of working with the public. "How do you do. I'm Allison Barker. And you are?"

"Diann Freeman. Mrs. Taggert Freeman."

"Who's the last person in the world you'd expect to see in Salt Lick?" Edwina asked.

The lanky brunette refilled everyone's glasses with sweet tea. No one made sweet tea quite like Vic, Debbie Sue thought, and he wasn't even a Texan. She finished chewing a bite of chicken Marsala excellently prepared by Vic, as usual, then dabbed at her mouth with a square of paper towel. "Russell Crowe."

"Dammit, I'm serious," Edwina said, her fist resting on a bony hip. "The very last person you thought you'd see in Salt Lick?"

"Oooh, I thought you said, 'Who would you most *like* to see in Salt Lick?' My mistake. I give up. Who did you see?"

"Russell Crowe?" Buddy said, spearing a bite of salad. "You mean that actor?"

Debbie Sue leaned and kissed his cheek. "He's not nearly as cute as you, honey bunch."

Buddy frowned. His black mustache twitched. "Cute?"

"It's driving me crazy," Edwina said. "I can't put my finger on who it was. But it was someone we know and the last person I'd expect to see. It was a gray pickup and it came so close to crashing into me, I damn near took out that Elvis Ate Here sign at Hogg's Drive-in."

"Oooh, no," Debbie Sue said, her eyes widening. "It'd be a shame to wipe out Hogg's claim to fame."

"Oh, I don't know," Buddy put in. "Their food's pretty good. They're well-known for that."

"I agree," Vic said.

"Anyway," Edwina said, "back to my question. I was kinda hoping y'all would supply something I could work with. Who do we know who drives a gray pickup?"

Debbie Sue mentally ran through a list of acquaintances, almost all of whom drove pickup trucks. She couldn't think of a gray one. "My crystal ball's plumb cloudy," she said finally.

"Mama Doll," Vic put in, patting Edwina's arm, "we

could play this game all night. Don't think about it. Just clear it out of your mind and the name will come to you."

"You're right. I'll think about something else." Edwina set the pitcher of tea on the table and reclaimed her seat at the table. Several minutes of eating passed before anyone spoke. "So, who do you think it was?" she asked.

Riding as Tag's passenger in his second unplanned trip to Salt Lick, Allison was more reflective than she had been on the previous ride. She didn't like admitting such a dark character flaw, but she was more than a little jealous of Tag's ex-wife. The blonde had taken his hand with unmistakable possessiveness. The ease and familiarity with which her arm slid around his waist sent a message loud and clear: *This is mine.*

Just as distressing was that the former Mrs. Freeman looked like the type of woman Allison longed to be—big, baby-blue eyes, blond layers and ringlets cascading like a waterfall down her back, and petite in stature, with a traffic-stopping body. If appearance dictated who belonged in the back of a convertible waving to an admiring crowd, Diann Freeman met all of the criteria. At that thought, Allison's dark side assumed an even stronger presence and she imagined how much better the woman would look *under* a convertible as it drove over her doll-like body.

Allison winced, disliking herself for the evil thought even more than she envied the ex–Mrs. Freeman.

In the backseat, Jill and her friends chatted and giggled, still exuberant and obviously overstimulated by the candy, soft drinks, and other teenage excesses of the evening. Their main topics were who had been wearing what and what boys were in the mall.

Tag, at total ease, talked and joked with the girls. A glance from his brown eyes came Allison's direction occasionally, but all she could return was a weak smile. She was afraid to say much, afraid the question "So you and your ex are getting back together?" would blurt from her mouth. She didn't want to make a total fool of herself, nor did she want to hear the answer.

"Did Quint ever mention that he was allergic to latex?" Tag asked her. "I've seen him have an allergic reaction to some foods, but he's never said a word about latex. Of course, that's not the kind of thing guys talk about."

"No, the subject never came up. But then, I hardly know him." She hesitated, debating if she should take advantage of the opening Tag had given her. The uncharacteristic jealousy she felt won the argument. "Was Quint's ex-wife friends with yours?"

"Not really. More like competitors."

From somewhere, Allison dredged up a silly titter. "What were they competing for? You and Quint?"

Tag's baritone chuckle filled the cab. Good. If he was laughing, hopefully that meant he hadn't noticed that she was prying. "They might've wanted the same fella a time or two, but the rodeo competition was the real contest. Both of them were barrel racers. And they both went for the Miss Rodeo America title. Diann lost."

"A beauty pageant? But I always thought beauty contestants were tall and willowy. Your ex can't be over five feet."

Practically a midget, Allison's evil twin thought.

"Five foot two to be exact. Miss Rodeo America's not your typical beauty contest. A gal's got to be more than pretty. She's got to be a hell of a horsewoman, too."

The bitter bile of jealousy filled Allison's mouth again, but, unfortunately, it wasn't harsh enough to make her shut up. "So don't leave me in suspense. They rode off into the sunset together." She frowned at her own cattiness.

Tag reached out and covered her hand with his own. "I know you must think a lot of Quint. All women do. But you don't have to worry about his ex-wife. She's been out of his bloodstream for a long time. I never believed he cared deeply for her anyway." He added a chuckle. "Most of Quint's affection is reserved for himself." He sighed then. "She was a beauty, though. You'll get no argument from me there. But her heart was black as tar."

Allison cared nothing about Quint's ex-wife's heart. She bit her lip and looked out at the Salt Lick city-limits sign zooming past the window.

She's been out of his bloodstream for a long time echoed in her head.

And how about you? she wanted to ask Tag. *Who's doing the backstroke in your bloodstream?*

Tag pulled in front of Allison's house and killed the engine, hoping it sent the message that he would like an invitation inside. He hated seeing the evening come to a close.

The girls piled out of the rear passenger seat and ran for the house. Jill had almost reached the front step when Allison called out, "Jill, come back here. Did you forget to thank Mr. Freeman for bringing us home?"

Jill stopped in midstep. She turned and walked back, smiling sheepishly. "Thanks for bringing us home, Mr. Freeman. And thanks for letting us eat at your restaurant and stuff." The girl looked at her mother for approval, then turned and dashed to the house again.

"She's a great kid," he said.

"Thanks. She *is* a great kid, but naturally, I think so. She's never in trouble, always minds, and always makes good grades. I wish I had a dozen like her."

"Really? You want more kids?"

"Oh, I don't think about it so much anymore. But I used to."

"A lot of career women don't want the bother of raising kids. Like it's beneath them or something." Tag played with the keys dangling from the ignition.

"Career woman? Me? Lord, I'm just trying to make a living. I've never thought of my job as a career."

"Well, you should. You've got a lot of responsibility and you're all alone. I know some pretty tough gals collecting six-digit paychecks who aren't doing it as well as you do."

Tag hoped his words rang true. Single mothers held a special place in his heart. His own mother had raised him and his younger brother alone and the memory of shared TV dinners, shared clothing, and nights hearing his mom cry in her bedroom still came back to him at odd times. Growing up in the Freeman house, there had never been enough of anything but hugs and kisses. Those his mother gave freely and often.

"Would you like to come in for a while," Allison asked. "Or do you need to rush back and pick up Quint?"

Damn, his eagerness to spend a few more precious minutes with Allison had made him forget he had to get right back to Midland. "I guess I could come in for just a few minutes."

He slid out, rounded the front of the truck, and collided with Allison. They both stepped back and laughed. Suddenly all he wanted to do was kiss her. He pulled her to him and was relieved at the eager response his lips found. As his passion rose he was interrupted by his cell-phone tone indicating a text message had been received.

He broke away. As he plucked his phone from his belt they stood as if in an intimate cocoon. He glanced down at the phone's tiny screen and saw the backlit message all too clearly. *Hey—redy 2 go. Where R U? Q.*

thirteen

For the second time in four days Quint found himself waking up in the afternoon with a killer headache. Alcohol and epinephrine did that to him.

This part of Texas was nothing but a damn disaster for him. In this place, he had endured as much pain and suffering as he had in the rodeo arena. Yet he kept getting sucked back here like a blade of grass in the path of an oncoming tornado.

He had heard Tag leave earlier in the morning. Having never held a regular job with a set schedule, Quint couldn't imagine getting up and going to work every day. Even his successful rodeo livestock company didn't require his daily presence at his office in Seguin.

He had Tag's home to himself. Padding barefoot across the Saltillo tile that covered the floors throughout the house, he followed the aroma of coffee into the kitchen. *Ahhh.*

Thank God, Tag had left hot caffeine waiting. That Tag was a good guy. Perhaps a little idealistic, but all in all, a real good guy.

Quint leaned against the counter and sipped coffee as he looked over the home's Southwest-style interior. Rough-hewn beams, rustic furniture, the scent of leather lingering in a subtle way. Original Western art hung on the walls. Manly, but not overly so. Tag must have hired a professional to do the decorating.

Taking his time, Quint refilled his cup. He had only one task for today and it was easy: drive to Salt Lick and deliver the information Debbie Sue had requested.

And maybe drop in on Allison. Visiting her today hadn't been his original plan, but now he supposed he should. He'd had two dates with her and hadn't seen either of them through.

When he saw Allison this time, things would be different. This time, he would take charge. No outside influences, no unexpected plans, and for damn sure, no kids. Meeting Allison's daughter's pushy little friend had been enough to remind him of the hazards of being around teenage girls.

Allison could think of nowhere she had ever been that was more relaxing than the Styling Station. Her tensions began to slink away as Edwina's brush slid through her hair and she listened to the words of "I Fall to Pieces" delivered by Patsy Cline's crystal-clear voice. "That's such a good song," she said. "It's a true classic."

"It sure is," Edwina replied. "Debbie Sue does have good taste in music."

Allison adjusted the plastic apron Edwina had draped over her shoulders. "I don't want to get too much hair on my clothes. I have to get back to Almost the Rage."

"Why, hon, it's late in the day. You should go on home." Allison's gaze caught Edwina's and they both looked into the mirror. "You know, you're about three weeks past needing a trim. Where've you been keeping yourself?"

"Oh, you know. Working. Seems like that's all I do anymore."

"Man, do I ever know. When I was your age I was alone with three little girls. I held down two jobs and took in ironing on top of that." Edwina laughed. Allison loved hearing her friend's robust laugh.

"I kept giving my ironing customers my own kids' clothes by mistake," Edwina continued as she ran a brush through Allison's hair. "I had to give up that ironing job when I realized buying new clothes was costing me more than I was making ironing. My poor girls. I can barely remember raising them. Seems like all I ever did was work while they raised themselves."

Allison looked at Edwina in the mirror. She had never heard anything but good about Edwina's children. "But they turned out all right. I mean, from what you've told me, it sounds like they have terrific lives."

"Oh, they're great. And yep, they're happy. All three married wonderful men. God love 'em, they turned out just fine. In spite of having me for a mom."

"Oh, Edwina, I know you're exaggerating. I've seen you from the store window, stopping to feed stray dogs and cats. I doubt you were anything less than a good mother."

"Well, maybe I'm stretching the truth a little, but looking back, I still wish I could have worked less and stayed at home with them more. They're only young once."

"And that time flies by," Allison said softly.

"And that time flies by," Edwina confirmed.

Debbie Sue came through the curtained door from the storeroom and saw the two women staring into emptiness with gloomy expressions. "What happened to y'all? I wasn't in the back more than three minutes. You look like you just found out George Strait was in town and you missed him." She walked over and switched on the CD player. George Jones came on with "The Race Is On." "There. That ought to liven things up a little."

Edwina sniffed and straightened her shoulders. "We're fine. Just talking. So you want just a trim, Allison?" She lifted a sheaf of her hair and let it fall. "I can't talk you into a manicure, too?"

"No, thanks, just a trim today."

Debbie Sue began restocking her beauty tray without entering the conversation, but she'd have had to be deaf not to have heard it. Talking about her children was one of the few times Edwina got emotional.

Debbie Sue couldn't contribute much to a discussion of offspring, but if Edwina and Allison thought having one grow up quickly was hard, they should know the pain in having one that never grew up at all. This year, her and

Buddy's little Luke would be eleven if he had lived. It dawned on Debbie Sue that she and Allison were almost the same age, and if Luke had made it this far, he and Allison's daughter might be friends. A rush of sadness sluiced through her.

"So," she said to Allison, trying to sound cheerful, "I hear you've been dating Quint Matthews."

"I wouldn't call it dating. We've had only a couple of sort of get-togethers."

"Quint and I go back a long way. Did he tell you?"

"He said y'all had been friends since you were kids." Debbie Sue listened as Allison told about being brought home twice by Quint's friend, then about Quint's allergic reaction to the latex balloons and how concerned she had been.

"Yep," Debbie Sue said, "I remember the night a couple of years ago when Vic nearly killed him with cheesecake and Frangelico sauce."

Edwina nodded solemnly. "That's a fact."

"It's kind of funny when you think about it," Debbie Sue said. "I mean, when have you ever met a more macho guy than Quint? He's tougher than a boiled owl, but he's allergic to damn near everything."

"Getting back to you and Quint," Edwina said to Allison's reflection. "Twice now you've started the evening with him and ended up with Tag? Why, girl, that's karma. Maybe you should heed the signs and shift your sights to Tag. I don't know him, but I can already tell you I like him better than Quint. Who wouldn't?"

"Now that's not fair," Debbie Sue said. "Not that Tag's

not a good guy. And not that Quint doesn't have a few short-comings, but—"

"Shortcomings? Is that what they're calling it these days when a man can't keep his pants zipped?" Edwina patted Allison's shoulder. "Listen to ol' Edwina, sugarfoot. Forget Quint."

"Why don't you like him, Edwina?" Allison asked.

"He's got one thing on his mind all the time. And that's taking care of himself and the little cowboy between his legs. Not that I have anything against a man with a healthy libido, but when he cares more about that than other people's feelings, then, as far as I'm concerned, he's a jerk."

"But he's been a perfect gentleman," Allison said.

"It's been two dates, right? I guaran-damn-tee you that by the next date he'll make his move."

"Ed," Debbie Sue said, ever compelled to stand up for a friend. "Quint just needs to find the right woman. For all we know, it could be Allison. After what happened with Eugene/Janine, he might have matured and grown past all that naked ape stuff."

"Who's Eugene/Janine?" Allison asked.

"It's a long story, hon," Edwina answered.

"He's somebody we ran into once who can't tell what sex he wants to be," Debbie Sue added.

"You mean he's gay? What does that have to do with Quint?"

Edwina flopped a wrist. "You don't wanna know. That's an even longer story."

"Well, Quint seems like a changed man to me," Debbie Sue said.

Edwina's jaw dropped and she gasped. "I'd believe a poker deck has five aces before I'd believe that."

"Okay, Texas Slim. I'll make a bet with you. If he's not a changed man, I'll kiss your butt and call you Shorty."

The sleigh bells on the doorknob jangled, interrupting the conversation. With Allison being the last customer of the day, a walk-in at this hour wasn't welcome. Edwina and Debbie Sue turned to look as Quint stepped into the salon.

"Well, if it's not the hard-on king," Edwina mumbled.

Debbie Sue shot her a murderous glare. "Come on in," she said to Quint, "and lock the door behind you. We're done for the day."

"You know, darlin', those are just the words I love to hear coming from a good-lookin' woman's mouth. 'Lock the door behind you.' " He removed his hat and was moving in Debbie Sue's direction when he stopped midstride. "Allison! Baby, I didn't see you sitting there. Lord, even with that plastic apron around your shoulders, you look pretty as a picture. Just how do you manage that?"

Allison smiled weakly. Debbie Sue saw a pinkish hue creeping up her neck. Edwina made an exaggerated gasp.

"Did you bring us the stuff we need to get started?" Debbie Sue asked, eyeing the tan tooled leather satchel he carried under his arm.

Quint's eyes went to Allison first, then to Debbie Sue and Edwina. "Can I talk to you in the back room?"

"Sure," Debbie Sue said, and started for the storeroom.

"Darlin', would you excuse us, please?" Quint said to Allison, lifting his Stetson.

Edwina walked to the storeroom doorway and pulled back the curtain for Quint to pass through. "Watch yourself, cowboy. I've got electric clippers here. Ever heard of a Brazil wax? You don't want to experience an Edwina buzz."

"Point taken, ma'am. You girls are in safe hands."

Inside the storeroom, Quint spoke in a low tone. "Listen, Allison doesn't know anything about my business here. I'd like to keep it that way."

"Why, Quint Matthews," Edwina said with an exaggerated lift of her chin, "we don't discuss our cases. We're fuckin' professionals. We've taken a hypocritic oath."

"Hippocratic oath, Ed," Debbie Sue said. "That's the one doctors take. I don't think it applies to us."

Edwina flipped a hand. "Oh, yeah. Well, whatever. No real difference, to tell the truth. We've worked for some pretty sick people, lemme tell you."

"Like I was *trying* to say," Quint said with strong conviction, "I'd rather Allison didn't know."

"Oh, quit worrying," Debbie Sue said. "We're not gonna blab your secrets."

"I want to know one thing," Edwina said. "Just where did a skirt chaser like you meet somebody as nice as Allison?"

"The same place I met Monica. Online."

"Good Lord, Quint," Debbie Sue said, "didn't you learn your lesson from that Monica?"

"Allison's different. She's stable. Grounded. Hasn't expected anything from me. So far, that is."

"And she won't, either," Edwina defended. "She's too good for that. It's too damn bad you didn't follow through with giving up women before you got to her."

"Look, you don't think I meant that, I hope. Hell, I'm not gonna live like a monk. I've got needs. And urges. Anyway, we understand each other about keeping my business private, right? That's all I wanted to say." He turned to leave, but stopped and looked back over his shoulder. "Y'all coming?"

"We'll be right behind you in a sec," Edwina said. "I gotta get something first."

Quint disappeared through the curtained doorway.

"What do you need, Ed?" Debbie Sue asked.

Edwina gave her a reptilian grin. "I just want to take advantage of an opportunity. I want to bend over and hear you call me Shorty."

Debbie Sue gave her an eye roll.

Edwina's expression grew serious. "You know we've got to protect Allison from him, don't you?"

Allison had been fidgeting in the styling chair, leafing unseeing through the pages of a *Glamour* magazine. Curiosity about what was going on in the storeroom was killing her.

Quint came back and she looked up, catching his gaze in the mirror. He intimidated her so, it seemed easier to talk to his reflection than to his face.

A sexy lopsided grin played across his face. "Hey, pretty thing, what time are we getting together tonight?"

She could feel his breath on her lips. She had never experienced a man as presumptuous as Quint. Still, as much as his boldness frightened her, it excited her. "Oh, Quint, I wish I could. But this is a school night."

"Not for you." He gripped the arm of the styling chair and turned it slowly until she faced him. He braced his hands on the chair arms, caging her, then leaned in close, surrounding her with the fragrance of his heavenly cologne. She felt trapped beneath the heavy plastic salon apron.

"Has anybody ever told you you've got incredible eyes?" he said in a low seductive voice.

Good grief! How she wished she were worldly enough to handle him. She gulped. "Sometimes."

"Can't your mom watch Jill?"

"That's not it. She doesn't need watching. I just want to spend some time with her tonight. Have supper together, help her with her homework or discuss school with her. Maybe I can go out with you another time?"

His lips brushed hers. "Another time, then. I'll be counting on it."

Just as she fought the urge to touch her lips with her fingertips, Edwina said from behind him, "It breaks my heart to interrupt you two, but, Allison, we need to do that haircut."

Quint straightened and glared at Edwina.

Allison breathed a sigh of relief. Her insides were trembling. "Yes, I really do need the cut."

"Yes, you do." Edwina edged Quint aside with her elbow. "Excuse me, Mr. Matthews, I've got work to do."

"Allison, I'll be in touch later," Quint said, and winked at her. He looked at Edwina. "Is Debbie Sue still in the back room?"

"She's still back there and don't forget what I said about the clippers."

Quint chuckled as he started back toward the storeroom.

Debbie Sue looked up when he returned. She was sitting in the comfy chair she and Edwina had dragged in and tucked into a corner so they would have a place to take breaks and get off their feet. She had already been scanning the information Quint had brought and had seen enough to discern how clever this thief had been in deceiving him.

"Hey," she said. "I thought you left. Listen, how're we supposed to know what this Monica looks like. Don't you have a picture of her?"

"The bank's faxing one to me tomorrow. It's one of those security-camera shots at an ATM machine. They said it was poor quality, but maybe it's good enough to use."

"That'll help." She tapped a finger on the sheaf of papers on her lap. "You know, we need to figure out a good trap to set for this girl."

Quint pushed his hat back with his thumb and planted his hands at his belt. "A trap? I don't get it. How do we trap her when we don't even know if we've got her real name?" He sighed and hung his head. "Maybe this mess can't be straightened out. Maybe I'm gonna have to learn to live with it."

Seeing him down and dejected was almost more than

Debbie Sue could bear. His cocky attitude was part of his persona. She got to her feet and patted his shoulder. "Now, now. You can't just throw in the towel. Give Ed and me a little credit. You might be surprised what we can turn up."

In truth, Debbie Sue herself would be surprised at what they might turn up, if anything. The investigation had scarcely begun, and already, rooting out someone who had committed fraud appeared to be a lot harder than spying on a cheating husband.

"Sorry," Quint said, sinking to the chair Debbie Sue had vacated. "The past four days have been kind of strange. What kind of trap do you have in mind?"

Debbie Sue began to pace, thinking aloud. "I'm thinking Ed and I could join two or three of these online dating services. You can tell us the kind of profile you posted that hooked this witch. If she hasn't retired she'll be trolling for another sucker." Debbie Sue grimaced at what she had just said and stopped and looked at him. "Sorry, I didn't mean—"

"Hey, that's okay. I was a sucker. Might as well say it."

"So what do you think of that plan?"

"Not bad. There is one hitch. Thinking back, she told me once she only writes back to men who post a picture. I don't know why it mattered to her. She obviously wasn't in for the long haul, so why would a guy's looks be important?"

"Hmm. Maybe she didn't want to make a mistake and accidentally meet someone she already knew. Or maybe she wanted the whole package, good looks to go with a thick wallet."

"Could be. But to make this scheme work, you'll have to post a *man's* picture."

"I'll figure it out. But right now I gotta get home. Buddy and I are going out for dinner. It's our anniversary."

He gave a sarcastic *pfft* and stood up. "Which wedding? The first or the second?"

Debbie Sue tilted her head and looked up at him, not liking the tone of his voice. "The first one, smart-ass."

He didn't grin at her sarcastic retort. His eyes held hers for a few seconds. "Too bad," he said at last. "You know, it could have been *our* anniversary."

She hesitated. When she had gone out with Quint before she remarried Buddy, he had never mentioned marriage. He had talked about her being his lover, his traveling companion, and his horse buyer, but never his wife. She smiled. "You wouldn't have married me in a million years, Quint. I know that. Let's just leave it at that, okay? What's going on between us now is strictly professional."

His sky-blue eyes drilled her as he lifted off his hat and reset it. "Fine. Suit yourself. But you don't know everything." He walked out of the storeroom.

Maybe not, Debbie Sue considered, but one thing she believed she did know was that Quint Matthews wasn't the marrying kind. He was just irked because he'd lost a contest to Buddy.

But she couldn't get into analyzing Quint's personality now. She was going home to her sweet baby, the best-looking—and most loyal—man in Texas.

She pulled a box from the shelf to her right and rummaged through it. Soon she found what she was looking for—a disposable camera she and Ed had bought for Domestic Equalizers business. She intended to take it with her tonight in case she wanted a picture of Buddy to remember their anniversary by. Nothing wrong with a girl wanting a picture of her husband to carry in her wallet or display in a frame. Nothing at all wrong with that.

She stuffed the camera into her purse and returned to the salon's front room. The shades were pulled and Edwina was sweeping up. "I'm outta here, Ed."

"Bye, doll, and happy anniversary. Tell that good-looking son of a gun you're married to I'm still waiting for him to get me a pair of my very own handcuffs."

Debbie Sue laughed. "I'm sure he hasn't forgotten. They don't use real handcuffs these days, you know. They've got those plastic things like you use to tie up garbage bags."

"If you look at it one way," Edwina said, "I guess it's the same thing."

On a laugh, Debbie Sue started for the door, but stopped. "Did Allison stick around and talk to Quint again?"

"Nah, she hightailed it out of here before he came back from the storeroom the second time. He makes her nervous. He makes me nervous, too. I gave Buddy my word that I wouldn't leave you alone with that character and here I've broken my promise the first rattle out of the box."

"I know you promised because you had to, Ed. When Buddy Overstreet wants you to do something, it's hard to say no. But you don't have to chaperone me and Quint. I'd never cheat on Buddy. Quint wouldn't try anything anyway.

His ego's so fragile right now, he couldn't take any more rejection."

"Just the same, I'd hate to be standing here looking like an idiot if Buddy comes through that door and you're in the back room with Quint. Good God Almighty, I don't even want to think about the explosion." She stopped her sweeping and leaned on the broom. "Now, tell me what kind of scheme you and Quint cooked up."

Debbie Sue filled her in on the conversation and the plan.

"So we're gonna stick some guy's picture on the Internet? On a *dating site* on the Internet?"

"I think it's a great idea, don't you?"

"It might be. If we had a willing, good-looking guy who'd go along with it."

Debbie Sue grinned. "Let me worry about that."

Edwina's jaw dropped and her mouth formed an *O* as a knowing expression came into her eyes. "Child, I don't like what you're thinking. Buddy's liable to lock you and me both up."

Debbie Sue adjusted her purse strap on her shoulder. "Listen, I gotta scoot. He's waiting for me. I'll remind him about those handcuffs."

fourteen

Nothing like starting the day with a grouch. Tag peered over the top of his newspaper at his houseguest, sitting on the other side of the table. His effort to talk to Quint had been wasted. The guy mumbled, grumbled, and kept his nose buried in the sports section.

Tag hid his amusement behind his own section of the paper. He didn't know what his old pal had done the previous evening, but apparently it hadn't gone well. "See Allison last night?" he asked finally.

"Nope."

"Gonna see her tonight?"

"Don't know."

"Get over to Salt Lick like you planned?"

"Yep."

"Then how come you didn't see her? You still like her, don't you?"

"I guess so. I haven't got to be around her much. Some damn foolishness happens all the time. Or her kid . . . wait just a damn minute." Quint laid the paper on the table and gave his friend a quizzical look. "You sure seem interested in what's going on with me and Allison. Or is it just *her* you're interested in? You've taken her home twice now. Is there something I oughta know about?"

"Just trying to figure out who put a burr under your saddle blanket." Tag sipped his coffee and avoided Quint's eyes.

"Uh-huh."

"Don't worry, buddy. The only way I'd ever see Allison is if you weren't interested in her. But you are, right?"

"Dink—"

"Drop it."

Tag was uncomfortable. He had hoped Quint would say she wasn't his type or even that he had something in the works with that blond paramedic, Olivia. Since Halloween night Tag had thought about little else than the kiss he and Allison had shared. That elusive thing people always talked about and looked for, chemistry, had been strong in the wind that night.

Then he remembered that in all the commotion after Quint's allergic reaction, he'd forgotten to tell him about Diann. "Did I tell you who showed up at the mall the other night after the ambulance hauled you off?"

"Who?"

"Diann."

"Diann who?"

"My ex, Diann. How many other Dianns do we know?"

"Oh. *That* Diann." Quint's eye twitched. He stood up, walked to the counter, and refilled his mug. "She still good-looking?"

"I couldn't tell you. She quit looking good to me a long time ago."

"Was she with somebody?"

Tag looked at his friend standing at the kitchen counter drinking coffee. "Now it's my turn to ask. You interested in her? 'Cause if you are, the best advice I can give you is to run the other direction and don't look back."

"I was just wondering who she's hooked up with these days, is all." Quint set his mug on the counter. "Listen, do you mind if I borrow your office for a little while? I'm expecting a fax."

"Naw, help yourself. I gotta go to town anyway." Tag rose and gathered and plumped the newspaper stack. He tossed it in the recycle bin as he passed through the kitchen on his way to the back door. "I'll see you later."

"Yeah. Later."

Once Tag was in his truck, he sat there letting the engine idle. At least Quint hadn't been out with Allison last night. Tag suspected he had asked her, but had been turned down. That accounted for his bad mood.

Tag sighed. All that meant was there was another night to get through.

Another day, another dollar. Hopefully.

Debbie Sue sat in her styling chair, her boots propped on her workstation counter, ankles crossed. No customers were due for an hour. One of the pleasures of arriving early was sitting undisturbed and collecting her thoughts before the day started.

The many pages of information Quint had left with her lay on her thighs. He must have printed out every online conversation he and Monica had conducted. Internet dating. Damn. She didn't know if she was capable of baring her heart and soul to the online personals. Oh, she knew plenty of people who had, women and men both, right here in Salt Lick. She heard their stories often enough from her styling chair. If she felt her options were exhausted she might do it, but thank God she didn't have to. She was so lucky to have Buddy. She couldn't imagine being single again or searching for someone with whom to connect.

She hummed to herself and sipped her coffee as she read, wondering if this Monica was an alias. Her last name might not be real either.

It was easy to see why Quint had been taken in. The woman seemed to be a willing, sincere innocent, not a con artist moving in for the kill. Her words seemed to reveal someone sweet but at the same time seductive. She had typed a positive response to everything Quint had said he liked. Every invitation he had extended, she had accepted. Yet the girl gave away nothing of herself. Not a clue to reveal her location.

As much as Debbie Sue wanted to find the woman who had stolen Quint's identity, she was more than a little curious to see the one who had stolen his heart. She couldn't help but feel compassion for him. She knew that underneath all that bluster and cockiness he was lonely. The memory of the look on his face when he first told her and Edwina the story made her want to cry.

In contrast to the pity she felt for Quint, she had a fair number of venomous emotions building for the crook who had taken advantage of him. She intended to get the opportunity to tell that woman what she thought of her.

The notion that this mystery was going to be hard to solve sneaked into her thoughts again. In a discussion of credit-card fraud with Buddy last night during dinner, he had pointed out the low percentage of arrests and convictions for such crimes.

The thought of Buddy made her think of last night's anniversary celebration. He had been surprised when she suggested dining at Tag Freeman's Double-Kicker joint. He thought she would want to go to Kincaid's in Odessa, the steak house they had labeled as "their place." He thought she would think it was romantic.

During the time she and Buddy had been divorced, he had taken his girlfriend to Kincaid's. Consequently the romantic aura Debbie Sue had attached to the place had been tainted. But Debbie Sue didn't tell him that. After all, hadn't she gone to Kincaid's with Quint? She had simply assured Buddy that dinner was the least romantic part of the evening and the best was yet to come.

Besides, she didn't get a chance to go to Tag Freeman's place often, and being an ex-rodeoer herself, she felt a loyalty to him.

In her rodeoing days she had known Tag, but not well.

Back then, sometimes when she hung out around the arena long enough to watch Quint make his ride, she would see Tag entertaining a crowd with magic tricks. Then, as soon as Quint won or lost, she would load up Rocket Man and head up the road to the next performance. That life had been hard and not for the faint of heart. She had been a kid and thought she was invincible. Sometimes she still thought about those days, but now the whole thing seemed more like a dream that had occurred long ago, one she had no desire to relive.

After a delicious barbecue meal, she had talked Buddy into posing for a picture beside the Brahma-bull statue that stood guard near the restaurant's entrance. He leaned an elbow on the bull's neck, pushed his Resistol to the back of his head, and gave her a huge smile, one that could melt a heart clear through the Internet's electronic highway.

The squeak of the salon's front-door hinges brought her out of her musing. The door opened slightly and closed again. She glanced in the mirror but saw nothing. She resumed reading, but heard the door open and close again. *Kids playing a trick.*

This time she left the chair and walked out to the salon for a closer inspection. She opened the door, and to her delight, she was greeted by her oldest—literally, her oldest—customer. Octogenarian Maudeen Wiley. Debbie Sue loved her with all her heart. "Maudeen! Hey, girl, what's going on?"

"Hell, I'm trying to get in this door. You got a dead body laying against it? The damn thing keeps closing on me."

Debbie Sue didn't have the heart to tell her no dead body was lying against the door, no extra weight had been added since the last time Maudeen had come to the salon. She took the wizened older woman by the arm and escorted her inside. Maudeen was under five feet tall and probably weighed less than a hundred pounds fully clothed. She looked to be shrinking with each passing year.

Today she was wearing jeans that appeared to be missing an ass and a Western shirt that appeared to be missing a bosom. The shirt was pink satin with pearl snaps and white fringe hanging from the yokes. Debbie Sue looked down and saw laced-up Ropers on Maudeen's feet. "Holy cow, girl, you're all dressed up like a cowgirl. Going to a rodeo?"

"What'd you say?" Maudeen asked, her voice slightly elevated.

Not only was the elderly woman getting weaker, she was getting deafer. Each of her visits to the shop seemed to require that Debbie Sue talk louder. "I said, what are you doing out and about so early?"

The elderly woman shuffled toward a styling chair, pushing a gnarly hand through her flame-red hair as she sank to the seat. Enormous diamond rings encircled four of her fingers, mementos from the men she had outlived. "I like to get out early and get my business done before the traffic gets heavy."

Debbie Sue grinned. In Salt Lick, more than a dozen vehicles were never on the road at any given time of the day. With the village's population of twelve hundred, the possibility of gridlock was remote.

"You don't have an appointment today, but I've got some time. Want your color touched up?"

"No, darlin'. That's sweet of you, but I came to ask a favor."

"You got it. Need a ride somewhere?"

"Nothing like that. I want to know if you'll let me borrow your shop for a couple of hours Friday night. I want to have a party and I don't want to use the Peaceful Oasis club room."

"How come? Don't tell me they charge you for using it."

"Naw, they don't charge. I just don't want to have to invite the whole damn place to my party. Half the ones you don't invite get mad and pout, the other half just shows up anyway. It's a losing situation. Like my love life."

The good news about Maudeen was that her body might be getting feebler, but her mind and tongue were sharp as ever. The only thing old about her was her birth date. "Of course you can use the shop. What time?"

"That's swell, honey. It'll be seven o'clock. Say, why don't you and Edwina come? I'm trying to win a trip to Branson. I get a point for every dollar you spend on stuff."

"I thought you'd been to Branson, Maudeen."

"Yes, but I went on the bus with a group from the home. This is a trip for two on an airplane and we get a fancy hotel room. I'd like to have some privacy with my boyfriend, if you know what I mean?" She winked a wrinkled eyelid.

"Which one is your boyfriend these days?"

"I haven't decided yet."

"Well, we don't want you to miss that trip. Buddy will be

out of town Friday and I think Vic's on the road, too. Ed and I'd love to come. Want me to drum up some more guests for you?"

"Lord, yes. The more the merrier. Don't feel like you have to buy something, but I'd sure appreciate it." She rose from the styling chair. "Well, I'd best run. See you Friday and thanks again, darlin'. Don't worry. I'll furnish the refreshments."

Debbie Sue stood in the doorway and watched as Maudeen shuffled to her '82 Cadillac Seville. Usually her granddaughter brought her to the beauty shop, and Debbie Sue wondered if Maudeen's family knew she was out driving.

As the elderly woman was about to pull out of the parking lot, it dawned on Debbie Sue she hadn't asked what kind of party Maudeen wanted to hostess. Debbie Sue yelled, but the roar of the V-8 engine drowned out most of Maudeen's reply. The only thing Debbie Sue heard her say was "toy."

Oh, toys. Yikes, Christmas was just around the corner. Debbie Sue had no need for toys, but she didn't mind buying one or two. She always made a donation to the toy drive the Baptist church sponsored every year.

fifteen

Allison had a habit of arriving at Almost the Rage early enough to inspect the merchandise and neaten the displays before starting the day. Business was definitely on the upswing and she didn't want to change her luck by varying her pattern. However, with her mom and Frank home from their trip, and knowing that Mom would be in the shop early, she had taken some extra time at home this morning.

Mom and Frank had been gone since Saturday morning on a four-day excursion to view the Hill Country's fall landscape. She envied but didn't begrudge the good time her mother was having. Her mom had been through some hard times, and if happiness was within her grasp, Allison wanted her to grab it.

Allison walked through the back entrance of the shop just in time to hear her mother ending a phone call.

"I'll tell her you called." A fit of giggling followed. "Now stop that. Okay, bye-bye."

"Who was that?" Allison asked, making her way to the front of the store. She stopped and straightened some capri pants on hangers.

Her mother assumed a smug expression. "That was a man, calling for you."

"Tag? Was it Tag?"

Confusion creased Lydia Barker's brow. "Tag? As in, 'you're it'?"

"Ha-ha. Funny. Tag, as in Tag Freeman."

Her mother's eyes popped wide. "You know Tag Freeman? Good Lord, he's a sexy man."

"Mom!"

"Mom what? Because I said he's sexy? I may be old, sweetie, but I can still recognize a man that fires the imagination. Frank's quit taking me to the Double-Kicker because he says he's tired of watching me drool in the coleslaw. When did you meet him?"

"Sexy, huh? Well, you should have been with me Saturday and Monday nights. He brought me home from dates I had with Quint Matthews."

"You don't mean the rodeo champion."

"Yes, Mother. The one and only."

"Good Lord. That was him on the phone just now, but he only gave me his first name. I've only been gone four days, haven't I?"

"How was your trip, by the way? How's Frank?" Allison busied herself readying the till for the day.

"Oh no you don't, young lady. You're not getting off that easy. Come over here and tell your mother what's been going on while I've been gone."

Allison closed the cash-register drawer, walked over to her mom, and gave her a one-armed hug. Then she related the events of the past four days. She omitted the part where she and Tag had kissed in front of his pickup. She didn't mind giving her mom details, just not *all* the details.

"What an awful thing for Quint, ending up in the hospital," her mother said, "but I'm glad Tag was available to bring you home. I can't help but notice that you haven't reacted to me telling you Quint called."

"Oh, I'm excited. Really. Quint's nothing if not exciting. I just wanted to bring you up to speed first. So what did he say?"

"Just asked if you were here. Then he asked who I was. We discussed the Hill Country. He has a ranch down there. Did you know that?" She took a piece of notepaper from her pocket and handed it to Allison. "Here's his cell number. He'd like you to call him. Now, why was your first guess that it was Tag I was talking to?"

"It doesn't really matter who it was, Mom," she lied. "I met Tag's ex the other night. She had her tentacles out like a giant squid." She turned and walked away before her mother could ask any more probing questions that might have painful answers. "I'm sure he's off the market by now," she mumbled.

★ ★ ★

The fax machine in Tag's home office ground and grunted as an image came through at a snail's pace. Fighting the urge to grab the paper and yank it free, Quint carried his coffee cup to the kitchen for a refill.

He hadn't seen Monica in months. He had so thoroughly convinced himself that it was she behind the theft of his identity, he wasn't sure what his reaction would be if he learned otherwise.

Returning to the office, he groaned to see the paper only inching its way forward. He cursed aloud, but on second inspection he saw that it was an important inch.

The top portion of a female face was visible. The print was black and white, but that didn't keep him from seeing that the dark hair pulled atop the head in a wispy fan was all too familiar.

Quint stood there transfixed as the picture became whole. The eyes, the full lips, even the necklace with the diamond heart he had given her, were visible and as close as his fingertips. He ran a finger down the woman's face, stopping at the lips.

It was her. To someone who didn't already know her, the image might be described as vague, but Quint was absolutely sure. It was her.

Edwina pulled her vintage Mustang to a screeching halt, grabbed her monster handbag from the backseat, and marched into the Styling Station. "Lock up the men and cover the children's eyes. I'm here." She struck a pose befitting the announcement.

Debbie Sue turned her styling chair a half circle to get a better view of her friend. "Well, aren't we full of it this morning? I'm sure I know why, too, but don't give me any details. I can barely look at Vic without giggling now."

"You couldn't be more wrong. Well, not *entirely* wrong, but that's not the only reason I'm happy."

"Do I have to drag it out of you? Tell me."

"I was just savoring the moment. You're the first person to hear." She sucked in a deep breath. "My baby girl called me early this morning. I'm gonna be a grandma."

Debbie Sue leaped from her chair squealing with delight. She enveloped Edwina in a big hug. "Oh my God, that is such great news!" They parted and Debbie Sue looked into her eyes. "Congratulations, Granny. I've been wondering when one of those girls of yours was gonna give you a grandchild. Which one is it, Billie Pat?"

"My baby, Roberta Jean. She took the home test this morning and called me right after." Edwina began sniffling. "My baby's having a baby. She's so young."

"Come on, now. She's older than you were when she was born. She's got a great husband and a beautiful home. She and Brandon will be wonderful parents and you'll be a wonderful grandma."

"Oh my God." Panic crossed Edwina's face. "I can't be a grandma. I can't cook, I don't knit, and I don't own any old-lady shoes. What kind of example would I be to my precious granddaughter?"

"You'll be a cool grandma. She'll—wait a minute. What makes you so sure you'll have a granddaughter? Roberta might have a boy. I hear the odds are still fifty-fifty on that."

"A boy! What the hell would I do with a boy? I raised three girls. I don't have anything in common with boys."

"You'll just love him, Ed. You'll just love him." Debbie Sue swallowed a lump in her throat. Then she forced herself to brighten, remembering she had to tell Edwina about Maudeen's party. "And you buy them toys!"

"That, I can do." Ed wiped a tear from her eye.

"Good, because I've told Maudeen we'll come to a toy party she's having Friday night right here in the salon. I told her you'd come, too. I hope you don't mind."

"Mind?"

"Be sure to invite all your customers. Maudeen gets points for people buying things. She's trying to win a trip to Branson."

"Wow, my first chance to buy something for her, uh, him? You know, I can see myself getting into this grandma thing. But there's one thing I refuse to do."

"What's that?"

"I refuse to wear one of those sweatshirts that has 'World's Greatest Grandma' blaring across the front."

"How about 'World's Hottest Grandma'?"

"Now you're talking."

Allison had tucked the piece of notepaper bearing Quint's phone number in her pocket while she contemplated if she should call. Half an hour later, she settled the debate and picked up the phone. It was past noon.

She felt certain he would invite her out for the evening and she didn't know what her answer would be. She had turned him down once. Could she do it a second time and expect to hear from him again? Did she even *want* to hear from him again?

A war between logic and emotion raged within her. The logical side that she so often turned to kept saying, *Are you nuts? This guy is loaded, handsome, and brimming with sex appeal. Go for it!*

But the side called emotion, the one with which she was scarcely familiar, demanded attention, too. It kept reminding her of how she felt in Tag's presence. She couldn't forget the way he had interacted with the children at the mall, the warmth that spread through her when he caught her eye and smiled and winked at her, and how her feet went numb when he kissed her.

A voice shot back, *And he's most likely getting back with his ex-wife.*

Yet another voice stepped up. *Why would you think that? The woman was awful. Have a little faith in Tag.*

She shook her head, obliterating the confusion and the voices as she heard Quint's cell phone ringing.

After four rings, she was about to hang up when a male voice said, "Tag Freeman."

Was she dreaming? Had she heard right?

"Tag? . . . Uh, hi. This is Allison."

"Allison! Man, this is a surprise. How are you?"

"I'm fine, thanks. Uh, I was returning Quint's call."

"Quint? I left Quint at the house this morning. Did he leave my number? Wonder why he did that."

"This is your number? That's odd. He gave it to my mom."

"Just a minute," he said.

Allison looked skyward, thanking whatever angel was hovering overhead.

After a few seconds, Tag came back on the line. "Oh, man, I think I know what happened. Looks like I've got Quint's phone. Mine has a deep scratch on the case, but this one doesn't. I must have grabbed his by mistake. He must have mine. Sorry, let me give you my number and you can call him."

She jotted down the new number, but instead of ending the call, to her delight, they fell into conversation. When they hung up, an hour and a half had passed, but it seemed like minutes. Most important, she knew Tag's ex-wife was out of the picture.

Edwina's words echoed in her memory. *Why, girl, that's karma.*

Quint was so excited he could hardly stand still. The woman who had disappeared into thin air was once again in his hands. Okay, so it was a photo that was in his hands, and not a very good one, but she was closer than she had been in months.

He had worried that the identity thief would turn out to

be a middle-aged woman with black roots showing through bleached hair, a cigarette hanging from her lips, and a baby propped on her hip. If that had been the case he would have packed and gone back to Seguin. He would have told the Domestic Equalizers to forget it, paid them for their trouble, and headed out. But it was Monica and he wanted to see her again. *Had* to see her again.

He grabbed the faxed picture and his cell phone. His finger slid down a long deep scratch on the phone's cover that hadn't been there yesterday. Fearing an accident might have rendered the phone inoperable, he flipped it open to view the faceplate. Thank God, the scratched phone wasn't his. Tag must have taken his by mistake.

He keyed in his own number and it rang only twice before Tag answered.

"Hey, looks like you figured out we've got each other's phones," Tag said cheerily.

"No big deal. Except that I've got to make some calls and the numbers I need are stored in my set. I'll come into town and pick it up on my way to Salt Lick. You at the restaurant?"

"I'm here. Always here. You're headed to Salt Lick, huh? Got a date with Allison?"

"Naw, it's business. I've got to get back early. Tonight I've got a date with that EMT I met Halloween night."

"Olivia? Oh, really?" Tag said on a chuckle. "So, you're not planning on seeing Allison anymore?"

"Allison's the real deal, but I don't think she can get away easily during the week, what with her kid and all. Gotta find something or someone to keep me occupied," he said on a lascivious laugh. "I'll see you in about twenty minutes."

Quint was determined to waste no time getting this faxed picture to Debbie Sue, and he didn't want her wasting any time either. He knew Buddy Overstreet wouldn't welcome his presence and he had figured out Edwina wasn't a big Quint Matthews fan either. On top of that, Allison was playing hard to get. None of it mattered. He was on a mission. The lovely Monica, who had tossed him aside like a wad of chewed gum, was going to see him face-to-face again.

sixteen

Allison's body was in Almost the Rage; her hands and fingers were sale-tagging fall dresses, but her mind was miles away. Sixty miles to be exact. All day she had found herself daydreaming and smiling like an idiot, thinking of something Tag had said. He was such an easygoing conversationalist. She could talk to him for hours.

Indeed Tag appealed to her far more than Quint, but how could she tell Quint? A simple explanation was needed, one in which she told Quint that while she was flattered by his attention, they weren't right for each other.

He had already said he planned on being in town only a short time. Was there any harm in ending things before they started? A to-the-point conversation could be cruel, but would it be any crueler than leading a man on while she secretly pined for his friend?

She had never been good at games of the heart. She'd had

too little experience with men to be practiced at it. All she had done most of her life was live in an unsophisticated small-town environment, work long hours to make a living, and raise a child.

A second thought came to her. What if Tag had no interest in her at all? What if all this time he had just been what it was clear that he was—a nice guy? What if she dismissed a suitable suitor like Quint too soon? She had been out with Quint only twice, really. Not often enough to make a determination. She did enjoy his company and she had to admit she did feel a little zing when he had talked seductively to her at the Styling Station. Perhaps one more evening with him would help her decide.

Damn, why did having a man enter your life have to be so complicated?

The inner debate raged on until she finally made a decision. She reached into her sweater pocket and retrieved the two pieces of paper that had phone numbers written on them, holding one in each hand. Oh, dear. She could no longer tell which was which and she hadn't taken the time to write a name for either number.

"Well, nothing ventured, nothing gained," she mumbled, deciding to go left to right. On a deep breath she picked up the receiver and keyed in the number she held in her left hand. One, two, three rings, followed by an automated answer in a monotone voice. "The party you're calling is unavailable. Please leave a message at the tone." *Beep.*

Deep breath. "Hi, this is Allison. I'd like to talk to you about something. Tonight, if possible. In person. I've got some feelings I think I should just put out on the table. Could you please come to my house for dinner? Say seven-thirty or eight o'clock? My mom and Jill both will be out for the evening and I'd like to take the chance to—" An ear-piercing electronic signal overrode the end of her sentence.

"Well, that's that," she said, hanging up.

The only thing left to do now was go home, fix some dinner, and hope her plan was the right thing to do.

She closed the store promptly at its designated time and rushed through City Market, picking up meat and vegetables. By seven-thirty, she had received no return call, even though she had knocked herself out and prepared a king's feast.

At eight-thirty, she found her gaze volleying between the clock and the pans of food warming in the oven, turning dry as cardboard. Doubt began to creep in. Why had she been so foolish as to forge ahead making a big dinner? Breaded pork chops, mashed potatoes, cream gravy, corn sliced from the cob, swimming in butter and cream, and frozen but freshly baked rolls. She sighed. It was beginning to appear as if she would have to dine alone tonight and put the leftovers in the fridge. At least she would have some good lunches at work the rest of the week.

Just as she reached into the cabinet for a plate the door-bell's chime echoed through the house. Her heart caught in her throat. God, how she hoped she had made the right decision.

She paused at the mirror beside the door just long enough to check her reflection, then reached for the doorknob and pulled . . .

"Tag!"

She stepped backward, her brain thrown into chaos as she tried to remember the phone number she had dialed. She thought she had called Tag's number, which meant Quint should be the one standing on her doorstep. She had prepared herself to tell Quint she wanted to pursue a relationship with Tag. Now here stood the winner of the debate she'd had all day with herself.

"Hi, Allison," he said softly, smiling and clutching the brim of his cowboy hat. "Sorry I didn't call you back, but I didn't have your home number and your dress shop was already closed by the time I got your message."

"Oh, the message. About dinner. Yes, I left a message about dinner, didn't I?" Her words sounded so dumb and dull they hurt her own ears.

"May I come in?"

"Oh, heavens, yes. Of course, what's wrong with me? Please do come in, Tag. Could I take your hat?"

"That'd be just fine." He handed over the hat and she placed it on the small table in the entry. He picked it up and turned it crown down.

Oops. From somewhere she remembered that cowboys always laid their hats upside down. "Oh, sorry. I forgot about that."

"That's okay. A lot of people who don't wear a hat don't know." He came into the living room slowly, looking around. "I like your place. It looks like a real home."

"Why, thank you, but it's my mom's house. I'm hoping to have a home one day for Jill and me, but for right now—"

Before she could finish her sentence, Tag interrupted her, his words tumbling from his mouth like an avalanche. "I'm sorry, Allison, but I've been driving around the block for fifteen minutes trying to decide if I should come in. I've never been one to take a friendship lightly and you and Quint seeing each other makes me feel wrong about being here. I was floored when I heard your message. It was like you had read my mind. Truth is . . . well, the truth is, I haven't been able to stop thinking about you since the first night I laid eyes on you."

He paused and looked at the floor. "I should have never kissed you while you're seeing Quint. I'm shamed about that. And I'm even more shamed because all I've been able to think about since then is kissing you again."

Allison stood glued to the spot. Her heart was racing. She was trying to think of a reply when he looked up at her and their eyes locked.

Suddenly she found herself in his arms and they were kissing passionately. He held her so tightly she was lifted from the floor, with only his body to support her weight, his desire pressing against her stomach. The feeling that they were one body overwhelmed her, and for lack of knowing what to do next, she clutched his muscular torso.

At last he broke away, putting space between them. They stared at each other, breathless. He laughed softly. "Lord, woman, what just happened here?"

"I don't know," she blurted, "but don't stop. Please don't stop kissing me."

A dam of pent-up emotions seemed to burst in him and he resumed kissing her lips while his hand slipped under her sweater and caressed her breast. Allison felt she might melt on the spot.

"I'm so glad I dialed the wrong number," she mumbled against his lips. "When did you and Quint exchange phones?"

Tag stopped, his lips suspended above hers. "What?" He pulled back and released her. "What do you mean?"

"I called your cell number thinking Quint still had your phone. I wanted to see him—"

His eyes narrowed and drilled her. "You called me by mistake? You thought you were inviting Quint to dinner?"

If Allison's head had been transparent, she was sure alarms and danger signals would be flashing in brilliant color. She was in trouble and had no clue how to get out. "No, no. I only wanted to tell him I had made up my mind. That I had chosen you and—"

"*Chosen* me?"

She had never heard his voice like this—cold, with a knife edge to it.

"*Chosen* was the wrong word. I only wanted to tell him how I feel. You don't understand."

"Oh, I think I do. I've seen a hundred of your type. Making one guy think he's gonna get lucky while checking out his friend behind his back. You're a little more subtle than most, but—"

Allison couldn't prevent the anger that spilled over. No one had ever accused her of such dishonesty, especially a man. "Don't you dare accuse me of that! You don't even have all the facts—"

His eyes burned with anger. "Standing in the middle of the cold hard truth is all the fact I need." He opened his mouth like he might say more, but shut it again. "What's the use of talking a thing to death? I should've known from the git-go that this was a mistake."

He marched toward the front door, picking up his hat and clapping it on his head on the way. Allison hurried behind him, but stopped in the doorway, watching as he stamped to his Navigator and climbed in. The door slammed, the engine fired, and he was gone, leaving a spray of gravel behind him.

"Fine! Just fine!" Allison slammed the door, tears already streaming down the cheeks that had been covered by his kisses just moments before. She broke into sobs and stumbled to the bathroom.

At last she calmed herself, splashed her face with cold water, and stared into the vanity mirror. "So, there," she mumbled to the tearstained image in the mirror. "That settles that. Having a crush on a dumb cowboy was a fool's errand in the first place."

It was her destiny to remain alone. She had proved she could do it. Not only that, she was damn good at it.

"Who's that?" Buddy asked, coming out of the bathroom, drying his hands.

Debbie Sue had been home for half an hour. She was in the same position in which she had been since arriving from work—plopped across the bed on her back, holding the picture of Quint's mystery woman. He had rushed into the salon late in the afternoon and presented it to her with both eagerness and reluctance, like he didn't want to let it go.

"It's a picture the ATM folks faxed to Quint. He dropped it off at the shop. His gut instincts were right. It's his girlfriend."

"Humph. Who isn't?"

The girl in the photograph wasn't as young as Debbie Sue had imagined she would be. Quint had always had an eye for the younger ones, so Debbie Sue had figured someone twenty, maybe twenty-two. Quint hadn't mentioned her age, but clearly she was no kid. Closer to thirty. Not old, for sure, but at least he hadn't been cradle robbing.

She was pretty, smiling, and, judging from the full-frontal shot of her face, unaware she was being photographed. On second thought, maybe she had been completely aware of the camera and was grinning anyway. Such a bold gesture could reveal volumes about the personality behind that smile.

Buddy lay down beside her on the bed and took the photo.

"Do you think she's pretty?" Debbie Sue asked him.

After a few seconds of inspection, he handed it back. "She's a real knockout. I'd like to shake her hand. That asshole Quint's been screwing people over for years. It's about time he got some payback." Buddy planted a kiss on her cheek, pushed himself up, and walked back into the bathroom.

Minutes later Debbie Sue heard the shower. She scowled at the picture. "She's cute," she muttered to the empty room, "but she's no fuckin' knockout."

"What?" Buddy called over the noise from the thrumming water.

"Nothing," Debbie Sue yelled. "I just said she's cute."

She shouldn't debate this subject with Buddy. He would only accuse her of being jealous, and since that was partially true, she had no defense.

She pushed herself to a sitting position and reached for the purse she had thrown on the bed. Keeping one eye on the bathroom door, she pulled out a packet of newly developed snapshots. She thumbed through them, looking for the one she needed.

Bingo. There it was. The picture of Buddy solo. All six feet and two inches of the most gorgeous man in Texas. Broad shoulders, narrow hips. Black hair, chocolate-brown eyes, and a thick black mustache. She had asked him to "pose sexy" and he had smiled for the camera as if it were his lover. Seduction oozed from the three-by-five print. Now, *that* picture was the one that was a knockout.

Her conscience tweaked her. Buddy would never go along with the plan she had hatched. There were two good reasons why. Number one, he would view having his picture blasted over the Internet without his knowing it as an extreme invasion of his privacy. Number two, he was a Texas Department of Safety trooper, with the goal of becoming a Texas Ranger. Having his picture on a dating Web site for millions of women, or men, to ogle was not something the average Texas Ranger would do.

On the other hand, if having it there meant catching a criminal, wouldn't that justify it? After all, this was kind of like working undercover, wasn't it? How could he get mad at that?

She could still hear the shower. She opened the nightstand drawer and pulled out a piece of notepaper and a pen. Keeping one eye on the bathroom door, she began to write:

West Texas Gentleman Looking for Someone to Spoil.

I'm a lonely man hoping to meet a woman to spend time and money on. Prefer someone in her late twenties. Dark hair is a real turn-on. This woman should be willing to accompany me to fine restaurants and exclusive weekend retreats. Be prepared to experience the good things money can buy. Please respond with photo and suggest a place we can meet.

Debbie Sue proofread the profile before folding the page and slipping it back into her purse. First thing tomorrow morning she would post the snapshot and the information on the same Internet dating site Quint had used when he met the mystery woman, and in a day or two the picture of her own sweet Buddy would be cast as the lure. She didn't doubt for a minute the mystery woman would bite. The ad was enticing enough, but beyond that, who could resist Buddy?

Just then he walked into the bedroom towel-drying his hair and smelling of musky body wash. He was wearing nothing but a smile and a hard-on. Debbie Sue gave him a leer. This was the perfect moment to test the bait.

seventeen

Debbie Sue arrived at the Styling Station the next morning excited. When she entered, Edwina was on the phone and gave her a nod and gestured a kiss. Debbie Sue waved the snapshot of Buddy in the air. "Hurry up," she stage-whispered. "I got Buddy's picture back."

Edwina nodded as she spoke into the receiver. "Okay, sugar britches, you take care of yourself. We'll see you tomorrow night." She hung up and motioned to Debbie Sue. "Let me see that."

"Who was on the phone?" Debbie Sue asked, handing Edwina the picture.

"Maudeen. She wanted to let us know the guest list for the toy party is getting out of hand. She's invited more than thirty people. She's hurrying around getting refreshments together. I told her we'd contribute to them. Our fridge is full of Cokes and 7-Up. Bless her heart, I don't think there's a chance in hell that many will come, but she's excited all the same."

"I've invited a few of my customers," Debbie Sue said. "Maybe they'll show up and Maudeen won't be disappointed. It'd be too bad if she doesn't win that trip to Branson."

Edwina studied the snapshot of Buddy. "Hmm-hmm. That Buddy is one good-looking man. I may answer that ad myself."

"Oh no you don't." Debbie Sue grabbed the picture from her friend's grasp. "You didn't tell Vic about this, did you? I know how you are with Vic and your oath to never lie to him."

"Nope, haven't said a word. If he doesn't ask me, then I can't lie."

"I need the computer," Debbie Sue said, urging Edwina up. She took a seat and adjusted the screen to her height. "I've got six sites in mind. We could have replies as early as tomorrow. I'm gonna be busy here for a while. Cover for me, okay?"

"No problem. What are you going to say?"

Debbie Sue dug the ad she had written from her purse and gave it to Edwina, then busied herself with logging onto the Internet.

Edwina giggled. "Sounds good to me, but you didn't really need to go to this length. With that picture of Buddy, all you had to say was 'Write me, I'm horny.' "

Debbie Sue giggled, too. "I know. But I wanted to be sure we draw her out."

"If she's out there and up to her old tricks, this'll work."

"Yeah. If she's out there."

Deep in thought, Allison braced her elbows on the dress shop's jewelry-and-accessory display case, studying a necklace-and-earring set that had just arrived, but her mind was on another subject. Relationships. When it came to relationships, she was worse than a virus. The surgeon general should declare a warning label be plastered across her forehead. In less than a week she had managed to meet and dispose of two men. Two fabulous men. One in particular. No wonder she was still single.

She didn't want to believe Tag would choose to never see her again. During their phone conversation a few days ago, he had opened his heart. Her own heart wanted to accept the idea that they had forged a bond, but her head wasn't buying it.

Forcing herself away from the display case, she mentally searched for a project that would keep her mind occupied as well as her hands, but her mind wasn't cooperating. Maybe she should make an appointment to visit the Styling Station. A hairdo and some of Debbie Sue's and Edwina's zaniness would lift her spirits.

The buzzer at the back door sounded, signaling that the door had opened. A few seconds later, Jill came in from the stockroom. "Hey, Mom. What's up?"

"Jill, sweetheart. What are you doing here and how did you get here?"

"Kay's mom's waiting in the car. I need some lunch money."

"Oh, I forgot to leave it this morning. Sorry." Allison walked to the office off the stockroom. As she lifted her purse out of a filing-cabinet drawer and dug out a five-dollar bill, she could feel Jill's eyes watching her. She handed over the money, but avoided her daughter's penetrating look.

"Mom? What's wrong?"

"Nothing, hon. Now run along to school." She looped her arm around her daughter's shoulders and kissed her cheek. "You have a good day."

"You seem sad," Jill said.

"I've just got a lot on my mind. Nothing to worry about."

Jill started out the back door, then stopped. "You know something, Mom? When I've had a fight with a friend, I don't wait for them to call me. If they're important to me I call them first."

She disappeared, leaving Allison standing in the office in wonder. It must be part of the maturing process to go from little girl, to mature woman, back to little girl, all in the span of a few minutes, she thought.

Well, she shouldn't let the wisdom of her child go to waste. She fumbled through her purse until she came up with the two pieces of paper with the phone numbers on them. She still couldn't tell which number belonged to whom, so she closed her eyes and selected one. She keyed in the number, took a deep breath, and waited. After several rings a familiar male voice with a distinctive Texas drawl answered. "Howdy. This is Quint Matthews—"

She disconnected. Okay, no automated machine recording, no monotone voice. At least she now knew for sure which of the two numbers was Tag's.

Returning Quint's number to her pocket, she held the other number to her heart and took an even deeper breath. For the second time in as many days, she keyed in the number.

Tag replayed Allison's message for the fourth time. Her soft voice, with a hint of a West Texas drawl, came on again. "Tag, this is Allison. I'm sorry I acted presumptuously. It was thoughtless of me to take your friendship with Quint for granted. Perhaps when his business is finished and he's returned home, you and I can work on being friends. I'd like that chance."

He felt like an ass and he didn't like it. In the first place, he shouldn't have gone to Allison's house and put her on the spot. He and Quint went back a long way. By showing up on her doorstep, he had betrayed a friendship that meant something to him. Any friendship was special, but one honed over time was especially so.

In the second place, he had been rude to Allison. Instead of giving her a chance to talk, he had followed his old pattern—go on the defensive, bluster up, act tough, locate the nearest exit, and split. Taking that route usually brought him a wave of relief at being able to breathe the sweet air of freedom again.

When he left Allison's home, there had been no air. It had been completely knocked out of him.

He pushed replay and listened again until he heard the click indicating the end of the message.

He sighed. Quint's behavior with women followed a pattern. He would soon leave the area and the woman. His leaving would be the signal that the field was open. Tag would just have to cool it and bide his time. He only hoped Allison didn't succumb to the Superstud's charms before then.

The following morning Debbie Sue left her house later than usual. Buddy departed for a seminar in El Paso and she'd had to give him a proper send-off. After all, he would be gone until late tomorrow night.

She was in a hurry. So much was going on. The publicity she and Edwina had reaped as detectives had boosted the salon's business, so Friday was always a busy day in the beauty shop, then there was Maudeen's party to prepare for at the end of the day.

And there were more Internet dating sites to join. Because she had been so much busier in the salon, she had succeeded in joining only two instead of the six she had planned on. Still, she had a gut feeling—one of those female-intuition things—that the thief of Quint's identity and his heart would answer. And it could be as early as today.

Solving the mystery this soon meant a loss of hours the Domestic Equalizers could bill to Quint, thus a loss of earnings, but sometimes friendship had to take precedence over money. She knew Quint well. Seeing that he was involved in this affair on a deeper level than his credit score made her hell-bent on finding who had screwed him over, and soon.

Pulling into her parking space, she wasn't surprised to see Edwina's Mustang already there. When Vic was out of town, Edwina was always up and into something at the crack of dawn. She liked to say that Vic's absences were the only time she got anything done, but Debbie Sue knew that Edwina flat-out missed his huge body lying next to hers, so she just didn't stay in bed.

Debbie Sue had no sooner walked through the door than an excited Edwina besieged her. "Damn, girl, I thought you'd never get here. Come look at this." She lifted a stack of pages from the payout counter. "Of the two lonely hearts clubs you joined, these are the replies that have come in."

Debbie Sue carried her purse and her lunch to the storeroom, speaking as she went. "Ed, don't call them lonely hearts clubs. That sounds so sad. They're Internet dating sites."

"And if not a lonely heart, what would prompt somebody to join such a site?"

"Well, not a lonely heart," Debbie Sue said, returning to the front room and looking over Edwina's shoulder at the computer screen. "Maybe a lonely—maybe, or it could be— oh, hell, you're right. Tilt that screen up a little, Miss Know-It-All, so I can see." Edwina complied. "Damn," Debbie

Sue said. "Fifty-two replies on the first day? I figured we'd get action, but this is unreal."

"That's not the best part. This is what I really wanted you to see." Edwina highlighted a line in a particular ad. "Here ya go, read this."

Debbie Sue began reading, her mouth moving with each word. Suddenly her spine went rigid. "What? Kathy Bozo? That good-for-nothing, lying, scheming, piece-o'-shit tramp?"

Kathy Boczkowski was the woman with whom Buddy had had a fling when Debbie Sue and he had been divorced. The very thought still made Debbie Sue's mouth water with venomous spit. The black-haired witch was living and teaching in Austin, the e-mail said. It also said, *Happy to see you finally came to your senses about remarrying Debbie Sue.*

Debbie Sue slapped the desktop with the palm of her hand. "Why, the nerve of her. I never did get to even the score on the lie she told me about her and Buddy being engaged. About fifteen minutes alone with her in the parking lot and I'd make that silly Yankee see stars over Texas she's never seen before."

Edwina looked up at her with a solemn expression. "I just hate it when you clam up and refuse to show your feelings. Mark my words, keeping everything inside is gonna make you sick someday."

Debbie Sue scowled. "You'd be the same damn way if someone like her made a play for Vic. You'd be worse." She urged Edwina from her seat at the computer. "Get up, Ed. I'm answering this one personally."

"C'mon, now, let it be," Edwina said, turning the desk chair over to Debbie Sue. "We've got a lot of ads to look at. Besides, you won him, didn't you?"

"It wasn't a contest, Ed. She looks down on me like I'm not good enough for Buddy. I have to answer her. If I don't, she'll always believe he didn't want me or that he and I didn't make it."

As Edwina stood behind her and watched, Debbie Sue's fingers flew over the keyboard. Minutes later, she finished. "Okay, read it. Make sure I haven't spelled anything wrong. The woman's a damn schoolteacher. I don't want her finding a mistake in my spelling. She always treated me like I was one of her slower students."

Edwina bent forward and began reading aloud.

Dear Kathy Bozo,

My partner Edwina and I run a successful detective agency in Salt Lick. We were written up in a little magazine called *Texas Monthly*. Maybe you've heard of it. We posted my HUSBAND'S picture trying to ferret out a low-life a-hole and who do you think answered first? It just goes to show you, you overeducated turd, you can fool some of the people all the time, you can fool some of the people some of the time, but there are some people you will never fool. And I'm one of them!

Yours truly,
MRS. JAMES RUSSELL OVERSTREET

Edwina returned to her full height and planted a fist on her hip. "I think you should tone it down."

"What? She tried to steal Buddy."

"I wonder about calling her names in writing. She could sue you."

"For what? . . . Okay, what can I call her?"

"Hmm. Let me see. I don't think you—"

Before Edwina could finish, Debbie Sue struck enter.

Edwina gasped. "It's comforting to know you find my opinion so valuable. Before you sent the thing off into cyberspace, I started to say I don't think you should be so civilized."

They broke into laughter.

"After this, Ed, I'm tempted to not charge Quint a penny. How often do you get the opportunity to tell off someone who deserves it? That's worth a heck of a lot more than money."

What a great way to start the day, Debbie Sue thought as she left the computer and began preparing her workstation. An old foe put down, a substantial pile of suspects for Quint's mystery woman, and laughter with a friend. Add the early-morning episode in bed with Buddy, and Debbie Sue had a clear picture of what heaven was going to be.

"Well, I want to charge him," Edwina said.

Allison moped around the kitchen going from the coffeepot to the sink in robot fashion. She had called Tag and apologized, had hoped for a return call, but had heard nothing.

Her mom sat at the table watching her. Finally she broke the silence. "Allison, I hate to see you so blue. There's lots of reasons he didn't call back. He's got a busy restaurant to run. Owning your own business takes a lot of your time. You know that. Besides, it isn't like you to be so negative."

Allison carried her coffee to the table and took a chair opposite her mother. She dumped artificial sweetener and cream into the mug and stirred, watching the cream blend. "I'm not negative, Mom. I'm actually quite positive. I'm positive I made a huge mistake and I'm *really* positive I'll never hear from him again. See? Positive."

Her mother sighed. "Did you remember that this is the weekend Frank is taking Jill and me to Abilene to the cutting-horse show? Why don't you go with us? We're leaving this afternoon when Jill gets out of school."

"I didn't forget. That's sweet of you to invite me, Mom, but if I go, who'll open the store tomorrow?"

"Just put a sign on the door. You're allowed a day off."

Allison shook her head. "Y'all go and have a great time. I'm looking forward to having the house to myself."

"Well, this is Friday night. Promise me you'll get out and do something. Something fun."

"I can't. I called Edwina yesterday to set time for a haircut and she invited me to a party at the beauty salon. She and Debbie Sue really want me to be there, so after Edwina trims my hair, I'm going to stay for it. Actually, she asked me to bring some cookies, but I told her I didn't have time to bake."

"What kind of a party is it?"

"Oh, it's one of those hostess things where they sell stuff and the party giver gets prizes. I think it's toys. One of the Styling Station's customers from Peaceful Oasis is having it. I don't know any kids to buy toys for, but I told them I'd be there. I can always get something and give it as a gift or give it to the church for their Santa drive. Christmas isn't that far off."

"Well, if Debbie Sue and Edwina are part of it, it won't matter what kind of party it is. I swear, those two could liven up an exorcism. You go and have a good time."

"I guess so. No need sitting here waiting for the phone to *not* ring."

"That's the spirit." Her mom reached across the breakfast table and patted her hand. "If you can't think of anyone else to buy a toy for, you can buy one for me. I happen to believe there is a little child in all of us."

Allison rose and went to her mother's side of the table. She bent over and placed a kiss on her mom's cheek. "I love you, Mom. I don't know what I would have done without you all these years."

"See, that's the little child in you. The one I miss. I love you, too. Listen, I've got an idea. Since I'm taking off tomorrow, why don't you take off today?"

"Oh, Mom—"

"Now, don't protest. You haven't taken a day off in ages. You can drop me off at the dress shop, then take my car and go to Midland for the day. Go to the mall or the movies or just hang out. You could stop in at Sam's Club and get a few things for the store. You could even pick up one of those giant packages of cookies from their bakery."

"Hmm," Allison said, tempted. She mentally ran through a list of needed supplies. "We do need some things. I *could* get some cookies. I could stop in a couple of shops at the mall and see the dresses they're showing for the holidays—"

"See? A business trip. Now, get ready for work and let's go."

eighteen

An hour later Allison was motoring toward Sam's Club in Midland, planning her day as she drove. Besides the supplies, she might even pick up some fresh-cut flowers for the house. Perhaps having flowers around would improve her mood.

At the giant warehouse retail store, she flashed her membership card and rolled an oversize shopping cart into the aisles. She had begun to feel relaxed and lighthearted. Her mom was right. She hadn't taken a day off in ages and it wasn't like her to mope around. Think positive and positive things will happen, she told herself.

Preoccupied with her list, she rounded a corner of a soaring aisle of merchandise and crashed into an empty cart. When she tried to pull back, she found the front wheels of her cart locked with those of the ownerless cart. She pulled harder several times with no results.

Finally, losing patience, she yanked with all her strength. The carts came apart with a metallic clatter. The empty cart jerked backward and crashed into a tall pyramid of family-size boxes of cereal. The entire stack tumbled to the floor, leaving her knee-deep in boxes of cornflakes.

"Oh, my gosh!"

She felt her face flush with embarrassment. She dropped to her knees and began to gather the boxes with shaking hands.

"Ma'am, are you okay?"

She looked up, shoved a shock of hair off her face, and found herself face-to-face with Tag Freeman. "Tag!"

"Allison! What happened?" He waded through the boxes to where she knelt, placed a strong arm around her waist, and helped her to her feet. "Are you okay?"

"I—I think so." She looked around to see who might be watching. "I'm so embarrassed. Just look at this mess."

"Don't worry about that—"

"But someone will have to clean it up—"

"Come over here," he said, leading her to a display of patio furniture. "Sit down for a minute."

She sank onto a plastic chair seat, again brushed her hair from her forehead, and sneaked peeks around her to see who might be watching. What was Tag doing here, for crying out loud?

He squatted in front of her. From somewhere he produced a bottle of water, which he opened and handed to her. "You should be more careful."

"I just wasn't looking where I was going." She took a tiny sip.

He chuckled. "Me, when I go into these joints, I try to avoid even getting close to stuff that might fall. Getting hit by it carries a price I'm not willing to pay again."

She shook her head. "Just look at this mess I've made. They're going to be so mad. I'll be banned from Sam's forever."

A young man wearing a Sam's Club vest approached. "You folks all right?"

Allison got to her feet. "We're fine. A cart got away from me and hit this display." She moved to help him pick up boxes. "Let me help you get these put back—"

"Oh, no, no, ma'am, it's all right. We'll take care of it. You sure you're all right?"

"Yes, yes, I'm fine."

"Okay, then. I'll get a ladder from the back and grab a helper. We'll be done here in no time. You and your husband go on with your shopping."

Husband? Feeling an uptick in her heartbeat, Allison swung her gaze to Tag. He gave her a wink.

"Looks like you've got everything under control," he said to the store employee. "My wife and I'll get out of your way and finish our shopping. Sorry about the mess." He took Allison's elbow and guided her away from the array of cereal boxes. "Wife, huh?"

"Sorry." She managed a weak smile and lifted her elbow from his hand. "You're the last person in the world I expected to run into here. Are you shopping for the restaurant?"

"Yep." He brandished a handwritten list. "And you?"

"Picking up a few things for me and Mom."

Tag glanced at his watch. "It's nearly lunchtime. You got time for some lunch?"

Allison's head was whirling, but her tongue worked independent of her brain. "Why, yes. Of course."

He grinned. "Good, then. Let's get this shopping done and find a place. I'll meet you at the front door."

For the next half hour Allison zigzagged around the megastore, tossing items into her cart. She was in such a state of distraction she wasn't even sure she needed some of them. At the bakery, she picked up a cardboard box of three dozen cookies frosted and decorated with turkeys and Pilgrims. Passing the deli, she saw large cheese and cold-cut trays for sale. If she knew Edwina and Debbie Sue, they would have a pitcher of margaritas at the party and the deli foods would taste better with tequila than icky-sweet cookies. "Why not?" she muttered, and added a deli party tray to her cart. When she saw Tag headed for the checkout line, she followed.

He looked into her cart. "You having a party?"

She laughed. "I'm going to a girls'-night-out thing in Salt Lick. I'm taking some refreshments."

"Oh," he said with a grin. "Just wondered. That's a lot of food. You should have called me. We do catering from the restaurant. We fix up party trays."

"I wish I'd known. I'm sure yours would taste much better."

Before he could reply, his turn came to check out and they each occupied themselves with making their purchases.

Outside, he pointed out a restaurant on the other side of the interstate. "How about OTB?"

"OTB?"

"On the Border."

"Oh, yeah. On the Border." *Drat*. Why did she have to sound so dumb?

They separated, and as Tag headed for his truck she watched him. His slight limp gave him a sexy swagger. Wearing Wranglers, a blue chambray shirt, a gray hat, and, of course, cowboy boots, he was so ruggedly handsome she almost sighed. She brought herself back to earth, made her way to her car, and drove across the freeway. He was waiting for her at the Tex-Mex restaurant's entrance.

Allison rarely had the opportunity to eat at the popular restaurant, but she loved Tex-Mex food and the Southwest atmosphere. Seated in a padded booth, they ordered iced tea and chicken fajitas for two.

As soon as the waiter left, Tag said, "Allison, I'm glad we ran into each other. I got your voice mail."

She felt a little jolt in her system as their last encounter and the reason for her leaving the message flew into her memory. "Oh . . . Well, I just wanted to clear things up and sort of start over. I did think I was calling Quint when I got you, but I wasn't calling him for the reason you thought."

"It doesn't matter. It's none of my business. I appreciate your calling back after I blew up and ran off like I did."

Before she could reply, the waiter returned with tall glasses of iced tea. They sat in awkward silence while he stirred two teaspoons of sugar into his tea and she dumped two pink packages of artificial sweetener into hers.

"Tag, I felt terrible—"

"I felt like an ass," he said at the same time. Then they laughed together.

"Anyway, I owe you an apology," he said.

She leaned back against the booth's back and swallowed a long swig of tea, attempting to contain her nervousness. His look came at her, direct and deliberate.

"There's something you oughta know about me," he said. "I'm not real good at communicating, especially with women. And I'm even worse with a woman I like."

Did he say "woman I like"? The tension simmering within her doubled. "Uh, I don't do a great job either. I haven't had much practice. In my life, there aren't many men to even try to communicate with. And there never has been."

"That's hard to believe. You're so easy to talk to. And so pretty."

She gave a silly titter, still nervous. "Thanks, but it's the truth. Lord, I've never lived anywhere but Haskell, Texas, and now Salt Lick, which is even smaller than Haskell. There isn't an overpopulation of available men in either place. You probably don't know where Haskell is. It's a wide spot in the road a ways east of here."

"I sure do. I've even been there. Or I should say I've been in that county bird hunting with some friends."

"Oh. Well, bird hunting's a big thing there. In fact, to some, it's bigger than ranching."

The waiter returned with a platter of sizzling grilled chicken strips, onions, and peppers. He filled the table with dishes—fresh guacamole, shredded cheese, sour cream, salsa, and warm refried beans veined with melting cheddar cheese.

"Yum," Allison said, picking up a soft tortilla and layering on spicy chicken strips and some onions and green peppers. "I can't remember the last time I ate here. In fact, until I met Quint, it had been months since the last time I dined out anywhere." She laughed as she topped her fajita off with some of everything from every dish. "I sound even more like a hick than I am. As you may have guessed, I don't get out much."

"Don't call yourself a hick," he said, busy constructing his own fajita. "Want to hear about a hick? I should tell you where I came from."

She looked into his eyes as he chewed. "Oh, would you? I'd love to hear."

He put down his fajita and paused, his eyes leveled on hers, as if he didn't quite believe her.

"Really," she said. "I'm interested."

He chewed a few seconds, then swallowed. "Well, I'm about as redneck as they come. I grew up here in Midland. My dad followed drilling rigs, worked as a roustabout mostly. Most folks called us oil-field trash."

The term *oil-field trash* was common in West Texas, used to define blue-collar workers who labored in the oil fields. She had assumed he came from a wealthy ranching family. "No kidding?"

He took another bite and dabbed at his mouth with his napkin. "Yep. Dad was always gone, working somewhere. My grandma and grandpa lived here in Midland, so Mom kept us here so we wouldn't have to be changing schools all the time. All she and Dad had was an old car and a trailer house with a mortgage on it. They had a hard time making the payments, but boy, was Mom determined to keep a roof over our heads. She worked as a waitress."

He gave a soft laugh and Allison was sure she could see in his expression that he was thinking of something from long ago.

"Anyway, when I got big enough, I dropped out of school to help them out. I went to work on a ranch a little piece out of town. So, you see, I never even graduated from high school. I am proud to say, though, that eventually I got a GED. I promised Mom I would."

Allison's own high-school years came back to her. Though she hadn't quit school to support a family, exactly, her senior year had been cut short by her pregnancy. She had graduated, though, and later educated herself by reading and taking correspondence courses. "But you've been so successful. And you're so smart."

"God gave me a lot of horse sense. And I've always been willing to work hard."

"Then working on a ranch is how you got so well acquainted with bulls?"

"I guess you could say that. When you work around cattle, you get acquainted with all of them. People call them stupid animals, but they've got personalities just like dogs or cats. Most domestic bulls aren't wild and crazy, you know. On the range, you can walk right up to most of them and rub their ears if you want to. Sometimes you run into a ringer, but on the whole, bovines are nonaggressive animals."

"Oh, I know. I had a friend in Haskell who had a pet bull. I grew up a town kid, so I was never around ranching directly, but almost everyone I knew was. How did you get into ProRodeo? That's an enviable accomplishment. It must have been hard."

"Not really. It just sort of happened. Working at the ranch, I always hung around the cowboys. I wanted to be one so bad. The local rodeo association must have felt sorry for me, 'cause they hired me to do odd jobs. I cleaned stalls, fixed up the bleachers, painted fences, that kind of stuff. I wanted to compete, but I never had the entry fees. I did the next best thing. I rode as pickup man for the bronc riders."

"Then how did you become a clown—er, a bullfighter?"

"I had a natural athletic ability, I guess, 'cause I could do things in the arena a lot of fellas couldn't. And you see, I wasn't afraid of it. That makes a difference. I kept hanging out and eventually I started filling in for the clowns." He ducked his head as if he were embarrassed. "I guess I liked the attention being a clown got me, so I started learning to do more little tricks and stuff. I got to be pretty good at magic tricks."

"From what I saw in the mall, you're better than good at it. Those kids adored you. How did being a clown become bullfighting?"

"Oh, the bullfighting thing came way later. It was almost a necessity when you think about it. Stock breeders kept bringing in bulls that were stronger and hairier, and pretty soon, just acting silly wasn't enough. Like I said, I wasn't afraid of the bulls, but I did respect their strength and the fact that they can be unpredictable in all that confusion in the arena."

"You mean the lights and the noise and all that."

"Hmm. You see, a lot of these young cowboys are so wet behind the ears they don't know that much about livestock, so they're a wreck waiting to happen. I decided I could make things a lot safer for cowboys and animals both if I took to just playing with the bulls and keeping their attention so the cowboys that got bucked off could get out of their way. Pretty soon, my little tricks and antics caught the eye of the pros and somehow I got hired." He grinned. "The rest is history, as they say."

"What a nice story," she said. "I can't believe how much I've learned about rodeos and bulls lately."

"Bulls are good animals. I like 'em. Just remember this. While it's not in the nature of most of them to hurt anybody, you never want to forget that they outweigh you by quite a bit and a pissed-off bull's a strong, powerful athlete."

"I guess I never thought of rodeo animals as athletes."

"Well sir, that's what they are nowadays. All the rodeo animals are. And as with any other high-bred animal, stock breeders try to concentrate all the good qualities, which include strength and aggressiveness."

She laughed around another bite of fajita. "I'll try to remember that the next bull I run into."

"So let's talk about you," he said, instantly switching gears.

"Hmm, well, what do you want to know?"

"Everything," he said with a big grin.

Among other things, Allison told him how she had come to meet Quint in the first place. He laughed at the story and appreciated Jill's effort. More than two hours later the waiter had cleared the empty plates from the table, repeatedly refilled the tea glasses, and presented the dessert menu for inspection twice. Allison and Tag had made two trips each to the restrooms. With the meal clearly over, Allison said, "Well, I guess I better go. Mom will start to think I've had a wreck in her car or something."

"I guess you're right. We stay any longer and they'll charge us rent."

As they walked outside Tag looped his arm around her shoulders. It felt good there, like the most natural thing in the world. At her mom's car, Allison unlocked the door, then peered up and shielded her eyes against the sun. "Thanks for lunch. And for entertaining me. You've made my day so much better." She rose on the tips of her toes and gave his cheek a peck.

He brushed her nose with his lips and opened her car door. She slid inside and lowered her window.

"Take my word for it," he said, his hands braced on the windowsill. "The pleasure was all mine."

She began to panic. Wasn't he going to ask her out? "Uh, maybe we can do it again sometime?"

"That would be great."

Allison waited for him to name a time and place, but he stared down at the ground, digging his keys from his pocket. "We seem to run into each other a lot. Maybe it'll happen again." He touched the brim of his hat. "Be seeing you," he said, and walked away.

She was disappointed, but she refused to be unhappy. Though she didn't know why he hadn't made a date with her, she was sure they had made a solid bond. They had told each other their life stories. She had to believe he didn't do that with every woman he met and she was dead certain she didn't tell every man. Telling Tag everything about her past hadn't bothered her at all. It had been easy. She might be unsophisticated where men were concerned, but something reassured her that this particular one was worth knowing.

nineteen

By late afternoon Debbie Sue and Edwina had viewed, read, and printed all the responses to the personal ads from the two dating sites. On the manicure table they had made three stacks labeled COULD BE, COULDN'T POSSIBLY BE, and HELL NO.

The COULD BES fell into the right age bracket and their pictures bore some similarities to the mystery woman's picture supplied by Quint. None was an exact match, though one in particular came close. Quint was the only person who could make that call.

The COULDN'T POSSIBLY BES were from Texas, but that was as far as their qualifications went.

The HELL NO bunch apparently didn't care about the seeker's desires. All were over forty, overdue a makeover, and, judging by the photos they had submitted with their replies, overly fond of their near-naked bodies.

"This is disgusting." Edwina stood up and stretched her back. "I'm glad I'm not single anymore. I don't think I could get into this Internet dating. I'd miss the old days and ways too much."

Debbie Sue, too, was feeling the pressure of sitting in one place too long. She rubbed her eyes as she bent side to side from the waist. "And the old ways would be?"

"Oh, you know. Walk into a bar, check out the men, point to one, and take him home. It was a lot more fun that way."

"And so much safer." After Debbie Sue and Buddy divorced, she had spent her share of time and two-stepped a million miles in raunchy West Texas honky-tonks, but she had always been afraid of the "pick up men in a bar" routine.

"Nothing safe is ever fun. Didn't your mama ever tell you that?" Edwina unwrapped a Tootsie Pop and stuck it into her mouth.

"Nope, my mama told me a lot of things, but never that."

The front door opened with a jangle and Allison struggled through it carrying a big flat box. "I'm a little early. I brought cookies and I've got a party tray out in the car."

She left the box on the payout counter and went outside. Edwina lifted the lid. "Oh, look. Turkeys and Pilgrims. I always wanted to nibble on a Pilgrim." She cackled as she picked out a cookie with thick orange frosting and a sugar portrait of a Pilgrim's face.

Allison returned carrying a round foil tray covered in

plastic wrap. Debbie Sue studied the assortment of vegetables, meats, and cheeses. "Good grief, Allison, this is enough food for an army. I know Maudeen said she's expecting over thirty people, but I'll be surprised if there's ten. Is your mom coming?"

"No. She and Frank took Jill to the cutting-horse show in Abilene, so I'm all alone."

"Ow, ow," Edwina said, stretching her torso again. "I don't know how people can sit in front of a computer all day long and not lose their minds."

"What are you doing in front of a computer all day?" Allison asked.

"Debbie Sue and I've been doing some Equalizer work. We're looking for—"

"Say," Debbie Sue interrupted, "you're the last customer today, Allison. How about we get primed for the party with a pitcher of margaritas?"

"That sounds so good."

"Now you're talking," Edwina said. "If it wasn't for Vic and tequila, I don't know if life would be worth living." She started for the storeroom.

"Ed, don't talk like that," Allison said, stopping her. "Stop and think about it. You've got plenty to live for."

"Yeah," Debbie Sue added. "Did you tell Allison your big news?"

Allison looked at Edwina with a questioning expression.

Edwina's red lips tipped up in a huge grin. "I'm gonna be a grandma. My first. Me, a grandma. That's a hoot, isn't it?"

"That's great," Allison said. "I think you'll be the best. Congratulations. Are you planning on buying the baby something tonight?"

"I guess so. I haven't bought toys in over twenty years. I wonder if they still make Betsy Wetsy."

Before either of the two women could answer, the sleigh bells jangled again and in walked Quint. Debbie Sue shot a glance at Allison.

"Evening, ladies," Quint said. "Hope I'm not breaking up—" He stopped talking when he saw Allison and lifted off his hat. He started toward where she sat in one of the styling chairs.

"My Lord, sweet cheeks," Edwina said, whacking him on the shoulder and looking him up and down. "You rub my fur the wrong way at times, but I'll say one thing for you. Wrangler's stock price must jump every time you put on a pair of jeans. We're just about to have margaritas. Care for one?"

Quint raised a palm in protest. "None of that tequila for me. I might have a cold beer if you've got it."

"I think we can find one in the back of the refrigerator," Debbie Sue said. "By the way, those job applicants you asked us to do a background check on are stacked on that little table if you want to take a look." She gave him her best arched brows and tilted her head toward the manicure table.

"What? Ohhh, oh yeah. The résumés I asked you to do a background check on. I'd almost forgotten. Thanks. I'll take a look while you're in the back."

Debbie Sue got to her feet and started for the storeroom. "Come with me, Ed."

"Not on your life," Edwina replied.

"Ed," Debbie Sue said firmly, grasping Edwina's upper arm. "Come with me." She dragged her along to the storeroom.

Allison was left alone with Quint as the two women disappeared behind the curtained doorway. Of all the people she might expect to walk into the Styling Station, Quint wasn't one of them. An uncomfortable silence ensued.

"I called you Wednesday and spoke to your mom," he said. "Nice lady."

"She told me. You didn't leave a number, so I called the one on caller ID. Didn't Tag mention it to you?"

"Tag? Why would he?"

"Because the number was actually his. Y'all had each other's phones for a while. I didn't know that until I called and he answered."

Quint's chin lifted as a knowing look swept across his face. He chuckled. "We *were* getting each other's calls for a while."

Allison searched madly for something to say. A tiny guilt at the way she had spent the afternoon pinched her. "Debbie Sue and Edwina are helping you screen applicants? What kind of job opening do you have?"

"It's, uh—it's in my office in Seguin. Bookkeeper. Last two or three haven't worked out, so I decided to get some help looking for somebody to hire."

"Did you use the Internet to look for applicants or just to check their backgrounds?"

"Both." He leaned toward her and cupped her chin in his hand. "You know, I've had pretty good luck looking for other things on the Internet lately. Thought I'd give it a try again."

Allison knew that line had to be meant to hit home with her, and it did. She felt her cheeks heat up. "I, uh, did quite a bit of interviewing for the doctor's office when I worked in Haskell. I'm a pretty good judge of character. Even if it's only on paper. Mind if I look at them?" She reached for the small sheaf of papers that had obviously just been printed off the computer.

Quint moved like lightning. Before she could touch a page, he scooped the papers up and held them close to his chest. "I wouldn't think of imposing on you like that. You girls have some plans for this evening and I'm butting in. Tell Debbie Sue I'm taking these with me and I'll get back to her later."

Arms full of loose papers, he started for the door.

"Let me get the door for you," Allison said.

Before she could open the door, Debbie Sue and Edwina returned, carrying margaritas and a Lone Star beer.

"Hey, cowboy," Edwina said, giving him a jab with her elbow. "Where do you think you're sneaking off to?"

Quint lost control of the papers and they slid from his arms to the floor.

"Oh, my goodness, let me help you." Allison squatted and began to pick up the scattered sheets of paper.

Quint squatted, too, and began to scoop up the papers in a disorganized pile. "That's not necessary. I've got it." He took Allison by the elbow and lifted her to her feet.

She glanced at the pages in her hand, at one picture of a scantily dressed woman with a come-hither expression and an explicit written message. She looked up at Quint in puzzlement. "I think this woman's looking for more than a job."

She fanned through a couple more pages, scanning the narratives accompanying each picture, struck by the revelation that Quint was still looking for someone. "These are personal ads." She leafed through more pages, aghast. "They're all personal ads."

The old feelings of inadequacy and self-doubt crept up her spine, into her brain. He was dissatisfied with her. All this time he had been courting her, he had continued to look for someone else. She felt like a fool. "I'm, uh—I'm so sorry. I had no right to read those. It's really none of my business." Avoiding Quint's eyes, she handed him the pages.

Quint's gaze darted between Debbie Sue and Edwina. In the thick silence, no one offered an explanation.

"Oh, hell, Allison," he finally said. "You're right. These are personal ads. I didn't tell you about my business here in Salt Lick because I didn't want to admit that I've been made a fool of again. I don't like what that says about me." He went into a long-winded tale of the identity theft for Allison. He even went all the way back to the fiasco with Eugene/Janine.

"So that's it. The whole unvarnished truth," he said in

conclusion. "I asked Debbie Sue not to tell you, or anybody, what they're doing for me."

Allison was moved by the soul-baring disclosure. What he had been through could have happened to anyone. Why, she and Jill were guilty of carrying on a ruse themselves, pretending she had been the one communicating with him instead of her twelve-year-old. She was overcome with sympathy, a good measure of guilt, and a little regret. For a second she contemplated telling him the truth about Jill's real role in their Internet meeting, but changed her mind. The poor guy had been deceived enough. She didn't want to add to his humiliation.

She moved closer to him and placed her hand on his forearm. "Please don't be embarrassed," she said softly. "Anyone can have the wool pulled over their eyes. Sit down and go through these pages with Debbie Sue and Edwina. The party doesn't start for two hours. I'll just sit on the other side of the room and drink my margarita."

Quint looked up at her. "Thanks, babe. I'll do that. But as long as you know what we're up to, you can help if you like."

As they perused the printed pages Edwina kept the margarita glasses filled. Quint had two more beers. The categorized responses had been jumbled together when Quint dropped them on the floor and each one had to be reexamined to match the picture with the profile.

"Here's a good one," Quint said, waving a page in the air. Leaning forward and resting his elbows on his knees, he read, "'I want to pour cake batter on your belly, and by the time we're finished, I promise you the cake will be done.' Whoa! Now that's a keeper."

"Stop it, Quint," Debbie Sue said, struggling to hold back a giggle. "These women are serious."

"I know that. But c'mon. Cake batter on my belly?"

Edwina appeared to be in deep thought. She pressed a finger against her cheek. "I wonder how that would work." Everyone hooted.

Debbie Sue rose, laid the pages on her salon chair, and took the drinks from Edwina's, Allison's, and Quint's hands. "Listen, y'all, we've got to get this place cleaned up. Maudeen and her group of li'l old ladies will be here soon. We don't want them to catch us whooping it up."

"Can I help?" Allison asked, hoping they would say no. Her eyes were almost crossed from the combination of the strong margaritas and studying the printed pages.

"Nope," Edwina said. "You stay right where you are. We'll get this joint shaped up in a matter of seconds. Wonder Woman's got nothing on us." She and Debbie Sue gathered the empty glasses and disappeared behind the curtained doorway again.

Allison laughed. These two were just what she had needed tonight and she was seeing a different side of Quint. Leaning over, she picked up the last couple of pages Debbie Sue had laid on the chair. "Why, good Lord," she exclaimed, stunned. "I can't believe this. I know this person."

Quint's eyes were trained on her. "You're kidding."

"No. I'm not kidding."

"Is it somebody from this town?"

"From Haskell. A girl I knew years ago. What are the odds? We were friends when we were kids. But we had a falling-out. She stole my boyfriend and I thought my world had ended. Monica. Monica Hunter." A frown tugged at her brow. "As I recall, she was never short of boyfriends. I wonder why she's looking on the Internet."

In an instant, Quint was out of his chair and leaning over her shoulder. "Lemme see?" He took the page from her hands and stood there staring at it. His facial expression and his body seemed to wilt right before her eyes.

"Quint? Are you all right? Is that her? Is that the woman? Have we found her?"

"It isn't her," he said, still looking at the printed page. "I thought maybe it could be. The person I'm looking for is also named Monica. The Monica I'm looking for is prettier than this."

"Lord, I can't imagine," Allison said. "She was the prettiest girl in town. In the county. Maybe in all of Texas."

Quint handed the photo back. "Sounds like you knew her pretty well."

"Only her entire life. I can't get over this. It's quite a shock seeing her in this venue." As she stared at the picture of the beautiful girl she had known for so many years, her chin quivered and she bit her lip to control tears. Liquor always made her overemotional and talkative. "A dozen times I've thought about getting in touch with her. Patch things up, you know? The boyfriend is long gone and the world didn't end, but Monica and I are still estranged." She looked up at Quint. "She hasn't left Haskell either. The last

I heard, she works at the courthouse and rents a house from the doctor I used to work for. I really should call her."

"Know what?"

"What?" Allison attempted to prop her elbow on the chair arm and almost tipped from the chair face-first.

Quint caught her arm. "Hey, you okay?"

She straightened and gave him a blurry stare. "I think so."

"Look," he said. "I'm gonna go and let you gals get on with your little party. Thanks for your help. Tell Debbie Sue I took all the material with me and I'll check back with her tomorrow."

"Okay. I'm sorry you didn't find the girl. Don't you worry, though. What goes around goes—" She stopped and frowned. "Phooey. I can't remember the rest of that." She shook her head, setting off a roar in her ears. "That's funny."

Quint bent and kissed the top of her head. "See you later. You better cool it with the tequila."

He opened the door and a woman who had to be ninety tottered through, carrying a platter of cookies. To Allison's shock, she also had a gallon jug of vodka hooked on one finger and a two-liter bottle of 7-Up tucked under her arm.

The little old lady looked up at Quint. "Hey, cowboy. You staying for the party?"

Quint lifted off his hat, shifting his armload of papers, and offered a hand to help her.

"Grab this jug," she ordered. "It's about to break my finger. I'd hate to see half a gallon of vodka kiss the pavement."

She looked at Allison through thick lenses that magnified her eyes. "Hi, honey. I'm Maudeen Wiley. I live at the Peaceful Oasis. You staying for the party?"

Good grief. Wasn't this woman too old to drink? "Uh, yes. Yes, I am."

Quint gingerly took the bottle from her and sat it on the payout counter. He gave Allison a dazzling smile and a wink, touched his hat brim, and walked out.

Maudeen looked after Quint as the door closed on him. "My, my," she said, lightly slapping her wrinkled cheek. "Now that's a good-looking man. I've seen him in here before. Nice package, too. I do love the sight of a good-looking man in tight jeans."

Nice package? Slack-jawed, Allison stared at the little old lady's flaming red hair and crepey skin, trying to guess her age. This woman was hosting a toy party?

twenty

Following Edwina from the storeroom, Debbie Sue saw Maudeen. Another half a dozen women had come into the front room. The door opened and still more came in, laughing and giggling. Soon the salon's front room was packed with at least twenty women who, Debbie Sue, Edwina, and Allison agreed, were new faces. A few of the others, Debbie Sue noticed, were Salt Lick residents and Styling Station customers she and Edwina had invited.

Last to arrive was Charlene Elkins, wife of Salt Lick's only auto mechanic. Where had she come from? She was a customer of the Styling Station's competition. Charlene dragged in a large insulated cooler and a grocery sack filled with packages of Styrofoam cups.

Not expecting so large a gathering, Debbie Sue looked at the group in horror. The Styling Station had only one bathroom. With the chair at the payout desk, the two hydraulic

salon chairs, and the three padded seats attached to the dry-
ers, plus the three folding chairs from the storeroom, she
could supply only nine seats. "I'm surprised so many are here
and that I know so few," she said to Maudeen. "Where are
all these women from?"

"Oh, they're from all over the county, honey. And some
came from over at Odessa. Most think it's better if they buy
toys out of town. I've been to lots of these parties. There's
always a good turnout. Jewel is the hostess. She's a real live
wire. All the girls love her. When she gets here things will
get going."

Why would someone prefer to go out of town to buy
toys? Oh, well, Debbie Sue decided, what difference did it
make? She searched her mind, trying to place this Jewel, but
failed. "I must not have met Jewel."

"Oh, she's from Odessa, honey. This is her first party in
Salt Lick."

Just then, the front door flew open and a bleached blonde
the size of an elf announced her presence. "Ladeeezz, Jewel's
in the building! Let's get this party started!"

Debbie Sue gaped. Jewel had to be in her seventies. She
wore a one-piece formfitting jumpsuit with a leopard-print
scarf tied at the waist and black ankle boots with faux-leopard
trim. An assortment of beaded bracelets encircled each wrist
and her hair was teased to football-helmet size, a do that
would make any Texas diva proud. Huge black-framed glasses
sat on the tip of her nose.

Meanwhile, Charlene opened the cooler, which Debbie
Sue saw was filled with crushed ice. The auto mechanic's

wife began to mix vodka and 7-Up in the Styrofoam cups. "Here y'are, girls. Step right up. Have a swig of the nectar of the gods." She tossed back a gulp of her own drink.

"Damn," Debbie Sue said. "I didn't know Charlene was a vodka guzzler. How did I miss that?"

Jewel went outside and returned, rolling in wheeled black suitcases. She opened one and removed a boom box. She set it on the payout counter, pushed a button, and the rhythmic thundering tune by Pink, "Get the Party Started," bounced off the walls of the salon's front room. Most of the women, cups of vodka and 7-Up in hand, began singing along and bumping and grinding to the loud music.

As Debbie looked on, growing more puzzled by the minute, Jewel, stepping and hip-swaying to the thumping beat of the music, moved through the throng with a small jar and a handful of Q-tips. She dipped the Q-tips into the jar and handed them out as she greeted each guest personally. "Hi, hon, I'm Jewel. Glad you could make it. Put some of this on your lips."

She danced over to Debbie Sue and handed her a Q-tip. "Here, darlin'. Just smear it on your lips." Debbie Sue didn't dare fail to follow the instructions. As soon as she swiped her lips they began to tingle.

"Feel the buzz?" Jewel said, stepping in time with the music. "Lips ain't where it goes, but you get the picture." She giggled and moved on.

Debbie Sue contorted her mouth. All of the women in the room were doing likewise and giggling.

"Oh, man, I want a biiig jar of that stuff," Bethany Nix said, and cackled.

Allison looked at Debbie Sue with a bewildered expression, passing her tongue over her lips. "This feels funny. What does she mean? Where does it go?"

Momentarily stumped about what to think, or more to the point, what to do, Debbie Sue shrugged. She, Edwina, and Allison appeared to be the only three who had expected something different from what they were witnessing.

"Don't worry," Jewel told her audience in an elevated voice. "All of our stimulants are edible and sugar-free." She let out a loud cackle. "No carbs."

"Are these diet products?" Allison asked.

"I don't think so," Debbie Sue said, and glanced at Edwina, who appeared to have been rendered speechless. A cookie had almost made it to her mouth, but had been interrupted by the Q-tip and remained frozen in midair.

Still stepping in time with the music, Jewel pulled out a portable clothesline and began hanging skimpy lingerie items. Allison gravitated to the garments immediately. One category of feminine attire Almost the Rage did not sell was lingerie. "Oh my gosh! These panties are missing the . . . the, the bottoms."

Debbie Sue yanked the hank of lacy fabric from her hands and hung it back on the clothesline.

Jewel started a new pass through the crowd, handing out creams and liquids that tasted fruity and generated sensations on the inside of wrists and on the backs of hands—warming lubricating jelly, fruit-flavored oils, vanilla-scented cream. "Don't forget," she shouted to the enthralled audience, "vanilla's a natural aphrodisiac. And all of our products are edible."

"Something tells me I missed something when I was discussing this party with Maudeen," Edwina finally said.

"Ladies," Jewel shouted, "are you ready for the good time?"

The crowd chorused an enthusiastic "Hell, yeah."

She danced her way back to her sample cases and opened one. She lifted out a large plastic bag and, continuing to move to the booming music, handed an item from the bag to each guest. "Here we are, girls," she yelled over the music. "Take a look. Substitutes for whatcha don't got at home."

The diminutive hostess danced past Debbie Sue, leaving her standing there agape . . . and holding an enormous rubber penis in one hand and a remote control in the other. And the thing was hot pink.

Debbie Sue looked around the room, stunned by seeing her most God-fearing, churchgoing customers playing with plastic and rubber sex devices. Every guest had a gadget in hand and was giving it a thorough examination. The word *toys* flashed in Debbie Sue's mind. *Sex toys! Oh. My. God.* Maudeen had tricked her. She crooked her finger at the octogenarian and said in her best Desi Arnaz voice, "Luuucy, you got some splainin' to do."

Maudeen clapped her hands and laughed. "Oh, my lands, isn't this a nice turnout? I'm so happy." She turned to Debbie Sue and gave her a little push toward the group. "Dance a little, honey. Mix it up. If you don't like that thing in your hand, find something else. Take a look at what Eloise is holding. Your ol' sweetie can put his thing in that when he can't put it in you. Keeps him out of a whorehouse."

"Maudeen," Debbie Sue exclaimed, looking closer at the object in Eloise's hands, which resembled a fist-size glob of translucent fuchsia jelly.

"I swanee," Edwina said, shaking her head. "The world we live in these days. Post your picture on the computer and meet a date. And now this." She pushed the switch on a purple plastic penis containing beads that began to spin and ripple with bright colors while it vibrated. "Would you look at that?"

"I can't stand to," Debbie Sue said. "It almost looks painful."

Edwina continued to play with her toy at varying speeds. "When I was single, you had to go out and strut your stuff for the real thing. Now they package it and bring it right to your door. Amazing."

"And in seven sensuous colors and sizes," Debbie Sue added, testing the remote control of the hot-pink penis. It began to work up and down in a rhythmic motion and she felt her face flame. "Look at this. I'm embarrassed to be holding it."

Edwina chuckled.

"Just stop laughing," Debbie Sue said. "If I know you, you've already got a list of what you're going to buy."

Edwina laughed again. "I see a few things I don't have. But then I don't need a lot. I've got the real thing at home."

Allison walked over, looking quizzically at the huge blue-

and-white dildo she held in her hands. "Do you know if this comes with batteries?"

"Can't say that I do," Edwina cracked, "but I'm pretty sure it will if you rub it long enough."

The three collapsed in laughter.

"This is terrible for someone like me," Allison said through tears of mirth. "I'm more celibate than a nun. I can't remember the last time I had sex or even with whom."

"Then you must be one of their target customers," Debbie Sue said, and they laughed more.

"How have these parties been going on and I don't know about them?" Edwina asked. "I'm supposed to be the Lance Armstrong of gossip in Salt Lick, and this has zipped right past my radar."

Jewel pulled even more rarefied "enhancement" accessories from her case and continued her spiel. Although she was by law, she went on, prevented from demonstrating the effectiveness of her stock, she managed to give a compellingly graphic description of each item. Debbie Sue noted that for those who had additional questions, Edwina was happy to join in on Jewel's pitch.

"Maudeen," Debbie Sue said, continuing to watch the guests play with and discuss the array of toys and the intricacies of each, "how did you get involved with this?"

"Oh, honey, I'm just trying to help Jewel out. Christmas is coming, you know, and she's got thirty-five grandkids. And land sake, she's lost track of the great-grandkids. It used to be she couldn't buy them all presents. Now she can."

"She makes good money at this?"

"Oh, my Lord, yes. That is, if she doesn't get arrested and have to pay a big fine. She was barely getting by on her Social Security. Now she's making about three thousand a month."

The word *arrested* set off an alarm in Debbie Sue's brain. "Arrested? Why would she get arrested? Is this against the law?"

Before Maudeen could answer, Allison piped up, "Three—did you say three thousand a month?"

"She makes more around Valentine's Day, when all the ladies try to add a little spice in the bedroom."

"I can see why you didn't want to have this at the Peaceful Oasis," Debbie Sue said, examining a deep purple contraption that resembled a dog's chew toy.

"Why, honey, the retirement homes are where the big bucks are. But the Oasis has a bunch of Bible-thumpers that threw a hissy fit when I tried to sign up for the rec room. I'm guessing they never liked sex when they were younger. Or maybe they never had it."

Maudeen took the device from Debbie Sue's hands and showed her the proper way to hold it. "This tickles your G-spot, honey. If your ol' sweetie can't find it, I guarantee you this thing can. And it comes in three sizes."

"Let me see that," Edwina said.

Quint Matthews's truck was idling at an intersection's red light. Aha! The prey was on the move. The driver of a tan

KIA sedan peeked over a candy display in a convenience store. The gray pickup of earlier use had gone bye-bye. It had proved to be too much to handle and too expensive to operate. The KIA driver exited the store.

The whereabouts of the Road Warrior, Mr. Matthews, had been unknown for the past forty-eight hours, but suddenly here he was. Call it karma or plain dumb luck. Whatever, the game was back on.

But something was different. An unmistakable urgency was visible in Quint's posture. He was hunched forward over the steering wheel, hands gripping the orb at ten and two, an expression of intensity on his face. He looked like an Olympic runner in the starting blocks, waiting for the sound of the pistol.

The light changed from red to green and Quint turned left, his diesel engine growling through the turn. Something was wrong. He wasn't heading southwest toward Salt Lick, or southeast toward his ranch in Seguin. No, he was entering the ramp onto I-20, going east.

The tan KIA's driver scooted behind the steering wheel, tossing lottery tickets and candy bars onto the passenger seat. The four-cylinder chugged and strained to catch up to Quint's big diesel.

To Quint's great happiness, the information operator had been happy to give him not only Monica's phone number, but her address as well. Ten additional minutes on mapquest.com and he had the directions to Monica, right down to every little yield and stop sign between here and her house.

She had sounded so calm and collected on the phone when he called and identified himself. No sign of surprise, not even the slightest hint of concern. He heard no sound of regret either.

In fact, she had been cordial, even playful. That was it: she had been playful. A titter, the likes of which only women were capable, had peppered the conversation too much. He had half expected her to beg for forgiveness. Instead, she flirted.

Well, putting on a good show with hundreds of miles between her and an old lover was easy. Things would be different when she found him standing in front of her, looking her in the eye.

Of course she didn't know he was on his way to visit her. Her last words on the phone had been "Maybe we'll see each other sometime."

Maybe, hell. There was no maybe about it.

Yep, when he showed up, she would cry. She would cave.

She had better.

At 9 P.M., Quint pulled into the hamlet of Haskell, population three thousand. He had driven in two hours and twenty minutes a distance that would have taken more than three hours if he had obeyed the posted speed limit.

Like most county seats in West Texas small towns, an old baroque-looking courthouse rose up in the center of town, filled an entire block, and lorded over the community. It had probably been built in the nineteenth century. And like most West Texas small towns, except for a cat crossing from one side of the street to the other, the place was dead—deader even than Salt Lick.

He didn't need to reread the MapQuest directions to find where Monica lived. The route was burned like a brand into his memory. Two turns and several blocks later he entered a modest neighborhood. It looked to have been affluent once, but now it was merely two rows of houses with For Sale signs posted in more than half the front yards.

He parked in front of a modest redbrick home. Still, in Haskell, it must have taken all the salary someone working at the courthouse could earn to pay the rent. "Maybe that's why she stole from me," Quint mumbled. She hadn't done it because she hadn't fallen for him. Naw, it couldn't have been that.

He looked in the mirror, adjusted his hat, and took a deep breath. He was almost happy for the first time in a long time. All questions would be put to rest in short order. This confrontation was what he had come for.

As the tan Kia passed Tenth Street the driver's peripheral vision caught a glimpse of Quint's big dually parked at the curb a few houses up. The sedan stopped and turned around.

The past two hours had been hell on the nerves. Driving

at speeds the economy rental car wasn't designed to travel was like sliding down a razor blade. Excruciating. The poor little sedan's chassis shook, shimmied, and whined. During the whole trip, the driver had anticipated an explosion or, at the very least, a complete engine meltdown.

Now Quint's truck door opened. The interior light came on. The man himself climbed down from the cab. He checked the tuck of his expensive shirt, dusted off one boot, and reset his Stetson.

Watching the good-looking devil stride up the sidewalk to the door, the driver sighed, then eased on past the house, turned into the driveway of a darkened house several doors up the street, and waited. The view was perfect. Whoever answered the door could be seen clearly.

After what seemed like an eternity, the front door opened and the driver got a good look. It was her all right. Monica. The hussy. Quint went inside and the door closed. Following Quint had finally paid off. Waiting was all that was left to do.

Ten, twenty, thirty minutes . . . All at once Quint bolted from the house. He didn't even close the front door. He quickstepped toward his truck, but was stopped for a moment by a man walking his dog. After a brief conversation, the man and dog walked on. Quint stood for a moment under the glow of an antiquated streetlight, yanked off his hat, and shoved his fingers through his hair. He glanced back at the house, then climbed into his truck, cranked the engine, and roared away.

The open door of the house he had just left loomed like an invitation. The opportunity was too good to pass up.

The tan KIA pulled to the exact spot just vacated by Quint's truck. The driver got out, took a quick look around, then walked up the sidewalk and into the house.

Little Miss Monica was in for another surprise.

twenty-one

Allison, unable to stop laughing, came to where Debbie Sue stood. "This is crazy, but I'm having so much fun. Jewel puts on a great party. The light show outside is so cool. I wonder how she does that?" She pointed to a flashing light suddenly brightening the salon in red, white, and blue.

"Light show?" Maudeen said. "She's never had a light—"

"Oh, shit," Debbie Sue muttered. "That's red and blues. It's the cops." Her thoughts flew to Buddy. *She* was the one who would soon have some explaining to do.

Sensing the alert, the reveling women stopped in their tracks. All at once the door flew open and banged the wall with so much force it bounced back and slammed shut again. Outside, two male voices could be heard arguing.

The door opened again more carefully. Sheriff Billy Don

Roberts stood in the doorway, hands on his hips. "Attention! All o' you, listen up!"

Deputy Harry Bridges, Billy Don's brother-in-law, barely five feet six in cowboy boots, stood just behind him. "This ain't no joke," he shouted, his wide-eyed stare swinging from the purple neon-colored dildo in Bethany Nix's hand to the vibrating pink penis Dorothy Tucker was operating at various speeds. "You've all violated the Texas Penis Code 43.21 for Public Indecency."

The guests' eyes darted from one to the other. Edwina was the first to break the silence with a low-key giggle. It soon erupted into a full-blown guffaw. Within moments the whole crowd was engaged in sidesplitting laughter.

Edwina waltzed over and threw a long skinny arm around the vertically challenged deputy's neck, her wrist reaching him midchest. Debbie Sue could see that the vodka on top of the several margaritas they had drunk earlier had driven out her partner's few inhibitions.

"Don't you mean the Texas *Penal* Code, Deputy Harry Britches?" Edwina said.

The room rocked with laughter again.

"Let's see how funny you think this is, smarty-pants." The deputy yanked handcuffs from his belt and hooked a link around Edwina's wrist. "Ever' one o' y'all's under arrest."

The room fell silent. All Debbie Sue could think was that Buddy Overstreet was not only going to divorce her the second time, he was also going to shoot her.

The sheriff strutted in front of them, his face grim, his

leather service belt and the half-dozen items attached to it
causing his pants to sag dangerously low. "*Now!* Have we
got your attention? . . . I'm gonna ask for your coopera-
tion. We don't have enough cuffs for everybody, but I guar-
an-tee you we'll use the ones we got if you give us any
trouble."

Jewel's voice piped up from the back of the group. "I've
got plenty of cuffs. You want fur-lined or rhinestone-
encrusted?"

Laughter erupted again.

The sheriff closed his eyes and clenched his jaw. "Dammit
all to hell, Harry, you can't reason with a bunch like this."
He threw a hand in the air. "Just take 'em in."

The crowd grew silent again as Deputy Bridges walked
behind them and motioned with his palms, as if to shoo
them through the front door.

The sound of a toilet flushing came from the storeroom,
followed by a female voice warbling, "Let's get this party
started." The curtain that covered the storeroom doorway
parted and Mrs. Billy Don Roberts stepped into the front
room, still zipping her jeans. She stopped and looked
around, then zeroed in on her husband. "What's going on,
boopsie?"

The sheriff's face turned three colors of red. "Velma! . . .
My God, Velma!" He stiffened his spine and squared his
shoulders. "I don't know what a fine churchgoing woman
like you is doing in this den of iniquity, but I can't make an
exception because you're my wife. Sometimes a man has to
make hard choices upholding the law."

Debbie Sue couldn't contain her laughter, even knowing how pissed Buddy was going to be. But surely Buddy would understand that this really wasn't her fault.

Laughter continued to plague the gathering until everyone was escorted outside. Parked on the far side of the parking lot, attached to the rear bumper of Deputy Bridges's old pickup, sat a cattle trailer with tall sides made of wooden slats. The tailgate had been dropped down to create a ramp. Typically, the ramp was used to load cattle. Edwina screamed with laughter again. "Billy Don doesn't have a paddy wagon in his budget. He's got a cattle trailer."

"Billy Don Roberts," Maudeen exclaimed, glaring up at him and shaking her bony finger at his nose. "Why, young man, I've known you your entire life. Why, your mama used to rinse your dirty diapers in my bathroom sink every time y'all's water got shut off. Why, if you think you're gonna haul me off to jail in that shitty old cattle trailer, you better retrace your steps and think again."

"Now, Miz Wiley," Deputy Bridges yelled, leaning closer to her face with his hand cupped against his mouth. "I cleaned it out before we came over here. I hung some o' them pine-scented air fresheners inside, too. You ladies will be real comfortable."

"Quit yelling in my face, you little idget!" Maudeen whacked him on the shoulder with her purse. "Why, I know your mama and daddy and I play poker with your grandma. Just wait till I tell her what you've been up to." She swung her purse at his head, but he ducked.

Billy Don intervened by gripping Maudeen's shoulders

and pulling her back several steps, where she could no longer reach his brother-in-law. "I told you to watch out for this
one," he warned.

Debbie Sue stepped up, angry now. "This isn't the first
fuckin' trailer I ever saw or rode in. But at least let Maudeen
and Jewel ride up front with you big tough men. I only hope
everyone in town sees us go by."

"Me, too," Edwina said, hoisting her chin and prissing up
the trailer ramp. She took a place against the sidewall and
clasped her hands around the slats.

"And me, too," sang out Allison, following Edwina and
taking a position beside her.

A roar mounted from the group. Charlene Elkins stepped
in front of them and thrust a fist in the air. "Let's go, girls.
Let's ride proudly through the streets of Salt Lick."

As the women dutifully crowded into the cattle trailer,
Debbie Sue didn't bother to remind them that there were no
"streets of Salt Lick." There was only *one* street that passed
through town and it was the state highway linking 302 to
I-20.

"I wanna ride in the back," Maudeen said, and multiple
hands lifted her into the trailer.

"Me, too," Jewel added, hanging on to her boom box.

The only one who climbed into the truck cab with Sheriff Billy Don and Deputy Bridges was Velma Roberts. Debbie Sue had seen her whisper in Billy Don's ear. Whatever
she said, apparently it was real enough to him. He turned
from red to white and handed the truck keys over to his
deputy.

As the truck and trailer pulled away from the salon with twenty-six women standing inside shoulder to shoulder, Jewel pressed the boom box's on button and turned the volume on high. The heavy drumbeat bounced off the pavement and filled the night air as they traveled the one and only main street.

From the very front of the trailer, behind the throng of women, a deep, mournful voice bellowed, "Mmmooooo," and the whole bunch broke into laughter again.

The drive to the jail took less than ten minutes. Apparently phones had started ringing throughout the town and county before the trailer had departed the salon and now a crowd of a dozen women was waiting at the sheriff's office. This show of support came as no surprise to Debbie Sue. Her customers were loyal.

Billy Don climbed down from the truck and confronted the clamoring crowd. "All y'all go on home now. This ain't got nothing to do with you."

"What'd they do?" someone called out.

"You don't wanna know," the sheriff replied. "Take my word for it, you don't wanna know."

"We wanna be arrested, too," someone shouted from the back of the crowd.

A chorus of "yeahs" followed.

"No, dammit," Billy Don shouted back. "I can't arrest every female in town. Just go on home now."

The din of feminine voices escalated.

"I mean it!" He jammed a fist against his sagging accessories belt and pointed toward the fire hydrant on the street corner. "See this fire hydrant? I'll get a hose and turn it on you! Harry, bring me that hose in back o' the jail!"

"Uh, Billy Don—"

Everyone turned toward Deputy Bridges, who had inadvertently handcuffed himself to one of the trailer slats. The crowd of women hooted.

Billy Don did an exaggerated eye roll and stamped over to the trailer. He fumbled at his belt for the handcuff keys, then unlocked his deputy. "Get 'em inside, Harry," he said. "I'll take care o' this out here."

Inside, the jail consisted of two six-by-eight cells and one bunk, each containing a commode. Deputy Bridges divided the group evenly, thirteen women packed into each cell. The music from Jewel's boom box caused the walls of the small frame building to vibrate.

Edwina sank to the bunk at the back of the cell. "Well, I don't know about anybody else, but I've been on my feet all day and I've had just about as much of this fun as I need."

With a sigh, Debbie Sue sat down beside her. "Buddy Overstreet is going to divorce me, shoot me, hang me, and leave me for the buzzards."

"I think that happened to somebody else," Edwina said. "I read about it when I was quitting smoking. I think it was Rasmusson."

Debbie Sue recalled that Edwina had used reading any and everything to distract her from smoking. Unfortunately most of the information she retained from the extensive reading she did was confused and incorrect.

"Don't you mean Ras—" Allison frowned and licked her

lips. "That stuff still makes my tongue feel funny. Don't you mean Rasputin?"

"Whatever," Debbie Sue muttered.

"Aw, c'mon," Edwina said. "This isn't gonna amount to much. If Billy Don charged these women with anything, their husbands would ride him out of town on a rail. And he could kiss his job as sheriff good-bye. Besides that, I'll bet a lot of bored husbands would get a kick out of some of that stuff at the party."

Allison came to where they were sitting and took a seat on the commode beside the bunk. "Do you suppose these parties were going on while Buddy was sheriff? Are they really against the law?"

"Hell, I don't know." Debbie Sue braced her elbows on her knees and dropped her chin into her palms. "All I know is if I survive Buddy finding out about this, I'm gonna have a long talk with Maudeen."

The sheriff walked into the room, looking authoritative.

"I suppose he's stopped the riot outside," Edwina mumbled.

"Bullshit," Debbie Sue muttered. "When Buddy was sheriff, he would've never done something this stupid."

"I betcha Billy Don wouldn't have done it either, if Buddy was in town. He probably knows Buddy's three hundred miles away."

The sheriff marched to the cell housing Jewel and her boom box. "Shet off that radio!"

"It isn't a radio," Jewel said, defiantly leaving the volume on high. Billy Don fumbled with a ring of many keys, finally found one, and opened the cell door. "Give it to me," he ordered.

"Make me," Jewel said, glaring up at him and sticking out her wrinkled chin.

Billy Don pried the boom box from her hands. The group didn't protest. They seemed to have sunk into a slump, no doubt the effect of the vodka and 7-Up starting to dissipate. Debbie Sue was starting to develop a headache herself.

The cell remained quiet as Billy Don walked back to the desk. "Now, you see, Deputy," he said to Deputy Bridges. "This is how you handle a riot. I've removed the source of, uh . . . the source of—hold on." He pulled a thick book from the shelf above his desk, leafed to a dog-eared page, and read briefly, his lips moving. He slapped the book closed and returned his attention to Deputy Bridges. "I've removed the source of agitation. Now the group is docile and ready to take the lead of the controlling officers." He pointed to his deputy, then to himself. "That's you and me."

"Ohhhh." Deputy Harry lifted his chin as if he had just seen the light. "I just figured the liquor was wearing off."

Billy Don tilted his head, his mouth twisted into a scowl. "Well, yeah, that's prob'ly true, too."

Idiot, Debbie Sue thought. "Where's Velma?" she called out. "Why isn't she in here with us?"

Murmurs rose from both cells.

"She's home. Took her m'self. We got young'uns she needs to be home tending. Now, I'm willing to let y'all leave on your own recognition—"

"Don't you mean recognizance?" Allison asked timidly.

The sheriff glared at her. "You know, Miz Barker, you oughta be ashamed o' yourself. You got a nice daughter and you're a businesswoman in this town."

"It was just a little good clean fun," Allison said. "What else is there to do in Salt Lick?"

The sheriff continued to glare at her, obviously unable to come up with a rebuttal. He raised his voice again, speaking to both cells. "Like I was saying, on top o' disturbing the peace and acting lewd and indecent, y'all all have been drinking. But I'm a fair man. I'll release you tonight if somebody picks you up and takes responsibility for you. So, if you got a cell phone, make your call. Those o' you that don't, I'll let you use the phone on my desk. Just keep it short." He started to walk away, but stopped and came back. "And no long distance."

Women began to paw in their purses for phones. Edwina dug out hers and looked at Debbie Sue and Allison. "Who do we call? It wouldn't do any good to call my guy. He's somewhere on the road between here and California."

"What about Buddy?" Allison asked.

Allison obviously didn't know just how utterly unhinged Buddy would become when he learned his wife was in jail and the reason. "Are you kidding? Buddy's at a DPS training seminar in El Paso. I'm gonna call him and tell him Billy Don Dipshit has arrested me for lewd and indecent conduct? Those are *real* cops he's with. They'd laugh him out of the meeting. I'd be better off to call my lawyer and have her start work on a settlement."

"Hey, maybe she could come pick us up," Edwina said.

"All the way from Odessa? It'd cost us a fortune. Allison, got anyone we can call?"

"We could call my mom, but she and Jill are out of town with Frank. I don't even know where they're staying. They were supposed to get in touch with me later this evening and tell me." She chewed on her thumbnail, deep in thought. "I suppose we could call Quint."

"Hell, yes!" Debbie Sue sprang to her feet. "Why didn't I think of him? He's the perfect person to call in a situation like this. If there's anyone who can't throw stones, it's him."

"That's good," Edwina said, "because we're sure as shit sitting in a glass house."

Allison dug in her pocket, produced the number for Quint's cell phone, and keyed it in. She held up a finger at each ring—one, two, three. "Oh, drat." She stared at the miniscreen. "'Call failed,' it says." She tried again to no avail. "I can't reach him," she said on a sigh. "Now what are we going to do?"

"Call Tag's house," Debbie Sue said. "Maybe he knows where Quint is. Or Quint could be there, but have his cell turned off."

"I don't have Tag's home number. Just his cell. But it wouldn't be a good idea for me to call."

Allison explained the situation she found herself in with Quint and his longtime friend. She recounted the angry scene in her living room and then the day's lengthy lunch that ended with an uncertain outcome. "So, see? I can't call Tag and ask for Quint."

"Well, I sure as hell can." Debbie Sue grabbed the phone. "Gimme that number."

Allison dug out the other slip of paper and read the number aloud as Debbie Sue entered it.

Several heartbeats passed. Then an answer. Debbie Sue blew out a breath in relief. "Hi, Tag. This is Debbie Sue Overstreet . . ."

Quint wasn't there, he told her after she explained their situation. On a good-natured laugh, he added that he would come to Salt Lick and bail them out.

"I can't tell you how much I appreciate this, Tag. I'll owe you, big-time. There's three of us, my friends Edwina Martin and Allison Barker and me. We'll be looking for you. And thanks again. And oh, by the way, where is Quint anyway?"

She listened, then folded the phone shut and handed it back to Edwina. "Tag's coming to get us. I can't believe he's gonna drive all the way from Midland. What a great guy."

"What about Quint?" Allison asked.

"He took off. Tag said he called information and got a number for some woman in Haskell. He placed a call, talked for a few minutes, then hightailed it out the door. What do you suppose that was about?"

Allison didn't answer. She just frowned and slowly shook her head.

That was a guilty look if Debbie Sue had ever seen one. Then she remembered, Allison used to live in Haskell. Did she know why Quint had gone there?

★   ★   ★

The tan Kia's driver, shaken and distraught, watched from a distance as a sheriff's department sedan, lights flashing, siren squealing, and a volunteer-fire-department truck came to a stop in front of the Tenth Street house. An EMT ambulance trailed them and pulled into the driveway. Volunteer EMTs rushed into the house. All of the colored lights in the dark night cast the scene in an eerie glow.

Minutes earlier the KIA's driver had placed an anonymous 911 call, then sat undetected and waiting. And was now watching as yellow crime-scene tape was strung around the redbrick home. This was not the way it was supposed to have played out. The planned outcome was for a civil discussion, compromise, and, finally, acceptance. What had happened instead was like a bad dream.

Neighbors began to congregate on the sidewalks and street. They stood in knots, talking in low tones. The sheriff and two deputies, probably Haskell's entire sheriff's department, moved in and out of the house.

After what seemed like forever, the EMTs emerged with a gurney. On it lay a shrouded body.

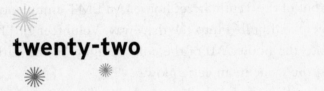

twenty-two

Allison had to share her suspicions with her friends. She pulled Debbie Sue and Edwina closer to her in a corner of the cell. "I think I know why Quint's gone to Haskell."

Debbie Sue and Edwina traded glances, then focused their attention on her. "So, tell us," Debbie Sue said.

For the second time Allison explained her relationship with the woman in the picture and described Quint's reaction when she told him she recognized Monica Hunter.

Debbie Sue crossed her arms over her chest and frowned. "I think you're right. I saw only one picture in the group that I thought resembled the photo the credit-card people faxed. God, what a small world."

"But why the secrecy?" Allison asked. "Why didn't Quint acknowledge to me that it was her?"

Edwina was pawing inside her purse. "Maybe he was afraid you'd call her and warn her."

"And because you two have dated a couple of times," Debbie Sue added, "he'd hate admitting to you he's got it so bad for her. Besides that, if we had found her, we'd have tried to talk him out of going after her and I think he already had his mind made up."

"Really? You think he's that hung up on Monica?" Allison asked.

"Like I've never seen him before," Debbie Sue said. "Listen, I know this man. I'm betting the whole reason he wants to find her is to try to win her back."

"Then why was he trying to date me?" Allison asked.

Edwina had found a stick of gum in her purse and begun to unwrap it. "Hon, you're using logic. You can't do that when you're talking about a man. They function from instinct, based on their egos and physical needs. They're only interested in"—she stuffed the gum in her mouth and counted on her fingers—"food, sleep, and sex. And not necessarily in that order."

"Quint has to have the attention of a woman," Debbie Sue said. "He's always been like that. I've always known the one he can't have is the one he wants the most."

Allison felt a mixture of disappointment and relief. "So Quint doesn't care about me? He's in love with someone else?"

"That's the way I see it," Debbie Sue said. "And I'm convinced, now that I know he's gone to Haskell."

With an untoward feeling of elation, Allison reached for her purse and fished inside it. She came up with a compact and lipstick.

"Why are you getting all dolled up?" Edwina asked. "It's the middle of the night."

Allison grinned. "You said Tag's coming, didn't you?"

Tag looked again at the picture Debbie Sue had sent him over the phone. She had sent it in response to his disbelief of the story she told him. The image was of her and another woman he had never met. She was taller than Debbie Sue, had coal-black hair, lots of makeup, and earrings the size of pancakes. Edwina, perhaps. The two of them were standing against the cell bars looking a little wilted. The back of Allison's head was visible in the frame.

He flipped the phone shut and returned it to his belt. His guess was that Debbie Sue had made the call because Allison was too embarrassed to do it herself. He had detected in her that concern over what people thought of her.

Public indecency and lewdness? He laughed. He couldn't wait to hear the whole story. For years he had heard about Debbie Sue ending up in oddball situations, but Allison? Understandably there were sides to her he didn't know—as well as the sides he would love to know—but this one was, by far, the most thought provoking.

He grabbed his hat and called out to his cook, Rafael, "Amigo, I gotta leave. If I can I'll come back later, but don't count on it. Everything okay here?"

"No problem, boss." The amiable young man grinned. "You got problems with your woman?"

Tag laughed and held up three fingers on his right hand. "Three of them."

"Oh, señor. Usted es absolutamente un hombre!"

Tag laughed and left the restaurant with *you're quite a man* echoing in his ears. While driving to Salt Lick he thought about what he would say to Allison. Different scenarios played out in his head. As he reached the Salt Lick city-limits sign he decided to let fate handle the situation. Right now he had to find the jail.

The chore was easy enough. Right on the main street, he saw a sign with SHERIFF'S OFFICE hand-painted in black. It was a strange sign for an official facility—a wrought-iron tripod supporting a WWII bomb casing suspended on chains. But then, much about Salt Lick struck him as strange. The sign was stuck in the ground beside the front door of a flat-roofed stucco building. In the minuscule parking lot, it looked like five minutes till closing at the only beer store in town. Cars were parked in every spot and at every angle.

Tag parked across the street and walked over to the small office. Inside, men, women, children, and dogs were all talking or barking—some doing both—demanding to be heard. The only men wearing badges had been pushed against the back wall and both looked to be on the verge of tears. *Chaos* was too mild a word for the scene.

Tag thought he understood what was going on. The mob merely wanted to get their loved ones out of jail. He looked around and spotted a straight-back chair in the corner. Dragging it to the center of the room, he stepped up on the seat.

Putting his fingers into his mouth, he gave a loud shrill whistle.

Dogs howled, but the din died immediately and all eyes turned in his direction. "Everybody listen up. You can't all talk at the same time or we'll be here all night. Line up behind me single file. Give the sheriff and his deputy the name of the person you came to pick up. You ladies," he said, pointing to the cell occupants, "when your name is called, step forward and leave with your ride. No talking, no fussing. Am I understood?"

A few mumbled and grumbled as all formed a line behind Tag.

"Sheriff," Tag said, "you want to unlock those cell doors now?"

As names were called women stepped from the cells and joined their benefactors. The three Tag had come for bid good-bye to their cell mates and followed him outside. He led them over to his white Lincoln Navigator.

"How appropriate," Edwina said. "My hero's riding a great white horse."

"Three hundred horses to be exact," Tag said as he opened the door to the rear seat.

Debbie Sue and Edwina pushed ahead of Allison and took seats in the back. Allison had no choice but to climb into the passenger seat beside him, and that suited him just fine.

"Take me and Ed back to the salon," Debbie Sue said. "We're parked there."

"You're okay to drive?"

"Are you kidding? All that tequila and vodka I drank is long gone."

"And you?" Tag said, leveling a look at Edwina. He had no intention of turning two drunk women loose behind the steering wheel.

"Oh, hell, hon, I only had three margaritas four hours ago. I'm sober as a nun. Or none too sober, I forget which."

He followed the directions to the salon. As Debbie Sue and Edwina disembarked he looked at Allison for the first time. "Is your car here, too, Allison?"

"No, my mom dropped me off hours ago. Guess you'll have to take me home. Again."

Tag smiled. "At least I know the way."

The drive was too short to start a conversation. He parked in front of her house. "Want to tell me how you got into that pickle back there?"

"Not really." She gave him a giggle and he wondered if she was still a little tipsy. "But I will. A customer of Debbie Sue's gave a sex-toy party and we got raided."

His brows shot up of their own accord. He was starting to see more unexpected sides of Allison with every hour. "Sex toys?"

"It's a big thing now. They have parties. Like Tupperware."

"Tupperware."

"Yes, you know. People come and buy items and the hostess, in this case Maudeen Wiley, gets free gifts. Maudeen's got to be in her eighties. I can't imagine what she buys at those parties, but—"

Tag couldn't keep from laughing. He had missed out on sex-toy parties.

"It isn't funny," she said indignantly. "A lot of women are sexually frustrated."

"Are you one of them?"

"No . . . Well, maybe."

Before he could say another word, she leaned across and smothered his words with her lips and he had no objection whatsoever to that.

"So what do you think?" she asked in a sultry voice. "Am I?"

"Feels like it to me." This time he kissed her. In no time, their kisses became more intense, their caresses more urgent.

"Tag," she whispered, "let's go inside."

He pulled away, his heart pounding. "But what about your mom and Jill? We could go to my—"

"My mom and Jill are gone until Sunday night. We'll have the whole place to ourselves."

He had often found fate to be smarter than he was. It had smiled on him tonight. He chuckled against her silky neck. "In that case, I'd be a fool to say no."

"Then don't," she said.

"You didn't bring any of those toys home with you, did you?"

"I didn't buy any."

"Good. 'Cause I don't think we're gonna need 'em."

★   ★   ★

Quint sat on the edge of a steel bunk waiting for a lawyer. The only one he knew was a corporate attorney who helped him in his business. Quint had called him, and like the good friend he was, he had arranged for a criminal lawyer.

A criminal lawyer.

Jesus Christ. Not in his wildest imagination had he expected to *ever* need a criminal lawyer.

All of the low points in his life seemed insignificant compared with the one he was experiencing now. He felt naked and vulnerable. Scared.

He had been told he was under arrest for the murder of Monica Hunter, but he wasn't buying it. They had to have the wrong Monica. There had to be more than one Monica Hunter in the world. The one he knew had been very much alive the last time he'd seen her, which was only a few hours ago.

He had also been told he was being held for pickup by the sheriff of Haskell County. After that, he had refused to speak without his attorney present. He wished he had waited a little longer before declaring this because when he clammed up, so did the cop who arrested him. None of it mattered. They had made a mistake. The Monica he knew had to be alive, and when his attorney arrived everything would be cleared up.

He had never been in jail. As depression settled within him, he looked around at his surroundings and thought about his circumstances. He had been on a one-man campaign to restore his good name. At the same time he had wanted to bring back the woman who had disappeared from his life. How was it possible that he found her and lost her in the same day?

And the loss was permanent? . . .

No, no way. Somebody had made a mistake, and when he got out of this damn jail, heads were damn well gonna roll.

The bedroom was dark, but morning light had begun to cast shadows against the walls. Allison stretched and smiled at the shape lying next to her. It had been years since she had awakened with a man and it had never been in her own bed. She hadn't approved of men sleeping over when she and Jill lived in Haskell. Now she was sharing a home with her mother and Jill was older, and allowing it just wouldn't be right.

But no one was home. She didn't have to worry about setting the wrong example or about how having a man in her bed looked. In fact, there couldn't possibly be anything bad about last night. It had been very, very right. She had never known she was capable of such passion, but she knew one thing for sure. Tag Freeman could easily become her drug of choice. And he was right. They didn't need sex toys.

Tag opened his eyes. "Hey, whatcha smiling about?"

She snuggled close to him and his thick arm came around her. "I might ask you the same thing," she said.

"Was I smiling? I must have been thinking about a dream I had last night."

"Oh, yeah?" Allison pressed closer to his big, solid body. She slid her hand down and felt his erection.

"Hmm, don't stop," he said, and gave a soft chuckle. "I

dreamed there was this beautiful—" Tag's cell phone chirped. He ignored it. "As I was saying, there was this beautiful roan mare—"

"Tag Freeman, are you comparing me to a horse?" She placed a kiss on his chest.

"I said it was a beautiful horse that—" The cell phone chirped again. "Shit. I should get that. Apparently somebody needs to reach me pretty bad." He sat up, swung his feet to the floor, and yanked the bleating phone from his belt on the floor.

The sexy moment lost, Allison threw off her side of the covers and sat up. "Coffee," she said, and grabbed a robe from the back of the door. As she made her way to the kitchen and started coffee, she listened to Tag's end of the phone conversation.

"Where is he now? . . . This is all crazy. What did they do with his truck? . . . Look, I'll get there quick as I can . . . Listen, tell him not to worry. It's gonna be all right. His friends are with him."

Allison went back to the bedroom and saw Tag's expression, grim and terrible. "What's wrong?"

"That was a lawyer. He's been retained to represent a friend of mine."

"Oh?"

He leveled a look at her. "It's Quint. He's been arrested for murder."

Allison couldn't hold back a gasp. Her palm flattened against her chest. "Is this a joke? Murder? My Lord. Who's he supposed to have killed?"

"A woman named Monica Hunter."

A roar began inside Allison's skull. Had her ears deceived her? Monica Hunter was dead? And Quint Matthews had been arrested for her murder? It couldn't be true. It made no sense. There had to be a misunderstanding. Quint was rich. He wouldn't kill someone over a few dollars' worth of credit-card charges . . .

Would he?

Allison dropped to the edge of the bed. The daze that had enveloped her lifted as she realized Tag was calling her name. She looked at him.

"Are you all right? You're white as a ghost. You're acting like you know something about this."

"I know Monica Hunter. Knew her, that is. We were sort of friends when we were kids. I know her whole family. Well, actually it was just her grandmother. Monica was wild as a weed. Her poor grandmother was never able to get a firm grip on her. The last time I spoke to the doctor I used to work for in Haskell, he told me he had rented his old house to Monica. He said she hadn't changed her ways at all. This is just so horrible."

Tag came to her side. "I'm so sorry. I wouldn't have blurted it out like that if I'd known."

"Did the lawyer say how—did he mention—"

"No, he didn't say. Is she the woman who stole Quint's identity? The one he hired the Equalizers to find? Oh, uh, you do know about that, don't you?"

"He told me about the identity theft, but I don't believe it.

Monica was spoiled and demanding, but I just can't imagine that she would have done such a thing."

Tag cleared his throat. "Uh, the lawyer says Quint thinks there's been a huge mistake. He wants me to call Debbie Sue and tell her to keep looking for Monica. Do you have her number?"

"Sure." Allison reached into the drawer of her bedside table and pulled out an address book. She called out the Styling Station's number as Tag keyed it into his phone.

While he spoke to Debbie Sue, Allison turned the pages in the address book to the Haskell phone number of Dr. Sinclair, only half listening to Tag. She intended to go to Monica's funeral. It was the least she could do for someone she had been friends with in high school. Besides, there would be few friends present. There would be no family present either. She would call Dr. Sinclair and ask to stay with him and his wife, Dot.

"You'll have to ask her," she heard Tag say. "No need. She's, uh . . . right here." Tag extended the phone in her direction. "Debbie Sue wants to talk to you."

Oh, no! Had Tag told Debbie Sue they were together? Staring into his eyes, she pressed the receiver against her ear. "This is Allison—"

Before she could say another word, Debbie Sue started. "This is the biggest bunch of BS I've ever heard. There is no way Quint Matthews would kill someone. Not for any reason. He can't even step on a bug. He's a bigger threat to himself than to anyone else. Tell me what you know about this Monica."

Though she had heard the gossip about this aggressive side of Debbie Sue and had seen a hint of it in the Salt Lick jail cell, Allison had never seen her on a mission. "I haven't been around her in years," she answered defensively. "Monica was smart and beautiful, but bored and spoiled her entire life."

"If anyone knows small-town cops, I do," Debbie Sue said. "This is their chance to hit the big time. They'll be pissing all over themselves."

"What do you mean?"

"Why, it's Quint Matthews we're talking about. What small-town prosecutor wouldn't want to convict *the* Quint Matthews. Poor ol' Quint's gonna need all the help he can get."

Poor ol' Quint, my foot. "Oh. Well, yes, I suppose he will."

"The Abilene cops won't transfer Quint to Haskell before Monday," Debbie Sue said. "We usually keep the beauty shop open on Mondays, but this is an exception. I'm gonna talk to Ed. We were sort of planning to go up to Haskell as soon as Buddy and Vic get home anyway."

"I should go to Haskell, too," Allison said as the reality of the woman's death continued to grow in her mind and heart.

"Do you want to ride with us?" Debbie Sue said.

"I don't think so. I may want to go sooner than Monday."

"Okay, let us know." Debbie Sue disconnected.

"You're going over there?" Tag asked.

Allison handed the phone back to Tag as she pulled her thoughts together. "I'd like to go tomorrow morning, but I need to get some work done to my car before I can make a road trip."

"Like what?"

"I need four new tires. And shocks and brake shoes. I think I need an oil change and a tune-up . . . Oh, yeah, and there's a leak in the radiator that needs to be fixed."

Tag's face held an expression of incredulity. "Did you overlook gasoline?"

"Oh, yeah, I need gas. I wonder if I can get all that done in a day."

"Gas, I guess. It'll be hard to get those kinds of repairs done on a Saturday. Can't you take your mom's car?"

Allison shook her head. "No, that would leave Mom and Jill without a car. She and I have been sharing her car since I haven't had the money to get mine fixed."

Tag stood up and paced around, pulling at his lower lip with his thumb and forefinger. "I'll just take you. I need to see Quint, too. Poor sucker's got to be feeling pretty low right now. I think he loved that little gal." Tag shook his head. "You know, he's not as tough inside as he is outside."

"Poor sucker? I appreciate your offer, Tag, but I don't want to see Quint. And I'm surprised you're supportive of him. He's been arrested for murder, not driving forty in a school zone."

"He's been *arrested,* Allison, not convicted. None of us have the facts. We're supposed to be his friends. Don't you think he deserves the chance to tell us his side of things?"

"What about *her* side? Who's going to represent that? All I know is that I told him who she was, even *where* she was. He left here and went directly to her. It's twenty-four hours later and she's dead."

"Quint Matthews couldn't murder anybody. He can't even put down a sick animal."

The words were almost an echo of what Debbie Sue had said a few minutes earlier, but Tag and Debbie Sue were prejudiced by their long friendships with Quint. Running her fingers through her hair, Allison walked to the window and stood, looking out but seeing nothing, trying to make sense of all that was going on around her. "They wouldn't arrest him without good reason. He had the motive. He even went so far as to hire detectives to locate Monica."

"You're not being fair," Tag said.

"A young woman has been killed and you're talking to me about what's fair? Quint Matthews told me himself that he was tired of people making a fool of him. I can see where words would have been exchanged, tempers could have flared. Anything's possible under those circumstances."

Tag walked up behind her and placed a hand on her shoulder, "I can understand why you're upset. But don't you understand why I have to go to my friend?"

"Yes," Allison replied icily, "and I need to go to mine. I need to make some phone calls now. You'd better go home."

"Allison—"

"I have a lot to do. Please. Just go."

She stood in the doorway and watched as he drove away. It wasn't that she didn't understand how he felt. She did, but it seemed like a further betrayal of an old acquaintance to feel sympathy or offer defense on Quint's behalf. She had to stay focused on righting a wrong.

twenty-three

Tag Freeman's conversation had left Debbie Sue's heart galloping through her chest. Despite a pounding headache and a mouth that felt like cotton, she wasted no time keying in Edwina's number.

After the fourth burr, a voice came on the line. "If this ain't an emergency, hang up." The line went dead.

Debbie Sue keyed redial. Two burrs later, Edwina's voice said, "What the hell do you want?"

"Ed, wake up. You won't believe this. Monica's dead, Quint's in jail, and Tag slept at Allison's house."

"Well, ee-i-ee-i-oh. Since those three things are in the same sentence, I know they must be related, but for the life of me, I can't see how. I must've had more tequila last night than I thought."

Debbie Sue repeated what she had just heard from Tag about Quint.

"My God, one just never knows," Edwina said. "Are we supposed to do something?"

"We have to help him, Ed. He's in denial. He thinks they've made a mistake. He thinks Monica's still alive."

"Well, is she?"

"No. Maybe. How the hell do I know? But he still wants us to find her."

"I don't know, Debbie Sue. Vic will—"

"Ed, Quint's depending on us. He *needs* us."

"And what about Buddy? He'll be home tonight. What are you gonna tell him?"

"Buddy wouldn't want an innocent man to sit in jail, accused of something he didn't do. Even Quint."

"I meant what are you gonna tell him about last night? If he hasn't heard the gossip already, he's bound to hear it fifteen minutes after he hits the city limits."

Debbie Sue scowled. What Edwina had said was true. Still, being arrested for lewd and indecent conduct seemed like small potatoes compared with murder. "I'll call him on his cell and tell him about the mess with the party. I'll save the news about Quint until tonight."

"Good idea," Edwina said.

"Did you talk to Vic? What did he say about last night?"

"He laughed. He wanted to know if I brought some of that stuff home."

"You mean you didn't?"

"Hell, I meant to get one of those purple G-spot things, but Billy Don showing up distracted me and I forgot."

"We've *got* to be in Haskell bright and early Monday morning, Ed. This news about Quint confirms it."

"You mean go tonight and stay over. I doubt if there's a decent motel in Haskell."

"No. I need to spend all day tomorrow doing something with Buddy. If we leave at five A.M. Monday, we'll get there by nine. That way we don't have to stay over. So we need to move our Monday appointments to today."

Edwina sighed. "Okay, I'll start calling. I don't know how I let you talk me into these things."

As Debbie Sue disconnected one of Buddy's remarks about Quint echoed through the halls of her memory: *Trouble follows him everywhere he goes. I don't want you getting caught in the middle of it.*

But how could she not help a friend?

"Shit, Quint," she mumbled. "You are so damn much trouble."

Allison stood at the phone mounted on the wall at the end of the kitchen counter, watching the clock and waiting for eight o'clock. Dr. Sinclair's office had always opened promptly at eight o'clock on Saturday and closed promptly at noon.

A woman she didn't know answered the phone and soon her old friend came on the line. "Dr. Sinclair here."

"Hi, Doc, this is Allison Barker."

"Why, Allison, what a nice surprise. Is something wrong, dear? You never call this early."

Allison knew his waiting room would be filling, so she got right to her reason for calling. She was near tears at the end and her voice had taken on a tremble. "So, you see, I feel I need to be there. There isn't a decent place to stay in Haskell. Would it be okay if I stayed with you and Dot?"

As he had done so many times in the past, Dr. Sinclair consoled her. "Of course you can stay with us. It'll be a treat to have someone in the extra bedroom again. The kids don't come around much. Live too damn far away and are too busy for us old folks. But Dot and I are going to exact our revenge. I'm selling the practice and we're buying one of those mobile RV things. We're going to go visit them and let them get a firsthand look at how we're spending their inheritance."

Allison knew he meant it. Time hadn't changed him a bit. She chuckled in spite of the circumstances. "Do you know where they took Monica?"

"They're doing an autopsy in Abilene. They'll be bringing her home sometime Monday."

Bringing her home. The words brought a lump to Allison's throat. "I'm not sure when I'll get there. I know you and Dot are busy—"

"Not to worry," Dr. Sinclair said. "If we aren't at home, just go in and make yourself at home. The spare key's where it always was."

"The fake rock in the flower bed?"

"Yep. That old piece of plastic has been sitting there so long it's actually turned to stone now."

Allison chuckled again, thinking how much she missed her former employer's sense of humor.

"I've got to run, dear. The girls out front tell me Mildred Hayes just brought one of her kids in. Looks like his tongue is stuck on an ice tray."

Allison hung up and reached for the phone book. She had to find someone cheap and available to work on her ailing '91 Crown Victoria this morning. Cost be damned, she was on her way to Haskell.

Charlene Elkins's husband was too busy to take on the repair on short notice. Option number two was a mechanic in another town, but even if she could find one on a Saturday, the car was in such bad shape she dared not try to drive it beyond the city limits. And she couldn't afford to have it towed.

Her third option was Mike Jones. He taught in the vocational-education department in the high school and sometimes placed kids who needed to earn extra money in odd jobs around town. In the past, when she'd needed help in Almost the Rage, she had called Mike. She knew the department taught a few of its students about auto repair. A kid from the high-school shop class had to meet two vital requirements: availability and a willingness to work within her paltry budget.

Later in the morning, a scruffy senior named Jesse Martin showed up at the dress shop to pick up her car keys. She squared her shoulders and looked him in the eye. "Listen to me, Jesse. It's very important that I leave town early tomorrow morning in this car. You're sure you can get it running and finish with it by tonight?"

"Heck, yeah, ma'am. I can make concrete run. And I've got friends who'll help me." He flashed a cocky grin. "I work on my dad's tractor and my mom's riding lawn mower all the time. I've got the highest grades in shop class."

"Shocks and tires? You can do that, too?"

"No problemo. My cousin's girlfriend's dad's got a salvage yard in Odessa. I can get my cousin to bring over everything you need really cheap. Trust me, you'll have a sweet ride when I'm done."

An instant of doubt and fear squiggled through Allison. Was a sweet ride necessary? All she wanted from the wreck was to get from Salt Lick to Haskell and back with no problems.

Deal with it, she told herself. She mustered a smile, made an agreement with the teenager, and handed him her car keys.

"This is what happens when your choices are few to none," she mumbled as she trekked back into the dress shop. "You just have to deal with it."

As promised, Jesse returned the auto to her home by evening and Allison realized she should have asked him his definition of a "sweet ride." Sitting in her driveway was the Crown Victoria.

Possibly.

It was the same color as her car.

Almost.

The back end was still white, but red and yellow flames blazed across the front fenders from the headlights to the doors. Besides that, it had been raised several inches. New oversize rims had been added to the wheels as well as over-size tires that looked like huge black bagels. Tires on steroids was her immediate thought. The license plates and the trunk were the only parts of the car that looked familiar.

"Oh. My. God."

"Sweet, ain't it?" Jesse said. "You oughta let me paint it purple." Purple would look cool with flames. He gestured dramatically to describe what he would like to do. "I'd do it cheap," he added.

"Uh, no thanks," she told him. "You've done more than enough."

After the teenager left, she stood on the porch studying the car, envisioning driving it back to her old hometown, the place she had imagined returning to as a success. Deal with it? She would need some fortitude to deal with this one.

Undaunted, before daylight Sunday morning, she was on I-20, driving east, the reason for the trip gluing her hands to the steering wheel. As the sun rose and brightened the day she kept her eyes straight ahead, refusing to acknowledge the stares of other travelers on the highway.

She had spoken to Debbie Sue and Edwina, explaining that she would be driving to Haskell before them and why. She had called her mother and reported the circumstances. Jill was ecstatic when she described the changes to the car.

At the last minute she decided to not call Tag. They hadn't parted on the friendliest of terms. With the loyalty he felt for Quint, staying away from him had to be the right thing to do. She wasn't emotionally prepared to discuss Quint further just yet. With so little to go on, the best thing was not to give in to assumptions and emotions.

Reaching Abilene, Allison began preparing herself for the task ahead of her. Haskell was less than an hour away. She concentrated on the last time she had seen Monica alive and was occupied with that thought when the dashboard displays lit up like a slot machine. Only lights racing around the steering were missing, but she was certain they would have been there if Jesse Martin had had more time.

She managed to steer to the side of the road. She had no sooner brought the Ford to a stop than it shuddered, let out one pitiful lurch, and coughed and died. Allison did what any sane single woman alone on the highway in a broken-down car would do. She cursed, hit the steering wheel with the heel of her palm, and kept turning the key in the ignition until the battery was completely dead. Then she broke into tears.

This was probably the very kind of situation her mother had warned her about when she'd chastised her for not having a cell phone. She had no one to call anyway. Still, just having a link to another human being right now would be comforting.

Early-morning highway traffic was light and what few cars there were didn't even slow down. Well, this was West Texas, where chivalry was still alive. All she had to do was make it clear she needed help. On second thought, the notion gave her pause. While gallantry might still be a part of the area's tradition, so, unfortunately, were abduction, rape, and murder.

Gathering her will, she left the comfort of her sweet ride, went to the front of the car, and raised the hood, the universal sign of distress. Then she got back inside and waited. Soon her early-morning departure caught up with her and she nodded off.

She awoke with a start and the sound of someone tapping on the driver's window. "Oh, thank goodness," she said, cranking the window down. "I'm having some—"

She halted midsentence, the words frozen in her throat as she looked into the face of Tag Freeman.

He smiled. "Trouble? You having some trouble?"

A more beautiful face she had never seen. "Uh, yes. I had my car worked on yesterday and—"

"This is *your* car?" His gaze roamed over the Crown Victoria from bumper to bumper.

She squared her shoulders, refusing to be intimidated by what must be his opinion of the car's appearance. "Yes. Yes, it is. A boy from the high school worked on it. He threw in the paint job for free."

"That's lucky. I was thinking you should ask for a refund. Nice tires. You oughta be able to just float on down the road." He made a forward-motion gesture with his hand.

Allison's lips twisted into a one-sided scowl. "Well, not everyone can afford a Lincoln Navigator."

"You're right," he said. "I shouldn't have popped off. Uh, why don't you try turning the engine over and I'll take a look." He walked to the front of the car and stood waiting.

Allison turned the key. The only sound the thing produced was a sickening click. He walked back to his Navigator and moved it alongside her car. Then he dug in the back and came up with jumper cables. "Let's give this a try," he said, and connected the cables to her battery.

Suddenly a single flash of real flame, accompanied by an ear-piercing roar, shot the Ford's hood ten feet into the air. A huge round disk sailed through the air behind the hood. Both objects landed with a crunch several feet away in the neatly plowed rows of a ripe cotton field.

Wide-eyed and shaking, Allison scrambled across the bench seat and out the door on the passenger side. She darted to the front of the car and clamped both hands against her jaws. "Oh, my God. What happened?"

Tag had already disconnected the jumper cables. She could see several wires twisted and singed.

"Blowback," he said. "A spark from the battery touched off the gas fumes."

She looked up at him. "Is it ruined?"

He looked back, biting his lip.

Allison broke into tears.

He looped an arm around her shoulders. "I'm sorry, sweetheart."

"That's my car," she wailed. "I'm going to be riding with my mom till I'm fifty. I should have already been in Haskell, but I couldn't leave Salt Lick till I had the car worked on."

"You can ride with me. I'm on my way there now. They've transferred Quint—"

"Quint." She gave him a look. "I'm not worried about Quint."

Her mind raced. What choice did she have? She *had* to

ride with Tag. She huffed out a breath. "I'll accept your offer for a ride, but I don't want to hear anything except facts about the murder, if you know any. Facts. Not opinions, not a speech about your undying loyalty to your friend. Just the truth about what happened."

She marched around the car and retrieved her purse from the passenger seat and her one piece of luggage from the backseat. Without another word she walked to Tag's Navigator and climbed in on the passenger side.

The driver of the tan KIA sat up the street from the funeral home, using an unfolded road map as a ruse. The real focus was the funeral home. Numerous phone calls had yielded the information that the body hadn't yet been delivered from Abilene.

The driver was about to give up and return to the motel when a shiny black hearse rounded the corner, pulled into the private driveway, and disappeared behind the building.

A tear slid down the driver's cheek.

Monica Hunter had come home for the last time.

twenty-four

swear to God, when I left she was alive. In fact, she was laughing."

Tag looked at his friend through the security window of thick glass in the visitors' area of the Haskell County Jail.

"That's the last thing I heard when I went out the door," Quint added. "Her laughing." His voice trailed off.

The room surrounding them was small and dismal. Kind of like Quint's chances at this point. "What about an attorney?" Tag asked. "Who are you using?"

"The only lawyer I know doesn't practice criminal law, so he called a buddy of his in Abilene. He came to see me when I was back there. He seems competent. He'll be here tomorrow when I go before the judge."

"Did he say what kind of evidence they've got?"

"All they've told me is Monica called a friend at eight-thirty and talked fifteen minutes. I got there shortly after that and stayed about thirty, forty-five minutes, I'm not sure. The coroner put her death between ten and midnight. I was there in that time frame. But, honest to God, Tag, I didn't do it."

"Oh, I know that. I never thought for a minute that you did. How did she—how was she—" Tag struggled with the question. Quint was already in obvious anguish. He hated adding to it.

"Electrocuted." Quint hung his head. He wiped an eye with his hand.

"Electrocuted!" Tag practically jumped from his chair. "How can they accuse you of murder in an electrocution? That happens often enough and I'll bet you not one is a murder."

"Apparently there was. Right here in Haskell. In the late seventies. A pregnant woman was sitting in the bathtub. Her husband dropped in a radio to keep her company. A *plugged-in* radio.

"The kid who did it walked, and some twenty years later a Texas Ranger working cold cases reopened the file and found enough overlooked evidence to not only prosecute the case, but fry the bastard's ass. It made the news, big-time. That DA's still here and has he ever got a hard-on to correct that oversight."

"I still don't see—"

"When I got there Monica was sitting in a hot tub out back on the deck. She was a little tipsy. She'd had several glasses of wine. I offered to join her in the hot tub, but she said no. Near the tub was this little cabinet with a counter made out of brick. She had one of those grilling machines plugged in. When she was found, the thing was in the tub with her."

"It couldn't have fallen in by mistake?" Tag asked.

"Not according to the sheriff. They said the only way it could be in there was to have been thrown or dropped."

"They're guessing," Tag said.

"That's what my lawyer said, but here I am all the same."

Tag remained quiet for several minutes, his mind trying to visualize the crime, but since he had never been in Monica's home, he couldn't see it.

Quint broke the silence. "Did Debbie Sue say when she was coming?"

"She and Edwina will be here tomorrow. They're taking on the investigation full throttle."

Quint huffed. "That woman's got a way about her. Haskell may never be the same."

"Her and her friend both are a pair to draw to, aren't they?" Tag looked down, then up again. "Allison's here, too."

"Who?" Quint asked.

"Allison Barker. She knew Monica, knew her family."

"Hell, I forgot about that."

Silence fell again.

"I sure appreciate your coming, Tag," Quint said at last, looking away. "Means a lot to me."

"Don't mention it. You'd do the same for me. I just wish there was more I could do."

"You going back to Midland today?"

"Uh, um, no, thought I'd stick around a few days. I haven't been out of the restaurant more than eight hours in a day since it opened. I can take some time off."

"There's no need to stay on my account."

"I came upon Allison having car trouble and gave her a ride into Haskell. I hate to leave her without—"

"I'm thinking you just plain ol' hate to leave her. Am I right?"

"Something like that," Tag said, looking at his friend. "I never planned—"

"Forget it. Allison and I never really had anything going on. Besides, I got bigger problems than that to worry about."

"Thanks. Uh, guess I'll see you tomorrow in court, eh?"

"You coming?"

Tag smiled, hoping to reassure him. "Wouldn't miss it."

"Well, you won't be able to miss me." Quint raised his arms, showing his jail garb. "I'll be the one in the black-and-white stripes."

Tag made a phony laugh at his friend's effort at humor.

"Listen," Quint said, "I'll be posting bail, so can you pick me up after the hearing? I don't know where my truck is."

"You bet. One of the reasons I'm here is to help you out." He started to leave his chair, but thought of something. "I forgot to ask. You were arrested the next morning, right? Who found the girl?"

"That's one of the strange parts. A 911 call was made that night from a public phone reporting a woman was dead."

"Man, that's important news. They tape those calls. Can't they tell from the recording that it wasn't you?"

"That's part of the problem. This is rural Texas, remember? They probably don't have the best equipment. Not only can they not determine the caller wasn't me, they're not even sure if it was a man or a woman."

Sunday evening found Allison at Haskell's only funeral home and mortuary. Dunnam's Funeral Home & Landscaping Service had set up a registry book and now housed the forest of flowers that had been pouring in all day. She had been here since Tag dropped her off around midafternoon. It would be a private service.

Allison's return held a note of nostalgia. Haskell was half the size it had once been. As the government had paid more and more of Haskell's farmers to quit farming, the old-time families moved to urban areas. In some cases, the government checks amounted to more than the farmers had ever made farming. Ranchers, finding it harder and harder to meet their expenses, had quit ranching and sold their land to bird hunters.

In the struggle for survival in a declining economy, the Dunnams had added a landscaping service to the mortuary business. It seemed like a natural follow-on, since they already had all of the equipment. The result was that the small town of Haskell had an incredibly beautiful cemetery shaded by trees not typically seen in West Texas.

Growing up, Allison had been inside the funeral home

when it was a crumbling Victorian mansion. In those days it had been the residence of a childhood friend, a descendant of one of Haskell's founding families. That family, too, had sold out and left the area.

The Dunnams hadn't found it necessary to spend much effort or money changing the mansion into a funeral parlor. The exterior already resembled a haunted house.

Inside, what was once the dining room was now the viewing room. The living room was furnished with chairs and couches of every form and fashion for the comfort of the bereaved. Also for the bereaved, the kitchen had been kept functional. Allison wondered how her former friends' old bedroom was being used, but decided not to think about it. Nor did she want to think about the current use of the other rooms in the house.

By nine o'clock, a horde of mourners had made their way in and out, paying their respects. Many she knew from the time she had lived here, many she had never seen.

With the dwindling crowd, she was finally able to sit alone with her thoughts. She couldn't keep them from drifting to Tag and the passionate night they had spent together. What was the matter with her? Here she was, engaged in a vigil for an old friend and her mind was lusting after a man.

She thought about the ride into Haskell after he had rescued her from the side of the highway. Unexpectedly he had reached across the space between them and taken her hand in his. "I'll take care of your car, Allison. Don't worry. I've got a friend outside of Abilene who's a mechanic, a *real* mechanic. I'll call him and have him tow it back to his shop.

He'll have it good as new by the time you're ready to go back to Salt Lick."

Allison opened her mouth to tell him she couldn't afford to have anything else done to her car, but as if he had read her thoughts, he said, "Don't worry about the cost. He owes me more money than he can repay in a lifetime. I'll just tell him to put the cost against that. I won't be out a dime. I was never going to see that debt paid anyway."

"I don't know how to thank you, Tag."

"You don't have to," he had said. "Let's just say I'm doing it for Jill."

The memory made Allison bite her lip. This trip to Haskell had been unplanned. She'd had neither time nor opportunity to put together her return to her hometown in a manner that reflected huge success. But here she was.

She had come back in the company of a handsome, successful man, something every woman dreamed of. And she was falling in love for the first time in her life.

Maybe she had returned in grand fashion after all.

"I thought we discussed dressing serious," Debbie Sue said to Edwina when she stopped to pick her up well before daylight Monday morning.

"I don't even know what that means," Edwina replied. "So, what? You don't want me going with you?"

Debbie Sue sighed. She was decked out in her knife-pleat Lady Wrangler dress khakis, starched white shirt, and a navy-blue blazer. She had pulled her long hair back and secured it at her neck with a red silk scarf. In her opinion, she looked every bit the professional investigator. "I just meant that we want to look like serious professionals."

"Hell, I'm wearing black. How much more serious can you get?"

Indeed. Edwina had on black capri pants and a black sweatshirt blaring the comment in pink capital letters I FOUGHT THE LAW AND THE LAW WON. As usual, her footwear of choice was matching black platform shoes.

"You're fine," Debbie Sue said, unable to erase the ring of resignation in her voice. "But could you just wear some different earrings?"

The two-inch miniature pistols hanging from Edwina's earlobes seemed inappropriate somehow.

"Abso-fuckin'-lutely. Just give me a minute." Edwina stalked into her mobile home and came back wearing two-inch silver hoops with a dozen dangling pink beads. "How're these?"

Debbie Sue sighed again. At least they were an improvement. "Great."

Once they were under way, the inevitable question came from Edwina's mouth. "How'd Buddy take it when he found out what we're up to?"

"He's trying to be understanding, but he doesn't like the idea of his wife getting involved in a murder investigation. You remember how he was about Pearl Ann."

What she didn't say was that as she had dressed this morning, Buddy had looked at her with a skeptical eye and reminded her he had been right about Quint: wherever the

ex-rodeoer went, trouble followed. But at least he hadn't ordered her to stay home. When she and Edwina solved the
mystery of who killed Monica Hunter, thereby saving Quint,
Buddy would have to take them seriously as detectives.

"Did you tell Vic? What did he say?"

"He was more direct. He said, 'You stumble across any
useful information, you pat yourself on the back, take it
straight to the police, then get yourself back home.' "

Debbie Sue gave a sarcastic huff. "Men."

They didn't talk until she pulled onto the interstate. The
pride swelling in Debbie Sue's chest could no longer be
restrained. "How 'bout this, Ed? The Domestic Equalizers
are on another murder investigation. Maybe we should
give up shadowing cheating spouses. Maybe murder is our
calling."

"Hmmph, let's just hope we don't end up being *its* calling.
We don't know what we're getting into. So what's the
plan?"

"Well, first thing, we'll have to locate the sheriff's office
and talk to him directly. He probably knows Buddy, so I'll
be sure to tell him I'm Buddy's wife. Networking, you
know. Then he'll want to see some identification and cre-
dentials so he'll know we're on the up-and-up. We should
tell him we've been retained by Mr. Matthews. Remember
that word, *retained*."

"Good idea," Edwina said. "If we say we're Quint's
friends, he's liable to think we're there to snoop or break
him out of jail. I'd hate for us to get tossed out on our
keisters."

"So then, we just start talking to people. Follow leads. You've been through the courses. You know the drill."

Her intention was to remind Edwina that they knew more than she was acknowledging. They had taken classes and passed tests to obtain investigators' licenses.

"Look, hon," Edwina said, "I know this is important to you. But snooping around and finding out if somebody's tearing off a little on the side is a lot different from tracking down a murderer. You don't want to forget that Alex Martinez might have put a bullet in you if Buddy hadn't arrived in the nick of time."

And Debbie Sue hadn't forgotten. Sometimes in the middle of the night she woke up thinking of the killer of her former friend and customer Pearl Ann Carruthers and how he had forced her into the West Texas desert at gunpoint. When she had those bad dreams, Buddy would hold her and pet her all night, telling her over and over she should leave chasing down bad guys to him.

But how could she? Solving the mystery of Pearl Ann's murder had launched Domestic Equalizers. "This is just another mystery. No different from what we did when we solved Pearl Ann's murder."

"Hmm-hmm. I'm thinking. Now, when are we gonna stop and get something to eat?"

A few hours, a lot of food, and several Dr Pepper and bathroom stops later, Debbie Sue and her reluctant partner entered Haskell. Since the sheriff's office was in the basement of the courthouse on the town square, they found it easily. Debbie Sue was glad to see the sheriff's car parked in its designated spot. She was anxious to get started and didn't want to waste valuable time chasing down the chief law enforcement officer of Haskell County.

When she and Edwina opened the door leading to the office area, they encountered two men, both wearing badges. The larger, round-bellied man she took to be the sheriff. He appeared to be reading the riot act to a much smaller man who stood with his head bowed. The hefty man glanced in their direction and held up one finger, indicating he would be with them momentarily.

"Merle, do you understand what you did was wrong?" he asked the smaller man, talking softly and slowly. Debbie Sue thought of the days when Buddy had been Salt Lick's sheriff and Billy Don Roberts had been his deputy.

"Yes, Sheriff Mike, I understand. But Jimmy said he had to get home and feed the cows. I didn't want them animals starving to death."

"Jimmy tricked you, Merle. You know he hasn't hit a lick of work in years. Poor ol' Justine does all the work around that place. No matter what the reason, don't ever unlock the cell door and let a prisoner out again."

"Even if he has to feed cows?"

"Even if he has to feed cows. Or kids or anything. You promise me, okay? 'Cause if you don't promise and if you do it again, I'll have to take back your badge and your radio."

"I promise, Sheriff Mike. Don't take away my badge. I do a good job for you, Sheriff Mike. Don't I?"

"Yes, you do, Merle. Now, run on. I'll talk to you later."

On his way out, the smaller man stopped, gave Debbie Sue

and Edwina a furtive look, and tipped his Lone Ranger straw cowboy hat, almost catching the sissy string on his chin.

The sheriff came over. "Sorry about that. I don't usually meet with people in the front office, but I'm acting as my own receptionist. The real one's running late today. Merle's a good man, but when I start explaining something to him, if I don't finish, he'll forget." He offered Debbie Sue his right hand. "I'm Sheriff Mike Jackson."

Debbie shook his hand enthusiastically. "How do you do, Sheriff Jackson. My name's Debbie Sue Overstreet. You may know my husband, James Russell Overstreet Jr.? He's a DPS trooper, but he used to be—"

"I know Buddy. He's a fine officer. I see him from time to time in my county." He offered a hand to Edwina. "Miss?"

"It's Mrs.," Edwina said, shaking his hand. "Edwina Perkins-Martin. My husband's a retired navy SEAL. He liberated Kuwait."

"I see," the sheriff said, continuing to look at her.

"Did I hear right?" Debbie Sue asked. "Your deputy let a prisoner go free? Isn't that dangerous?"

Sheriff Jackson released Edwina's hand and turned back to Debbie Sue. "Trust me, Merle will never do it again. His main objective in life is to do a good job here. Now that he's been told that what he did was wrong, he'll never do it again. Luckily, Jimmy was only in jail for peeing in public. Again."

"Merle seems real nice," Debbie Sue said, for lack of anything else to add.

"You'll never find better. He's not a fully appointed deputy. He's my assistant and my wife's cousin. He's a little slow.

But if there's anything unusual going on in town, he's the first to let me know. I wouldn't trade him. Now, how can I help you ladies?"

Debbie Sue took the floor, explaining their presence. She finished by saying they had been retained by Quint and asking to see him.

"Lady detectives. Sure, I heard about y'all. I was just going upstairs for Matthews's bond hearing. You're welcome to come if you want."

They tramped up aged steel-stepped stairs with baroque wrought-iron railings and walked along the wide, high-ceilinged hallway of the old courthouse, their voices echoing and their steps causing the well-seasoned oak floor to creak.

"I won't stop you from doing what you think is your job here," the sheriff said, "but I gotta tell ya, this case against Matthews is airtight. It's a heartless thing he did to that poor girl."

For the next few minutes the sheriff filled them in on the details. "So you see," he said in conclusion, "he was there during the time frame when the death occurred. He had the opportunity and I believe he had the motive."

"You didn't mention witnesses. Did someone place him at the crime scene?"

"Yes, ma'am. Old Harry Perkins was walking his dog around nine-thirty. As Matthews was leaving the decedent's home the two of them had a conversation."

"Is Mr. Perkins an upstanding citizen?" Debbie Sue asked. "How did he know he was talking to Quint?"

"Oh, heck, don't ask me to vouch for upstandingness." The sheriff chuckled, causing his round belly to jiggle. "When you've done this job as long as I have, you learn that even the best of folks have a few dark little secrets. Ma'am, there's no doubt Matthews was at the scene."

"And you know that because . . . ?" Debbie Sue said, pushing the issue.

"He gave Harry an autograph. Got it right here in an envelope."

The sheriff picked up a manila envelope from the receptionist's desk. He reached inside and pulled out a sealed plastic bag containing a piece of paper embossed with *From the Desk of Quint Matthews, World Champion Cowboy III.* It took Debbie Sue a few seconds to make out the scrawling signature *Quint Matthews.*

For the first time in a while, Edwina opened her mouth. "Great day in the morning. That boy's ass is toast."

Debbie Sue glared at her.

Sheriff Jackson arched his brow and nodded. "Could be."

In the courtroom Quint gave a loud "not guilty" when asked how he pleaded. The judge set bail at $3 million. Quint spoke to his attorney and, within the hour, walked out of the jail a temporarily free man.

Tag Freeman was waiting out front in his Navigator. No one paid them any heed, which was a blessing, Debbie Sue thought. If the townspeople knew Quint was the accused murderer of one of their own, things could play out differently. Before they could drive away, Debbie Sue arranged to meet them for coffee at Esther's Café.

They spent the next hour in a sober discussion of events. The only thing close to an alibi that Quint had was the man walking his dog. When Debbie Sue had first learned Quint had left an autograph behind, she had been dismayed, but thinking on it more, she was glad. What kind of idiot would commit murder, then stop and sign an autograph on his way out of the victim's house?

She brought up the point. Quint dashed her euphoric moment by saying his attorney had told him that the prosecuting attorney would make an issue of that also—just before he sold the jury on the notion that that was exactly what the perpetrator had counted on.

Throughout the conversation, Quint refrained from tossing out the usual sexual innuendos. He had no glib quips to offer. He just wasn't himself. Debbie Sue couldn't help but feel sadness.

twenty-five

Allison awoke to the enticing aroma of coffee and the muffled sounds of Dr. Sinclair and his wife, Dot, talking in the kitchen. Good grief, what time was it? The funeral-home director had driven her back to the doctor's house at nine-fifteen. She must have fallen into a deep sleep. She put on her robe and slippers and entered the kitchen.

"Allison. I hope we didn't wake you," Dr. Sinclair said. "We were trying to be quiet." He came to her and gave her a hug.

"Allison, sweetheart, how are you?" Mrs. Sinclair asked. "Did you sleep all right? Was it too cold? There are extra blankets in the linen closet at the end of the hall." Dot Sinclair's instincts for Southern hospitality were impeccable.

"I slept fine. Don't worry about me." Allison scanned the kitchen for sign of a clock.

"It's ten-thirty," Dr. Sinclair said, interpreting her action.

"Ten-thirty! Good heavens, I never sleep that late."

"There's coffee," Mrs. Sinclair said. "Help yourself. You know where the cups are."

"We didn't see your car out front," Dr. Sinclair said.

As Allison poured a cup of coffee she related the catastrophe with her car and the fact that a friend had given her a ride into town.

"Oh, bless your heart," Mrs. Sinclair said. "Bob, give her some money."

"Heavens, no," Allison said. "It isn't your fault I hired a mechanic who should stick to repairing tractors and lawn mowers. I'm just grateful to have a place to stay."

"You can drive my car while you're here." The doctor pulled a ring of keys from his pocket and began to remove two. "Dot and I'll share."

Allison did need transportation and renting a car was beyond her means. "Well, if you're sure it isn't too much trouble." She took the keys.

"If y'all will excuse me," Mrs. Sinclair said, "I'm going to take a shower." Stopping by Allison's chair, she placed a weathered hand on her forearm. "The bereavement dinner is at six at the church. You're planning on being there?"

"Oh, yes." She took a seat opposite Dr. Sinclair at the table. "I don't know how to tell you—"

"Excuse me just a minute, Allison." Dr. Sinclair cocked his ear as if he were listening for noises from the bedroom. "I'll be right back," he said, and left the kitchen. He returned carrying a computer disc in a clear plastic case.

"Sorry, Allison," he said. "I wanted to make sure Dot was

in the shower." He offered the disc. "I want you to take this to Mike Jackson as quickly as you can. This morning. Don't say anything to anyone about it. Dot doesn't even know it exists."

Allison took the disc. She had never seen him so intent and serious about anything.

"Of course, but what—"

"A little over a year ago someone broke into the house we're renting, er, or *were* renting to Monica. Mike said it was apparent the would-be thieves were looking for drugs. Everyone thinks doctors carry a pharmacy around with them."

"Yes, I remember when that happened, but—"

Dr. Sinclair raised his palm. "Let me finish. My insurance agent advised me for my own safety and protection against litigation to install a video security system. You know, proof that someone actually broke in to steal the drugs instead of me selling them."

He shook his white head. "What a world we live in. Anyway, I bought a system and had it installed without telling Dot. I knew it would unnerve her. She thought the tree-mounted cameras were motion-detection lights. They take shots at quarterly intervals, front north and south, then rear north and south. Each disc stores a month of activity. I changed discs before Dot and I left on Thursday. It's possible that on this disc is Monica's . . . is the incident."

Allison felt a flutter in her heart at the realization of what she had in her hands. "Oh, my gosh. Then it's possible—"

She held her breath for a moment, then laid the plastic

case on the table and folded her hands in her lap, saying a silent prayer that he wouldn't ask her to view the tapes.

"I want Mike Jackson to view it," Dr. Sinclair said. "Would you please take it to him? I can't—"

"I'll get dressed and do it right now."

The doctor opened his briefcase and removed a catalog-size mailing envelope. He picked up the disc, dropped it inside the envelope, and handed it to her. "Thanks," he said. "Oh, and let me get your cell number."

She had never longed for a cell phone, but on this trip, every time she turned around, she needed one. She ducked her chin. "Gosh, I don't have one."

"Then take mine. I'll use Dot's." The doctor removed a cell phone from his briefcase and handed it to her. He also handed her a business card. "The number's on this card."

"Thank you, Dr. Sinclair."

Allison carried the cell phone and the precious parcel into the bedroom, set it on the dresser, and stepped away, staring at it. She suddenly wished that Tag were here. She felt a desperate need for a stronger hand than hers to carry out this request.

She dressed in a denim dress she had brought from Almost the Rage and was gone from the house before Mrs. Sinclair came out of the bathroom.

It would be good to see Mike Jackson again, she thought as she drove to the sheriff's office. They had always been friends and she hadn't seen him since she left Haskell more than two years ago.

The first thing she noticed when she pulled up to the

courthouse parking lot was the empty parking place reserved for the sheriff's car. Betting to herself that he just might still be there, she went in and was met by Lantana Tanner.

Allison made a silent groan. The three-hundred-pound receptionist hadn't changed. Lantana had had that job for more years than Allison had been alive. The woman knew everything that went on in the county, and what she didn't know she made up. Allison would have to be very careful what she said to this human gossip disperser.

Lantana let out a shriek as if one of her family members she hadn't seen since birth had arrived. "My Lord, would you just look who's here? Allison Barker. You back for the Hunter girl's funeral tomorrow? Wasn't that just the most horrible thing? You've put on a little weight, sugar, but you're still just as pretty as a new baby calf. I've never thought weight was such a terrible thing for some women. You're one of the lucky ones that can carry it well. Big-boned women are so fortunate.

"How's your mama and that poor little girl of yours? Did you ever figure out who her daddy is? Did he ever come back and offer to help you with her? It was so brave of you to stay here and have that child the way you did, what with everybody talking about you and all. I couldn't have done it myself. But then, I've always placed too much emphasis on being proud.

"I love that little dress you've got on, sugar. I swear, some people are just able to wear a feedsack and look just fine. What can I do you for?" She smiled like the Cheshire cat.

Allison had forgotten about Lantana's machine-gun delivery of insults. How she could say that much without taking a breath was baffling. Allison wasn't quick enough to put her in her place, but then that was impossible because Lantana felt her "place" was wherever she stood.

Choosing to ignore all the questions, Allison looked over Lantana's head and around the room. "Is Mike in?"

"No, sugar, he just left. Had to go up to Wichita Falls. He'll be back about six. Is there something I can do for you?"

Allison was thinking in triple time. What should she do? She wanted to be at the church by six o'clock. Yet she didn't want to appear too evasive to Lantana. The gossipmonger would land on that like a horse on hay.

"It's really nothing," she said, going for aloof. "I found this disc in some of my stuff that I never got around to unpacking and realized it belongs to Mike. It's just some of the high-school football games from back in '92. I had them put on a DVD disc. I figured he might like to have it back."

"Too bad we don't have a DVD player here. We could watch it. I'd almost forgotten he played football. He was such a good-looking boy. Now he's big as a buffalo and nearly as hairy. But then I guess he was already fat when you left Haskell, wasn't he?"

Allison leveled a glare at Lantana. "I'll just put it on his desk."

"I'll be happy to do that—"

"No problem, Lantana. I'll do it. I might not get to see him before I leave town and I want to write a note to him."

Stepping around the woman, Allison walked into the sheriff's private office, wondering where she had found the nerve to defy Lantana Tanner. She grabbed a piece of paper from a little square leather box of blank notepaper and picked up the pen lying on the desk blotter. She wrote a note explaining what the disc was and its potential, then folded it, placed it in a legal-size envelope, sealed it, and wrote MIKE JACKSON across the front in bold letters, underlined for emphasis. She slid the smaller envelope inside the larger one Dr. Sinclair had given her, licked the flap, and sealed it. She placed the large envelope squarely in the middle of the desk blotter and walked back to the reception area. "I'll call Mike this evening and ask if he got the disc and the *sealed* note I left."

"Well, I'm sure he'll be glad to hear from you. He doesn't get a lot of calls from women. You'd think he would, being divorced for all the years he has been."

Allison remembered when Mike Jackson and his wife divorced. Her leaving him for a Coca-Cola truck driver from Abilene had been one of Haskell's scandals. "Yes, well—"

"And him having such a good job and all, too," Lantana went on. She shook her head and sighed. "He's probably got money in the bank, too. Did I say he's fat as a hog?"

"Yes. Yes, you did. I'll be sure to mention that to him, also."

Allison left. She would call Mike before she left for the church, but she wasn't worried that the tape and note wouldn't find their way into his hands. Lantana Tanner might act like a fool, but she wasn't one.

★ ★ ★

Peeking between the venetian blind's aluminum slats, Lantana watched Allison get in her car and drive away. When her car was out of sight, she went to the sheriff's desk and examined the manila envelope.

Darn, it was sealed. But it was still moist in places. She slid a letter opener along the edge of the envelope's flap. Inside was a DVD and another envelope too tightly sealed to tamper with.

She removed the disc and looked at it. It looked homemade all right. Hmm. She would love to watch it, but a movie of some old football games and some high-school memories wasn't worth her job. The only other job in town that was frequently available was at the Dairy Queen. At her age she wasn't about to start flipping burgers.

The sheriff had already had a stern talk with her about prying and gossiping about what went on in his office. She was on her last leg with him. She decided to leave the disc alone, but good grief, the manila envelope had been opened and closed so many times the adhesive was gone and the flap was bent and wrinkled.

She laid the tape and envelope containing the note in the middle of the desk blotter and crumpled the larger envelope into a ball. She would just pick up another manila envelope on her lunch hour. Thank goodness she had time.

Merle was hungry and tired from patrolling the area all morning. His mom had put a sandwich in his backpack and some chips. He sure would like a Dr Pepper. There were cold drinks in the icebox in Sheriff Mike's office and he had said they were for everybody.

Merle had waited until he knew Miss Lantana would be gone to lunch. He didn't like her. She teased him and asked him questions that made him nervous. She also laughed a lot and sometimes he thought she might be laughing at him. He tried his best to stay away from her.

He stuck out his left arm to indicate a left turn. He was a good driver and always obeyed the highway safety rules. It didn't matter that he didn't drive a car. It was still important to let others know your intentions.

He parked his pride and joy near the sheriff's-office entrance, then took a chain out of the basket and threaded it through the spokes. Sheriff Mike had told him if he did that no one could take it again.

Some mean person had stolen his bike before and left it on the train tracks to be run over. Sheriff Mike had bought him a brand-new one. He had even gone to the auto department in Wal-Mart and bought paint the same color as the county vehicles, and all by himself he had changed the bike to look like an official deputy's car. Merle had completed the project by duct-taping a CB antenna to the rear fender. He had never been so proud in all his life. He knew he wasn't a deputy. He wasn't smart enough for that job, but he was the sheriff's helper and he took great pride in that fact.

He took his cold drink and sandwich to a chair close to Sheriff Mike's big desk. He would never sit in the big chair with rollers on the legs. Only Sheriff Mike could sit in that chair.

Before he had taken a bite of his sandwich, he saw a DVD and an envelope. Uh-oh, he was in trouble. Once before he had brought his portable TV with a DVD player to the sheriff's office at night to watch some movies. He had only done it so he would be close at hand in case he was needed. When he told Sheriff Mike what he had done the sheriff told him he didn't want him coming into the office at night again. If someone saw the lights they might stop and ask for Merle's help and that would make it look like the sheriff wasn't doing his job.

Merle would never make Sheriff Mike look bad and he had never come in at night again, but apparently Sheriff Mike had left a movie behind and Miss Lantana was going to get him in trouble. She had written a note. He didn't read well, but he could make out the sheriff's name on the front and it was even underlined.

Merle broke out in a cold sweat. He had to do the right thing. He would never let Sheriff Mike down. Not ever. He placed the DVD and the note in his backpack. He would return the movie to the video store after lunch.

Miss Lantana might think she was smart, but he was smarter. Way smarter.

twenty-six

At a quarter to six, before leaving for the bereavement dinner at the church, Allison made a call to the sheriff's office. Perhaps Mike had returned early. The recorded message instructing her to leave a number told her otherwise. She sighed. She couldn't be comfortable until she knew Mike Jackson had the surveillance DVD in his possession.

"Hi, Mike, this is Allison Barker. I'm staying at the Sinclairs' house. Please call me tonight. It's extremely important." She left her temporary cell number and disconnected.

For all she knew, Mike was watching the DVD this very minute. Perhaps he was even on his way to apprehend the murderer. Or, in the worst-case scenario, the camera had missed the event altogether. Lord, she missed the dull, drab life she used to have.

Coming to a stop in the Great Hope Baptist Church's parking lot brought back a flood of childhood memories.

Years of Sunday school, vacation Bible school, and singing in the choir. During her childhood, what the schools didn't provide in entertainment, the church did. Times were so different now.

Allison entered the church basement to an array of food laid out on folding tables. The ladies of the church auxiliary customarily prepared a meal for grieving families. She hadn't eaten all day and was starved. There was a large platter of ham and several green-bean casseroles with broken bits of canned onion rings swimming in mushroom soup. A variety of Jell-O dishes in various stages of unjelling were overshadowed by a bounty of desserts.

Guests were gathered in little knots discussing the events that had unfolded over the past few days. Low conversations came to a halt when Allison neared. She felt lonely and isolated. She was an outsider, no longer part of the town.

She overheard a couple say that Quint Matthews had posted bail earlier in the day and had been released to await a trial date. He was later seen having coffee with two women and another cowboy in a local restaurant.

Quint had to have been having coffee with Debbie Sue, Edwina, and Tag. She had to tell Debbie Sue and Edwina about the video. She reached for her cell phone as she looked for an exit from the church. Outside, she dialed Tag's number.

"Yo. Tag Freeman."

Allison gripped the phone and spoke. "Tag, this is Allison, I need to tell you something."

When she had finished the story about the surveillance

DVD, Tag said, "My God, Allison, we've got to make sure the sheriff gets that envelope *tonight*. Where are you now?"

"I'm at the church, at the bereavement dinner. Do you know where the sheriff's office is?"

"Yeah, I was just there this morning."

"Meet me there in fifteen minutes." Allison closed her phone. It started ringing immediately.

Hoping that Tag had forgotten to tell her something endearing, she flipped open the phone and spoke softly. "This is Allison."

"Allison Barker," Mike Jackson said. "What a surprise. How long has it been?"

Allison smiled. "Too long, Mike. I wish I had called you under more pleasant circumstances, but I have to know something. Have you been to your office this afternoon?"

"That's where I am now."

"Great. Have you had a chance to look at the DVD I left for you?"

Silence. Too long a silence for Allison's blood pressure.

"What DVD?" he asked.

Allison felt she might faint. She told Sheriff Jackson the story, concluding with, "And when I left your office, it was on your desk."

The playful classroom buddy of old was gone and in his place was the voice of authority. "How far are you from here?"

Allison told him she was at the church.

"Great. Come to my office as quick as you can."

When Allison reached the courthouse, an entourage was

waiting—Debbie Sue, Edwina, and Tag. She left Dr. Sinclair's car and walked toward them.

"Good God, sugar," Edwina said, "you look like death chewing on a biscuit."

Allison couldn't hold back tears. Between gulps she told the trio what had happened.

"Well, standing out here isn't getting anything done," Debbie Sue said. "Let's go see what the sheriff's got." She started for the sheriff's office.

Sheriff Jackson looked up when they entered. "I've already called my receptionist, Lantana Tanner, and told her to get down here. She was here all afternoon. She's got to know something about the envelope and the DVD. I could've asked her over the phone, but if I had, everyone in town would know about it before I hung up."

"Did he say Lantana Tanner?" Edwina whispered to Debbie Sue.

"Shhh," Debbie Sue replied.

Just then the giant woman threw back the door and huffed in, obviously more irritated than curious or nervous. Pink foam curlers were attached to her head, an enormous aqua chenille robe covered her bulk, and Dallas Cowboy slipper socks covered her feet.

"Sheriff, I'm here. What's going on? I was right in the middle of *American Idol* and you know I never—"

"Cool it," the sheriff said sternly, his hands planted on his belt. He began to grill her about the envelope.

She reported that the envelope had been on his desk when she went to lunch. When she returned it was gone. "I didn't touch it. I assumed you'd canceled your trip or had come back early and taken it. I had no reason to think otherwise. Am I going to get paid overtime for coming all the way down here?"

"Go home," the sheriff said. "Thanks for coming in."

He waited until she was well gone before speaking again. "There's only one other person I can think of who might know something. Y'all excuse me, please, but I have to ask you to leave so I can conduct some business." He stood up and made an attempt to herd the group toward the door.

"Wait a minute," Debbie Sue said. "We're not going anywhere. We have an obligation to our client to locate this DVD or whatever it is."

"Miss—" the sheriff started, but was interrupted by Allison taking hold of his arm.

"Mike, please help us. We all want the same thing. The truth about who murdered Monica. These are friends of mine and *their* friend is in trouble. If I'm responsible for the DVD disappearing, I'm in trouble. Please let us help you. We won't get in your way." Allison's voice broke. "I should have never let the DVD leave my hands until I handed it to you personally."

The bull of a man crumbled. "Now that's nonsense. You left it in the office of a sworn official of the law. You had no reason to think anything would or could happen to it. You did exactly right." He looked at each of them. "You can come along, but you'll have to follow me in your own rigs. And don't forget, I'm in charge. You'll all do as I say. Understood?"

★ ★ ★

Merle had made his usual stops, checking to see that every-thing was quiet and peaceful in his hometown. Some tacky person had thrown out some trash and he stopped to pick it up. He didn't like it when people threw their trash out of their car windows. As his mom would say, that wasn't nice.

He pedaled three times around the downtown square and was seven blocks from the courthouse when he spotted the tan car inside the cemetery.

It was the same car he had seen parked on the road near Dunnam's. That day, the person inside was trying to read a road map, but he was really spying on the funeral home the whole time. Merle knew that for sure, because he had watched the car.

Because people treated him as if he were invisible, Merle was always able to see a lot. Everybody assumed he was in-capable of figuring anything out, but he did figure out things. He took longer than others, but he could figure out lots of things.

He had figured out for sure that the tan car wasn't a Haskell car and it didn't belong there in the cemetery. There was never a car in the cemetery this late. He knew he needed to see what the occupant of the car was doing, but he didn't like to be in the graveyard at night. It was dark and scary.

He had almost talked himself out of riding around the low gray wall that encircled the plots when he noticed the shadowy figure standing near a freshly dug grave. He didn't think it was a ghost. He didn't believe ghosts cried. And this person was really crying.

The person was standing beside the new grave where Monica Hunter would be put tomorrow. The man who dug the grave had said a bad person had killed Miss Monica.

What if this was that bad person?

Merle couldn't decide what to do. Should he ask the person what they were doing here crying? He was confused and scared. He wished Sheriff Mike was here. He would know what to do.

Merle started back to the courthouse. He stood on the pedals and pumped hard so he could go faster. He was almost there when the familiar blue-and-brown sheriff's car came toward him.

Sheriff Mike pulled to the side of the road and motioned for Merle to stop. Another vehicle, a red pickup carrying people he didn't know, pulled alongside him. Merle had to squeeze his bicycle between the sheriff's car and the red pickup.

"Merle," Sheriff Jackson said, "got a second to talk?"

"Sheriff Mike! You gotta come quick! Somebody's in the graveyard crying!"

"Merle, there's no law against being in the graveyard crying. Now listen to me, I need to ask you something."

"But they're crying! They're standing there, looking at that place Miss Monica's going to be laying for eternity in peaceful rest. And they're crying!"

"I want you to calm down. It's a real sad thing about Monica passing on. There are a lot of people who'll be crying. Settle down and answer a question for me."

Merle knew it was his duty to tell the sheriff. He pushed on. "It's the car that was parked and spying at Dunnam's yesterday."

Debbie Sue decided to take matters into her own hands. Sort of. She reached out and touched Merle's arm and gave the sheriff a wink above the cyclist's head. "Tell you what, Merle. My friends and I'll drive to the cemetery and see what's going on. You stay here and talk to Sheriff Mike. Would that be okay?"

Merle switched a look between her and the sheriff. "I guess so."

Debbie Sue smiled and eased her foot off the brake. "Where's the graveyard, Allison? Let's just drive over there so the sheriff can talk to this guy and find out about the surveillance video."

Following Allison's directions, Debbie Sue drove a few blocks out of town to the county cemetery. The moon had risen and some of the headstones shone in its reflection. Debbie Sue had never seen so many trees that weren't mesquites all in one place in West Texas. Their dark silhouettes lent an air of eeriness. God, no wonder Merle had been afraid. Debbie Sue wasn't usually afraid of anything living or dead, but her palms had gotten a little moist.

"Look, there's the car he was talking about," Edwina said.

As Debbie Sue steered left to get a better view of the car, her headlights spotlighted the person standing at the open grave. The person turned and looked into the bright beam, frozen by the sudden light.

"Holy fucking shit!" Debbie yanked the steering wheel, making a sharp turn and throwing up a barrier against the tan sedan's exit. She shoved the gearshift into park and leaped from the cab.

"I'll be a son of a bitch," Edwina cried, opening her door and following Debbie Sue.

Allison was stunned. She looked at Tag.

"Are we supposed to yell an obscenity and jump out of the truck?" he asked. "There does seem to be a pattern here."

"We've got to help them." Allison yanked on her door handle, only to find it locked.

"Forget it," Tag said. "This is a crew cab. You can't open these back doors if the front doors are closed."

"What? Can't you open the front doors?"

"I could. If I was an acrobat."

Allison's heart began to pound. "You mean we're trapped?"

"Let's wait a minute. If they don't come back, maybe you can reach the front door and open it. You're smaller than I am."

"This is insane," she said, her voice growing more strident. "My Crown Victoria might have been junk on wheels, but at least I could get out of it."

"Now calm down. I don't think they're in harm's way."

"But we don't even know what they're chasing."

"I'm not so sure they do either."

He pointed at Debbie Sue, who was running between two rows of tombstones like the headless horseman. Only her light-colored khaki pants could be seen in the night. The pants stopped once beside a headstone, then took off again.

Edwina was closer to the truck. She made three little steps, stopped, leaned on a headstone, and adjusted her shoe. Five more steps and she stopped and pulled at her bra strap.

"What are they doing?" Allison asked.

"Damned if I know," Tag answered, shaking his head.

To Debbie Sue's dismay, the person who had been targeted in her headlights was nowhere in sight. "Ed, where the hell did he go?"

Complete silence. Except for the rustling of dried leaves. The sound surrounded Debbie Sue, almost like a whisper. The clouds had moved over the moon and left the landscape in pitch-black darkness. A shiver ran up Debbie Sue's spine. "Ed? . . . Ed? Where are you?"

She began to walk gingerly. She couldn't see a thing, including Edwina. "Ed, don't pull this shiiiii—*oomph!*"

Debbie Sue landed on her tailbone. She got to her feet, the smell of dirt all around her. She dusted her bottom and her blazer sleeves and bent her arms, checking for injuries. Her elbows bumped a wall.

A wall?

She could see nothing, so she reached out with her hands, feeling what was beside her. Bare dirt. She looked up and all she could see was a three-by-six slice of sky slightly lighter than her surroundings. *Shit!* She had fallen into an open grave. "Damnation! Son of a bitch!"

A voice beside her said, "You left out fuck."

Debbie Sue jumped so high she shinnied a good two feet up the dirt wall before Edwina said, "That won't work. I've already tried it."

"Dammit, Ed, you scared the living shit outta me! Why didn't you say something?" Debbie Sue bent forward, catching her breath and waiting for her heartbeat to slow.

"Oh, I'm so sorry," Edwina replied, exaggerated civility and sweetness hanging on each word. "What was I supposed to say? 'Hi, Deb, glad you dropped in. Can I get you something to drink?' "

Debbie Sue looked toward the voice, but could barely see Edwina's outline. "This is no time for sarcasm. How the hell are we gonna get outta here?"

"This is the perfect fucking time for sarcasm. Of all the lousy places I've wound up in my life, and you know there have been some doozies, this one takes the cake. Thank God Tag and Allison are in the pickup. They'll get us out."

"Not for a while, they won't. Not unless they figure out how to open the friggin' doors."

"What is that supposed to mean?"

"You can't get out the backseat with the front doors closed. Tag might be able to reach them, but he'll have to break both his legs first. He's a pretty big ol' boy."

"That's crazy. Putting doors like that on a pickup makes no fucking sense."

"Tell it to Ford. You're talking *sense* to me from the bottom of a grave, in the middle of the night, in the middle of fucking nowhere?"

They stood there in silence, listening to each other's breathing.

"I guess we better start being nicer to each other," Edwina said. "Seeing as how we're gonna be *laying together for eternity in peaceful rest.*"

Debbie Sue couldn't hold back a snicker. "That Merle's something else. I couldn't believe it when he said that. He's worse than Billy Don."

Edwina began to laugh and Debbie Sue joined her. They both bent double in laughter, gasping for breath. The giddy moment had almost passed when a human voice from above silenced them both.

"Here. One of you reach up for my hand and I'll pull you out."

Debbie Sue looked up and saw the outline of a human against the black sky. "Eugene!" She thrust her hand upward.

"Janine!" Edwina said.

Once they were aboveground, Edwina whacked Eugene/Janine's shoulder. "You're the one that nearly ran over me in Salt Lick."

Eugene/Janine ducked and raised his arms in self-defense. "Stop. Don't hit me. I bruise easily."

Without warning, Eugene/Janine startled and disappeared behind a tree trunk just before Sheriff Jackson, Merle, Tag, and Allison walked up.

"Sorry we weren't any help, but we were trapped in the truck until the sheriff arrived," Tag sheepishly offered. "Are y'all OK?"

"What happened?" the sheriff asked.

"We fell in an open grave, but Eugene pulled us out," Debbie Sue said.

"Janine saved the day," Edwina said, wiping her feet on her pant legs. She had been forced to remove her shoes to shinny up the grave wall.

"Who's Eugene?" the sheriff asked.

Eugene prissed out of the shadows. "That would be me, Officer."

"Who's Janine?" Allison asked.

"Ditto!" Eugene/Janine said in a falsetto voice.

Even in the dark, Debbie Sue could see Allison's jaw drop. Tag and the sheriff likewise.

"Are you having trouble, Sheriff Mike?" Merle asked. "Do I need to call 911?"

"No, Merle," the sheriff answered patiently. "I'm not in trouble. I *am* 911, remember?"

"Oh, yeah. I forgot."

The sheriff turned his attention back to the little group. "Somebody needs to start explaining things to me. We're all gonna take a little trip back to my office right now." He looked at Eugene/Janine. "Miss, uh, I mean, sir, you ride with me and Merle. Allison, you and your band of clowns follow us."

"Did he call us a bunch of clowns?" Edwina whispered to Debbie Sue as they tramped back to the pickup.

"Shut up, Ronald McDonald, and just do as he says."

twenty-seven

Debbie Sue and Edwina followed the sheriff. At his office, he motioned for Merle to help him and they began dragging chairs from the reception room into his private office. Allison and Tag soon appeared.

"Now. Is everybody here?" the sheriff asked, placing the last chair. The chairs were arranged in a semicircle, each facing his desk.

Looks switched among the assemblage. Like sheep, they responded in unison to the sheriff's gesture for them to sit down. He took a seat behind his desk. "Now," he said, sweeping a hand past Debbie Sue and Edwina, Tag and Allison, and Merle, "I pretty much know their story and how it fits into the evening, but I don't know anything about *you*." He pointed a finger at Eugene/Janine.

Debbie Sue was still muddling through what Eugene/

Janine was doing in Haskell, Texas, when he was supposed to be in Las Vegas.

Eugene/Janine squared his shoulders and lifted his chin. "I'm not speaking without an attorney present. I have rights. I haven't done anything wrong and you had no reason to arrest me." His voice became higher with each sentence.

"No one's being arrested," Sheriff Jackson said in an even, calm voice. "Yet."

Debbie Sue and Edwina traded glances.

"Just settle down," the sheriff continued. "I'm gonna get to the bottom of this here and now." He turned to Tag. "You seem to be a normal kind of fella. You tell me what's going on."

"I wish I could, Sheriff," Tag said. "I only came up here to see my friend Quint Matthews. I gave Allison a ride when her car broke down outside of Abilene. I'm pretty much in the dark about anything else."

Eugene/Janine pursed his lips and glared at Tag. "So you're a *friend* of Quint's," he spit out spitefully.

Debbie Sue wished Eugene/Janine would just shut his damn mouth. She rolled her eyes.

"He's always gone for the pretty boys," Eugene/Janine added.

Tag half rose from his chair. The sheriff's voice boomed. He glared at Eugene/Janine. "I've had enough of this. I gave you a chance to speak your piece. Now it's too late. Merle, bring in that TV set we went to your house and got." He pulled a disc from his jacket pocket and held it up for all to see. "Y'all excuse me while I watch a movie."

"The surveillance disc," Allison cried, coming to her feet.

"So that's the video," Tag muttered.

"There's a video?" Eugene/Janine's eyes went wide. He looked scared and nervous for the first time.

"He's gonna watch a movie? Now?" Edwina asked.

"And he called *us* clowns," Debbie Sue grumbled.

As soon as the sheriff and Merle left the room, Debbie Sue pounced on Eugene/Janine. "How the hell do you figure into this mess?" She poked his shoulder with her finger. "I thought you were having a sex-change operation in Vegas." She looked him up and down. "Looks to me like you've still got all your old parts."

"Well, thanks for bringing that up, Debbie Sue." Eugene/Janine sniffled into a handkerchief. "Like I don't have enough to worry about, you have to remind me of that."

"Seriously," Edwina said, "what happened to your sex-change operation?"

"That doctor I paid all that cash to went to Brazil with my money. He took money from several other unsuspecting patients, too. He's hiding out, the bastard." He dabbed his eyes. "The Las Vegas police wouldn't help me at all. They treated my claim like a big joke."

"Hmmph," Edwina said. "I guess it's just as well. You might've had to tell them where you got the money in the first place."

Debbie Sue gave Eugene/Janine a look. "So the money you stole from the Carrutherses for your operation got stolen from you? Where I come from, that's called poetic justice."

"No, it's not! There's no justice when justice isn't due! I didn't hurt anyone!" He began to wail.

On a sigh, Debbie Sue put her arm around his shoulder. "There, there. Are you still taking hormones?"

"Yesss," he whined. "I really don't know why I want to be a woman. The mood swings are ridiculous. And I'm retaining enough water to float a boat."

Debbie Sue shot Edwina a glance as she pulled Eugene/Janine closer. "Eugene, did you have anything to do with Monica Hunter's death? In case you haven't figured it out, that video the sheriff's looking at might show what happened. You wouldn't happen to be the star player, would you?"

Eugene/Janine bit down on his knuckle. "Oh my God. I only wanted to confront her about how she treated Quint. I can't go to prison. I'm too fragile." He broke into even louder sobs.

Twenty painful minutes ticked by, the silence broken only by Eugene/Janine's sobs and sighs. Finally Sheriff Jackson came back into the room wearing a grim expression. "Folks, I'm gonna call the district attorney and have him get in touch with the district judge." He looked at Tag. "Mr. Freeman, was it? Do you know how to reach Mr. Matthews?"

"Yes, I can call him now."

"Good. Get in touch with him and have him get here as quick as he can. Tell him to bring his lawyer."

Tag left the room. When he returned, he reported that Quint and his attorney would be in the sheriff's office within the hour.

"Oh, no," Debbie Sue cried out. "Quint did it, didn't he? It was on that tape, wasn't it?"

"No, ma'am," the sheriff replied. "Monica Hunter was very much alive when Mr. Matthews left her."

All eyes turned on Eugene/Janine. He squirmed in his seat.

"He didn't do it either," the sheriff said. "It was an accident."

"An accident?" the group chorused.

"But I thought they determined the grill couldn't have fallen off the counter," Allison said.

"Well, they were right about that. It didn't fall off, but it was an accident all the same."

The group glued their collective gazes on the sheriff. "There's quite a bit of the tape showing Mr. Matthews talking to Monica. Mind you, there's no audio on the tape, but it appears he did no harm. In fact, he got down on one knee and handed something toward Monica. It appeared he was asking her to marry him."

"Oh God," Debbie Sue said softly, almost in tears. "Poor Quint."

Edwina shook her head. "Bless his heart."

Eugene/Janine leaped to his feet and stamped his foot. "That ass!"

The sheriff pointed a finger at him and growled, "Now you just sit down before I change my opinion."

Clearing his throat, the sheriff continued. "Monica started laughing at Matthews and he left." He glared again at Eugene/Janine. "That's where *you* come in. At first I didn't recognize you, but it's you all right. Long red hair, tight green dress, high heels."

"That sounds cute," Edwina whispered to Debbie Sue.

Eugene/Janine gave her an appreciative smile. "The shoes are brown with little green bows on the toes. I got them at Nordstrom's while I was in Vegas."

"Knock it off," the sheriff boomed. "Like I was saying. I've got you on tape."

He turned back to the group. "Mr., er, Miss, well, this person"—he pointed at Eugene/Janine—"looks like he's chewing Monica out, but good. She came out of the water and tried to reach a towel that was lying on the counter. It was a little too far away, and when she stretched for it, she accidentally pulled that plugged-in grill into the hot tub. Y'all know the rest."

Eugene/Janine broke into loud sobs again. "Oh God, that's exactly what happened. It was awful . . . Even—even the cat got upset . . . It yowled and ran out of the room." He dabbed his eyes with a ragged tissue and blew his nose. "I never meant to hurt her, honest. I only wanted to tell her to leave Quint alone."

Tag pulled a handkerchief from his back pocket and offered it. Eugene/Janine took it and boo-hooed into it. "Quint's never known what's best for him . . . I knew she was using him, the hussy. When she and Quint were dating, when he wasn't in town, I followed her. I heard her tell a friend in the ladies' room that she had caught a big fish and was going to reel him in and take him for all she could. The little tramp." Eugene/Janine blew his nose with a loud snort.

"You're the one who called 911?" Tag asked.

"Yes. I couldn't just leave her . . . like that."

"Why didn't you just tell us it was an accident?" the sheriff asked. "Why did you run? Man, er, uh, ma'am, er, uh, hell, you could've been shot."

Eugene/Janine's gaze darted around the room, perspiration showing on his brow. "I'm under a restraining order. I'm supposed to stay away from Quint. I only wanted to tell that little, that little—I didn't dream he'd be accused of murder. I wouldn't have let it go to a trial. Honest, I wouldn't have. I would've confessed."

"Well, I guess it doesn't matter now," Sheriff Jackson said. "Mr. Matthews's legal problems are over."

"Yeah," said Debbie Sue, rising to her feet, "and his *real* ones are just beginning."

"Again," Edwina added. She, too, stood.

"Did I hear somebody say my legal problems are over?"

All heads turned toward the voice at the door and Quint Matthews.

"Ah, Mr. Matthews," Sheriff Jackson said, getting to his feet. "Come in. I didn't think you'd get here so quickly or I would've waited."

"I was still at the truck stop diner, not that far away."

"I was just explaining to the group here the action on the surveillance disc at Miz Hunter's home."

"DVD? A *surveillance* DVD?" A muscle quirked in Quint's jaw. He took a menacing step toward the sheriff. "My lawyer never mentioned this. Did you know about this disc all along?"

"Whoa, now." The sheriff thrust his face forward, obviously not intimidated. "Just hold everything, cowboy. Nobody's hidden anything from you. Nobody knew what happened. If it wasn't for Allison Barker, we wouldn't know now and your butt would still be parked in my jail."

Quint looked at the group for the first time, his eyes landing on Eugene/Janine. "You? Why, you little bastard. It's you who's been following me, isn't it?" His right hand curled into a fist. "I oughta take you apart—"

Eugene/Janine shrieked and darted behind Edwina's back. "Don't touch me!" He peeked around Edwina's side. "Sheriff, don't let him near me."

"Don't get me in the middle of this," Edwina said, and stepped aside, exposing Eugene/Janine.

Tag stood up and put his hand on Quint's shoulder. "Quint, calm down, buddy. Everything's working in your favor here. Don't screw it up with an assault charge."

Quint's posture relaxed. "Okay, okay, I'm fine. I'm not gonna hurt the . . . the—you say everything's working in my favor? How?"

"Why don't you just have a seat, Mr. Matthews, and I'll explain what's happened."

Quint sank to a chair in front of the sheriff's desk, but

perched on the edge of it like a coiled diamondback. The sheriff, too, took a seat. For the next ten minutes he outlined how events had unfolded up to the present.

Eugene/Janine timidly stepped toward Quint and placed a hand on his forearm. "See? You're not in trouble at all. You've been cleared. Isn't that good news?"

Quint yanked his arm away from Eugene/Janine. "You ever lay a hand on me again and you'll scratch your ass with a stump for the rest of your life."

Eugene/Janine winced, then scurried behind Edwina again.

Debbie Sue sat down beside Quint and leaned toward him. "I'm so sorry about all of this, Quint. You must be heartbroken, having offered Monica a wedding ring and all."

"Wedding ring? Is that what you thought? Babe, you of all people know me better than that. I offered her a hotel key. I stopped and got a room."

"What's that supposed to mean? I thought she was the one. I thought you loved her."

"That might have entered my mind at first. But she wasn't as important as my freedom."

Debbie Sue recoiled. Edwina stepped forward. "Sheriff, shoot him! Aim carefully and just shoot him."

Quint laughed. "Edwina, looks like you're gonna have to put up with me a little bit longer." He stood up and gave his shoulders a shimmy. "Now, if all of you will excuse me, I've had the weight of the world lifted from my shoulders and I'm getting the hell outta here."

"You going back to Midland?" Tag asked.

"Naw, man, I'm going home. Back to Seguin, and I might not leave there for a while. The fact is, I may never come back to West Texas again."

Quint lifted his gray Stetson and looked at the occupants of the room again. "Thank y'all for everything you did for me. Allison, something tells me you and Tag need me to get out of your hair. I wish y'all luck. Debbie Sue, send me a bill. Add a tip." He pointed to Eugene/Janine. "Sheriff, I want you to arrest that man. I've filed protective orders in two counties on him. Tarrant and Guadalupe. The paperwork is in the glove box of my truck. It won't be hard for you to verify it. I expect to see him locked up tonight."

Eugene/Janine bravely stepped from behind Edwina's shadow. "Excuse me, but I am not going to jail. I only wanted to tell that woman that what she was doing to you was unforgivable. I haven't—"

He stopped when Quint took a step toward him, but the sheriff grabbed Quint's arm and steered him toward the door. "Ma'am," he said to Eugene/Janine, "if I were you, I wouldn't say another word. I think the safest place for you tonight is in my custody. Merle, keep an eye on him while I step outside with Mr. Matthews."

Merle snapped to attention and saluted. "Yes, sir."

Edwina turned to Debbie Sue. "Guess our work here is done. You want to head on back tonight? Vic will be at home waiting for me."

"Sure, no need to stay. Allison, you want to ride with us?"

"Well, I, uh, don't know. I'd like to go to the funeral tomorrow and my car . . ."

Tag placed a protective arm around Allison's waist and pulled her close. "I'll stay over. You can go to the funeral, then I'll give you a ride back to Salt Lick. We'll stop and check on your car on the way."

Allison's face broke into a beaming smile. "You remember the way to my house?"

"Yes, ma'am. I most assuredly do."

epilogue

All charges against Quint were dropped. He was free to resume his life, though he faced a relentless barrage from a merciless media. Monica Hunter's death and the run-up thereto contained all that readers and viewers craved—celebrity sex and scandal and a fair amount of redneck humor.

Despite the publicity, Quint's reputation as a lover didn't take the hit it had a few years back. Perhaps it had even been enhanced. He was now the man that no woman—or man—could resist.

Eugene/Janine had violated a restraining order against stalking Quint. He received an eighteen-month jail sentence. While confined, he made good use of his time. He wrote a tell-all book about the death of Monica Hunter and his relationship with a three-time world-champion bull rider. The book, entitled *What I Did for Love,* was an instant must-read. It became a *New York Times* bestseller.

Upon his release six months early because of good behavior, Eugene/Janine became a media darling, giving interview after interview detailing the story of his/her affair with Quint, his/her brush with the law, and the grisly story of Monica Hunter's electrocution. He was invited to be a guest on *Oprah, Leno,* and *Letterman,* and all of the morning talk shows.

Tag and Allison dated for ten months, then married. Allison and Jill moved from Lydia Barker's small cottage in Salt Lick into Tag's 4427-square-foot home in Midland. As Mrs. Tag Freeman, Allison realized a dream of opening a dress shop in the mall. She added maternity wear within the year.

Tag expanded his business, opening a chain of barbecue joints. He penned a cookbook and landed a TV cooking show called *Cooking Cowboy Style.* He was on the road to being famous again, but this time he wasn't alone. With a wife, a daughter, and a son on the way, life held new meaning and purpose.

Sheriff Jackson recognized the potential for real harm from Merle's good intentions. He gave him "the most important job in the county"—feeding and loving all stray dogs and cats in the county. The job came with a uniform, a badge, and a whistle. Dr. Sinclair retired and donated his office building to the county with the proviso that it be used as a safe haven for lost animals. Merle was surrounded by greetings of love and kisses every day, and he gave back freely. He had never been happier in his life.

Edwina and Debbie Sue continued as usual—looking for trouble, getting into trouble, and explaining their way out of it. As Debbie Sue said often, "Well, somebody's gotta fuckin' do it."

Quint made fewer trips to West Texas, but he kept in touch with the Freemans and the Equalizers. He had learned something from his experience: life might be there for the taking, but real friendships were there for the lucky.

A+
AUTHOR INSIGHTS, EXTRAS, & MORE...

FROM
DIXIE CASH
AND
AVON A

Edwina's "Advice to the Lovelorn" column in the Salt Lick Weekly Reporter *has been wildly successful. It seems that when it comes to relationships, most of the newspaper's readership (approximately 900) has come to rely on Edwina's wisdom. She's thrilled to pass on what she's learned from the four marriages that produced her three daughters—Billy Pat, Jimmie Sue, and Roberta Jean—each named for her respective father.*

Dear Edwina,

Bobby and I have been married for a year. Everyone says that we're just the cutest couple ever! My problem is my mother-in-law. Every day, while Bobby and I are at work, she comes to our condo and lets herself in with a key my husband gave her. She cleans, does the laundry, irons, cooks a wonderful meal, and has it waiting for us when we get home from work. Along with supper, we find money she has left on the kitchen table. She never bothers us otherwise, but I'm fed up and ready to say something to her. What do you suggest?

Fed Up in North Dallas

Dear FU,

How about "thanks" for starters?

Yours truly,
Edwina *"Watchdog-for-lost-souls"* Martin

Ed,

My parents have always given me every little thing I ever wanted. I've just graduated from high school and now my mom is saying she wants me to go to college in the fall and prepare to stand on my own two feet. I'd rather travel around the countryside experiencing life and finding myself before settling down to the mundane existence of earning a living. Would you back me on this as soon as possible? I want to charge a trip to France while my mom still has enough credit left on her MasterCard.

Thanks,
Not Your Ordinary Debutante

Dear Yes You Are,

While you're out there looking for yourself, see if you can't find another version, one with a little common sense and appreciation for what your parents have done. As for going to France, keep that money in the good ol' USA where it'll do some real good.

Edwina *"Dipped-in-red-white-and-blue"* Martin

Dear Ms. Martin,

My girlfriend doesn't want a CZ for her engagement ring. She wants the real thing, a diamond. I say you don't need a real ring for real love. Do you agree with her?

Leroy

Dear Leroy,

Is a snake's ass close to the ground? When you asked for her hand in marriage, did she give you a *real* answer? When you ask her to forsake all others, do you want the *real* truth? Don't start your life together with something fake, or she might fake a lot of other things, if you get my drift.

Edwina "*Keep-it-real*" Martin

Dear Edwina,

My husband and I are discussing a much-needed vacation. I want to lie in the sun, he wants to go to the mountains and ski. Can you offer a compromise?

Needing a Vacation

Dear Needing,

I tried snow skiing once, and after my experience, here's what I suggest. Go on the ski trip. After you've broken your leg, you can lie on the beach and sun.

Edwina *"Been there won't go back"* Perkins-Martin

Dear Edwina,

I need help. I want to wear my hair in one of the new cute short styles. The problem is that my boyfriend insists that I wear it long. He says he loves the way hair feels gliding through his fingers. How can I get him to see things my way?

Hair to My Butt and Hating It

Dear Hairy Butt,

This is one of the easiest problems someone has asked me to solve in a long time. Just stop shaving your legs. You can save yourself the expense of buying razors and save the time spent shaving. This will give him more time to run his fingers through it. A win-win situation if there ever was one.

Edwina *"There's a solution to everything"* Martin

Having been in the beauty business for several years, tomboy Debbie Sue has gone through an evolutionary change and developed some beauty tips.

Debbie Sue Overstreet's Beauty Tips for All Stages of Life

1. If you're between the ages of 21 and 30, enjoy yourself. Your beauty is a work of God and nature, and you might never be prettier than you are right now. Remember, that glow comes from within.

2. If you're between the ages of 31 and 40, cleanse properly, always use a moisturizer, and stay out of the sun. The West Texas sun can turn your skin to leather quicker than a saddle-maker.

3. If you're between the ages of 41 and 50, eat healthy, exercise, and get at least eight hours of sleep each night. This isn't easy if you're married, but it's worth striving for.

4. If you're over the age of 50, enjoy yourself. Your beauty is a work of God and nature, and you might never be prettier than

you are right now. Don't get on that extreme makeover wagon. It's more dangerous than riding a Conestoga moving west.

5. Debbie Sue adds to all of the above, the advice Miss Sophie Tucker gave fifty years ago: *From birth to age 18, a girl needs good parents; from 18 to 35, she needs good looks; from 35 to 55, she needs a good personality; and from 55 on, she needs cash.*

RECIPES

Tag Freeman spent years perfecting the mouth-watering real Texas barbecue he serves in Tag Freeman's Double-Kicker Barbecue & Beer. Though his recipes have heretofore been secret, to do Debbie Sue and Edwina a favor, and because they're friends of Allison's (not to mention taking the opportunity to gain publicity for his restaurant), Tag has agreed to allow these culinary gems to be presented for the first time, in his own words, in this book.

Tag Freeman's Barbecue Rub

I believe that no self-respecting barbecue would call itself "barbecue" without a good pre-cooking rubdown. So here's how it starts:

Put into a food processor the following:

¼ cup each: paprika, salt (kosher, preferably), and brown
    sugar
2 tablespoons each: chili powder, garlic powder, onion
    powder, ground cumin, and ground coriander
1 tablespoon coarse ground pepper
1 teaspoon dry mustard

Pulse it all once real quick, just to mix it good and refine it.

Then you need a prime cut of meat and a dose of vinegar. Any old kind of vinegar will do, but I prefer the apple cider kind. Rub down the meat with the vinegar. Don't marinate, don't soak. Just rub down and massage. Follow with rubbing in the spices.

Cook real slow over hot mesquite coals in a smoker for a real long time, basting with a mix of Tag Freeman's Barbecue Sauce, a little water and a tiny bit of that vinegar. Cooking time depends on the size of the chunk of meat. If it's a big chunk, cooking might take all day, in which case you want to have plenty of cold beer on hand. If it's a little chunk, a couple of hours will probably do it.

This will give you a tender, succulent piece of meat, and the aroma while it's cooking will have your taste buds jumping for joy.

Serve it up with my secret sauce (recipe to follow), some fresh ears of corn steamed to tender, golden perfection and bathed in butter, a little tangy coleslaw tossed with my secret pecan dressing, and have yourself an eating orgy.

Tag Freeman's Secret Barbecue Sauce

Saute: 3 cups coarsely chopped onions, 1 tablespoon finely chopped fresh garlic in ½ cup olive oil, just until the onions are translucent. Takes about five minutes.

Add: ¼ cup coarsely chopped fresh hot red chilies, including the seeds

¼ cup chili powder (any kind you like, but I like the dark red kind)

2 teaspoons ground cumin

Simmer for another minute or two, then add 1 or 2 tablespoons of grated ginger

Follow up by adding: ⅓ cup vinegar (again, I like the apple cider kind)

1 can tomato paste
1 cup strong coffee
½ cup soy sauce
½ cup molasses
⅓ cup orange juice
2 tablespoons prepared mustard
1½ teaspoons salt

Simmer uncovered for 15 or 20 minutes, or until very thick.
Use to baste meat during cooking, then serve on the side. Hmm-hmm. Larruping.

Cole Slaw with Tag Freeman's Secret Pecan Dressing

5 or 6 cups shredded cabbage (add some purple cabbage for color)
½ cup diced celery
½ cup thinly sliced carrot

Dressing:

Stir 1 tablespoon sugar into 2 tablespoons half-and-half until sugar is dissolved. Add: ½ cup mayonnaise, 1 tablespoon sweet pickle relish, 1 tablespoon honey mustard, ½ cup toasted chopped pecans, a smidgen of salt and black pepper, and a whisper of cayenne pepper. Pour dressing over salad just before serving. Garnish with a handful of dried cranberries.

© Rash Photography

DIXIE CASH is the writing team of Jeffery McClanahan *(right)* and Pamela Cumbie *(left)*. They grew up in West Texas during the great oil boom, an era filled with "real-life fictional" characters whose stories scream to be written. Pam has always had a zany sense of humor and Jeffery has always had a dry wit. Surrounded by cowboys and steeped in country-western music, when they can stop laughing long enough, they work together creating hilarity on paper. Both live in Texas—Pam in the Forth Worth-Dallas Metroplex and Jeffery in a small town near Forth Worth.